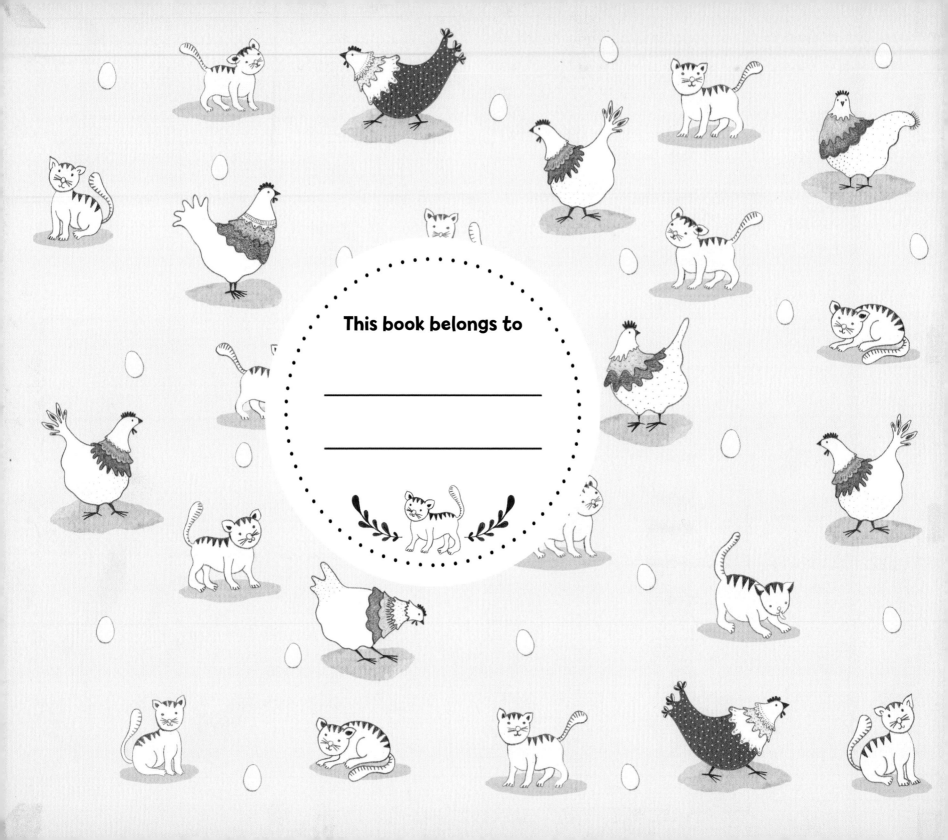

This book belongs to

_____

_____

AN EGG FOR SHABBAT

Mirik Snir

Illustrated by **Eleyor Snir**

KAR-BEN
PUBLISHING

KAR-BEN PUBLISHING®
An imprint of Lerner Publishing Group, Inc.
241 First Avenue North
Minneapolis, MN 55401 USA
Website address: www.karben.com

Main body text set in Billy Infant semibold.
Typeface provided by SparkyType.

Library of Congress Cataloging-in-Publication Data

Names: Snir, Mirik, author. | Snir, Eleyor, 1975–illustrator.
Title: An egg for Shabbat / by Mirik Snir ; illustrated by Elyor Snir.
Description: Minneapolis : Kar-Ben Publishing, [2021] | Audience:
    Ages 4–7. | Audience: Grades K–1. | Summary: Young Ben,
    eager to help his mother, rushes to the chicken pen Sunday
    through Friday mornings and each day learns a new lesson
    about carrying an egg.
Identifiers: LCCN 2020014833 (print) | LCCN 2020014834 (ebook) |
    ISBN 9781541596641 (library binding) | ISBN 9781541596658
    (paperback) | ISBN 9781728417622 (ebook)
Subjects: CYAC: Stories in rhyme. | Eggs—Fiction. | Helpfulness—
    Fiction. | Jews—Fiction. | Mothers and sons—Fiction.
Classification: LCC PZ8.3.S4686 Egg 2021 (print) | LCC
    PZ8.3.S4686 (ebook) | DDC [E]—dc23

LC record available at https://lccn.loc.gov/2020014833
LC ebook record available at https://lccn.loc.gov/2020014834

Manufactured in the United States of America
1-47730-48179-5/7/2020

For Sol, Eliana, Gala, and Emilia
Love, Imma Eleyor and Savta Mirik

SUNDAY

"This looks like a ball,"
he thought right away.

He couldn't resist.
He wanted to play.

And then . . . **oh no!**

**With a big *smash,* the egg came down —*crash!*

The boy came home.
His eyes were sad.

He told his mom.
Would she be mad?

"Oh, Ben, my dear. Oh, son of mine. You learned a lesson, and that's fine."

MONDAY

"I'll give it a try . . ."
the little boy said.

"I can carry some things
on the top of my head."

And then . . . **oh no!**

Hop, pop, kerplop!
The egg did drop.

The boy came home.
His eyes were sad.

He told his mom.
Would she be mad?

"Oh, Ben,
my dear.
Oh, son of mine.
You learned a lesson,
and that's fine."

"I will hold the egg tight,
bring it home in one piece.

Not a dent, not a crack,
not a scratch or a crease."

And then . . . **oh no!**

Clickety-clack!
The egg
did crack.

The boy came home.
His eyes were sad.

He told his mom.
Would she be mad?

"Oh, Ben,
my dear.
Oh, son of mine.
You learned a lesson,
and that's fine."

WEDNESDAY

"I'll take this home!"
He ran and skipped.

Too fast went Ben—
until he tripped.

And then . . . **oh no!**

Ben thought to himself,
"I'll just peek inside . . .

and look for the chick.
Where does it hide?"

And then . . . **oh no!**

**Flickety-flake!
The egg did break.**

The boy came home.
His eyes were sad.

He told his mom.
Would she be mad?

"Oh, Ben,
my dear.
Oh, son of mine.
You learned a lesson,
and that's fine."

Ben held the hen
up to his cheek.

"What have I learned
so far this week?"

"I will not toss eggs in the air!

No eggs on head. I wouldn't dare!

Won't squeeze them tight, won't try my tricks!

Or run too fast!

Or check for chicks."

On Friday night, their eyes were bright.

The challahs gleamed with special light.

SATURDAY

**And on Shabbat,
the day of rest,
they gathered strength
. . . for what?**

You guessed!

Might Mom need
his help again?

Sunday   Monday   Tuesday

Wednesday   Thursday   Friday   Saturday (Shabbat)

MILLER'S

Treasure or Not?

HOW TO COMPARE & VALUE

AMERICAN
ART POTTERY

DAVID RAGO & SUZANNE PERRAULT

MILLER'S

Treasure or Not?

HOW TO COMPARE & VALUE

AMERICAN
ART POTTERY

DAVID RAGO & SUZANNE PERRAULT

We would like to take a moment to thank a handful of friends who, for nearly 30 years, have supported our involvement with American art pottery. These include, but are not limited to Jordan Lubitz, Robert and Rosaire Ellison, Dr. Eugene and Carolyn Hecht, Bob and Betty Hut, Dr. Martin and Ester Eidelberg, Bill Feeny, Dr. and Esthey Meyers, Lynn Kelman, and Bob Sears.

Miller's Treasure or Not?
How to Compare & Value
AMERICAN ART POTTERY

A Miller's-Mitchell Beazley book
Published by Octopus Publishing Group Ltd.
2-4 Heron Quays
London E14 4JP
UK

Mitchell Beazley Production Director: Julie Young
Mitchell Beazley Deputy Art Director: Vivienne Brar
Miller's Commissioning Editor: Anna Sanderson
Miller's Art Editor: Rhonda Fisher
Miller's U.S. Project Manager: Joseph Gonzalez

Produced by Saraband, Inc.
9 Hunt Street
Rowayton, CT 06853
USA

Editor: Sara Hunt
Series Editor: Deborah DeFord
Volume Editors: Robin Langley Sommer, Deborah DeFord
Graphic Design: Dutton and Sherman
Editorial Assistants: Erin Pikor, Nikki L. Fesak
Proofreader & Indexer: Matthew Levine

ISBN 1 84000 382 0

Set in Bembo 9.5/12
Produced by Toppan Printing Co., (HK) Ltd.
Printed and bound in China

On the cover: Pedestal Compote, Tiffany Pottery; back cover: St. George Slaying the Dragon, Batchelder Tile Co.

Contents

An Introduction to
American Pottery

How to Use This Book

The unique compare-and-contrast format that is the hallmark of the *Miller's Treasure or Not?* series has been specially designed to help you to identify authentic pieces of American art pottery and assess their value. At the heart of this book is a series of two-page comparison spreads—60 in all. On each spread, two examples of a pottery's work, related by type or design, are pictured on facing pages and carefully analyzed to determine not only the market value of each vessel or tile, but *why* one is more valuable than the other.

With this approach, you'll be able to consider the context in which the pieces were created, their intended uses and relative condition, and their importance in today's pottery market. By comparing and analyzing a variety of examples, you'll gain the knowledge and skills you'll need

to find and evaluate American art pottery pieces and assess their worth with confidence. The illustrations and call-outs, below and opposite, show how the various elements on a typical two-page comparison work.

The book's introductory chapters offer an overview of the American art pottery market and practical pointers on the care and display of your acquisitions. A fascinating region-by-region primer on the development of art pottery in the United States is illustrated with a superb array of top-of-the-line pieces.

And finally, at the back of the book, you will find further information on where to see and buy American art pottery, other sources of information that may advance your knowledge and understanding of the field, a glossary of pottery terms, and a detailed index.

The *introduction* presents an overview of the featured pottery or pottery line, its style and design, and its place in the art pottery market today.

The *featured wares* include one good example of a pottery's ware and one relatively better example.

The *call-outs* highlight the "value features" of each piece—the key design and condition factors that account for the relative market value of a pottery vessel or tile.

The small *value boxes* (blue for the good piece, pink for the better piece) contain the size and potential value range of the featured vessel or tile.

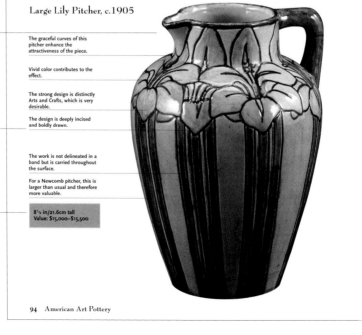

Newcomb College Pottery

The pottery produced at Newcomb College in New Orleans, La., has been a collector favorite for three decades. Soft, attractive, feminine, the ware was usually glazed in shades of blue, covering natural designs of indigenous flowers, nightscapes, and occasionally, creatures of the bayou.

One of our true Arts and Crafts potteries, Newcomb College was founded to introduce Victorian women to the applied arts. While its curriculum included bookbinding, metalwork, and needlework, it is best remembered for its decorative and highly popular works in clay, each of which was a one-of-a-kind example.

Newcomb pottery was always hand-thrown (or, in the case of tiles, hand-built). The decoration of early pieces was painted on the surface. Over time, gentle incising was used to emphasize the design more strongly. Eventually, decoration was modeled into the raw clay, providing more depth and detail.

Early pieces from Newcomb—those most sought by modern-day collectors—are covered in mirrorlike glossy finishes. Colors on these early pieces were usually blues and creams. Pieces with yellow decoration command the highest prices. Such pieces were distinctive and unique, with themes varying greatly from one piece to the next.

The biscuit used was fairly dense, and most pieces have remained intact but minor damage is acceptable.

Large Lily Pitcher, c.1905

The graceful curves of this pitcher enhance the attractiveness of the piece.

Vivid color contributes to the effect.

The strong design is distinctly Arts and Crafts, which is very desirable.

The design is deeply incised and boldly drawn.

The work is not delineated in a band but is carried throughout the surface.

For a Newcomb pitcher, this is larger than usual and therefore more valuable.

8½ in/21.6cm tall
Value: $15,000–$15,500

94 American Art Pottery

The *headline* is a brief descriptive title for each featured item, followed by an approximate date of creation.

Flower Band Pitcher, c.1905

The curving form is less graceful than that of some of Newcomb's comparable work.

The piece is smaller than Newcomb's average size of 8in (20.3cm).

The flowers are tightly drawn, but not lush and large.

This design is restricted to a band.

The decoration is crisp, though not brightly colored.

This high-glazed finish is typical of Newcomb's early work and is very desirable

Size: 6½ in/16.5cm tall
Value: $6,000–$7,000

The *bulleted points* highlight important design and production characteristics and other value points of a featured ware or line

• *All Newcomb College ware was made by hand, most of it thrown by Joseph Meyer. Even the tiles were hand-built, as seen by the HB cipher.*
• *Newcomb is a soft and feminine ware, with curving forms covered with tones of blue and green. The forms are unforced, or easily thrown on a potter's wheel.*
• *Most pieces of Newcomb pottery are under 8in (20.3cm) high. Taller examples, some over 20in (50.8cm), are known to exist; pieces taller than 10in are considered "large."*
• *Newcomb is one of the only potteries whose value has never decreased over the last 30 years.*
• *Some damage is acceptable to modern-day collectors, partly because of the uniqueness of each piece.*
• *Flowers are the most common decoration, followed by native landscape and bayou scenes. Insects, quadrupeds, and birds are the rarest of Newcomb subjects and always sell for a premium.*

The *Key Facts* boxes provide further background information on the featured pottery and its founders and major potters.

Key Facts

Newcomb College pottery was the brainchild of Ellsworth Woodward, an important New Orleans artist and an excellent teacher. Founded in 1896, the college's mission was to give students "practical information as to a method of learning a living through the curriculum." Other skilled teachers joined the staff, including Paul Cox, Mary Sheerer, Leona Nicholson, and Frederick Walrath.

During the early period, many of the pottery decorators were undergraduate female students. They were able to sell some of their pieces in the campus store and could keep a percentage of the profit generated. The pottery's early high-glazed work was phased out by about 1910. A transitional period was characterized by soft, "waxy" finishes, mainly in blues and soft greens. By about 1914, nearly all Newcomb's work was covered in the soft matte finishes for which the studio is now best known. Later work, from about 1935 until the mid-1940s, was again finished in high glaze. This, however, has little of the quality and charm of earlier efforts which is reflected in its value.

Newcomb College Pottery 95

Sicardo Embossed Vase

This is an example of Weller's Sicardo line.

Although Sicardo ware was usually only hand-painted, this piece employs a design that is both embossed and hand painted.

Bold iridescent metallic colors of magenta and silver enhance the value of this piece.

The work represents a bridge between Weller's early hand-decorated ware and its later production pottery.

Jacques Sicard was regarded as highly for his painting on pottery as for his glazing, making this an unusual design for him.

Size: 12in/30.5cm
Value: $6,400–8,600

• *Production pieces were almost always molded.*
• *Weller attempted to compete with Roseville's popular production ware, but the firm seldom matched its rival's designs and production standards.*
• *Included among Weller's most popular production lines are Coppertone, Woodcraft, Selma, and a series of curious and large lawn figures.*
• *An artist routinely added colors to the molded decorations on the production pieces.*
• *Production ware almost always bore one of the company's numerous marks.*
• *Because these pieces were created with molded, repeated designs, even minor damage greatly reduces value.*
• *Generally, production lines with animals and creatures are*

◁ *While the embossed grapes and leaves shown here were part of the molded form, the rich, lustrous glazes that cover them came from the hand of master designer and decorator Jacques Sicard.*

Sometimes, a Key Facts box is replaced by a *detail* that offers a close-up view and further description of a featured ware.

Weller Pottery—Embossed Decoration 157

Understanding the Market

For the benefit of the ever-growing number of collectors, there are hundreds of books now available on art pottery, ranging from cross-continental surveys to monographs, from hair-splitting explorations of basic production ware to the individual masterworks of such ceramic luminaries as George Ohr and Henry Mercer. During the 30-year revival this market has enjoyed, museum shows have helped to establish the credibility and reveal the beauty of this all-American art form. The collector base has never been larger nor better informed, whether the individuals participate online, bid in person at live auctions, or buy at galleries and antique shows nationwide.

Yet despite this groundswell of interest and academic availability, the element of risk involved with buying art pottery seems greater than it needs to be. Bound up with collecting ceramics are issues relating to condition, restoration, authenticity, and the establishment of honest value. This last, curiously, is the most difficult to determine, even though the necessary information has never been more readily available.

Prior to about 1982, only a handful of art pottery "specialty" auctions had occurred, managed by collectors or dealers of decorative ceramics, each offering several hundred lots in a single sale. These groundbreaking auctions focused mainly on commercial ware, and were presented—if at all—mostly in catalogs without photos. Since that time, however, an average of 5,000-plus pieces of ceramic art ware have crossed the live auction block every year. If we add to this the thousands of objects sold

◀ *$10,000–$12,000*
Aerial Blue bisque beach scene, 13in/33cm, c.1895. Designed by W.P. McDonald. Rookwood Pottery.

▼ *$4,000–$6,000*
Jack-in-the-pulpit painted matte, 9in/22.9cm, c.1905. Designed by Sallie Toohey. Rookwood Pottery.

publicly online, either with fixed prices or through interactive auctions, the total may well exceed 20,000 items annually. This is significant for many reasons, not the least of which is the pricing information it makes available to the general public. Prior to 1980, the only way to know what that piece of Roseville Blue Pinecone or that Grueby floor vase was worth was to sell it and see what price it brought.

Now, between online research and the perusal of auction catalogs, accompanied by postsales results, dealers and collectors alike have at their fingertips price results for more pieces than any individual could handle personally in a lifetime. In the last decade alone, more than 150,000 pieces of art pottery of all types have sold in a verifiable public forum. The more industrious among us can even trace similar (and in many cases, the very same) pieces from one sale to the next, watching how the prices change (usually upward) from year to year. In spite of this, most people remain relatively uninformed about current value. Complicating the matter are such real issues as how various types of damage affect pricing and the uncertainty of many buyers regarding their capacity to determine fine artwork from excellent brushstroking.

Our own approach in this book has been to explain, as clearly as possible, the criteria we use to determine estimates in our auction, private, and online businesses. The market for American art pottery is like any other—at best, a moving target. Your interests are best served if you abandon expectations of understanding all prices and values at all times, and hope instead to achieve an overall knowledge of pottery's worth and salability.

Consider this, for example. Through the 1960s and most of the 1970s, people thought that Rookwood was the only really important American pottery, and that the company's early work was its only significant contribution. Brown-Glazed or Smear-Glazed anything was easy to sell and difficult to overprice, as long as it was perfect.

This changed toward the end of the 1970s as an understanding of Art Nouveau and the Arts and Crafts movement grew among American collectors. Early

▲ *$20,000–$25,000*
Early high-glaze vase with
yellow and blue flowers,
9in/22.9cm, c.1900.
Newcomb College Pottery.

▼ *$20,000–$25,000*
Early high-glaze charger
with crabs, 12in/30.5cm
diameter, c.1905
Newcomb College Pottery.

20th-century innovations such as Rookwood's Iris and Sea Green pieces, with their whiplash curves and vibrant colors, were suddenly among the most prized. And work by the Grueby Pottery—oddly vegetal, green-glazed stuff, with stylized leaves and a quiet intensity—went from an obscure curiosity to a chic collectible.

The Pricing Game

Prices mirrored the mindset. A Rookwood Standard 8in/20.3cm vase, decorated with flowers, sold for about $100 in 1975. By 1980, it was worth about $200. In 2000, the same piece would bring about $450. However, an Iris vase of the same height, with the same decoration, has experienced a very different growth rate. It would have sold for about $75 in 1975 and maybe $150 in 1980. By 1990, it would have soared in value to about $800. And by 2000, it would have crested at about $1,250. The prices for Sea Green, always higher, would have risen from about $250 in 1975 to about $4,000 at this writing.

Grueby's price development was even less predictable, especially considering the tremendous growth in awareness of American Arts and Crafts, of which this pottery was the leading exponent. Prior to 1975, we regularly traded 8in/20.3cm Grueby vases for about $175–$250. By 1980 the same pieces were bringing about $350–$450. Prices for this ware increased slowly through most of the 1980s, with a hefty rise occurring in about 1987, when our 8in/20.3cm vase was worth about $1,000–$1,250. Then prices stagnated again until about 1995, when they suddenly exploded. That vase went from $1,000 to $1,500; a year later, from $1,500 to $2,000; and in the year 2000, the same piece was worth about $3,000.

More than fashion is at work here. While changing tastes play a part in every market, education and sophistication constitute major factors, as well. There are hundreds of books on art pottery available for today's collectors, while in the 1970s, there were perhaps a dozen. Instead of surveys featuring only the major pottery producers, a number of monographs provide in-depth information about many of our smaller, although

▼ *$6,000–$8,000*
Decorated vase with stylized grape vines, 7in/17.8cm, c.1915.
Marblehead Pottery.

▲ *$4,000–$6,000*
Decorated tapering vase, 6in/15.2cm, c.1915.
Marblehead Pottery.

influential, makers. In addition, sweeping retrospectives exist that bind all the information together, providing the insights and perspectives needed to make sound decisions about what is important and why. In the pages of this book, you'll be able to compare the fine points of a given ware and their impact on value. We've tailored the approach to appeal to a wide and discerning audience. This is a very mature market.

Today, we have a sense of how much collectible material is available. One of the nagging questions asked years ago was, "Why should I pay so much for that when I don't know if five more will turn up tomorrow?" We don't hear that as much these days because we've already seen the majority of what has survived years of neglect and abuse. Through my association with "Antiques Roadshow™," on which my wife, Suzanne Perrault and I have appeared as appraisers for the last 5 years, we have seen tens of thousands of objects pass before us. As a kind of social X-ray, this has provided us with tremendous insight into just how many, or how few, of these precious objects remain undiscovered. There aren't many.

Further, we've had the opportunity to see tens of thousands of pieces, in person and in hand, as they crossed the threshold of the auction and private-dealership marketplace. Our auctions alone (David Rago Auctions, in Lambertville, N.J.) sell more than 6,000 pieces of art pottery a year. While we would never assume we had seen or known about every piece of art pottery extant, a great deal can be determined from handling and viewing over 100,000 pieces in the last 30 years.

The Informed Collector

The amount of information available helps to explain the relative sophistication of modern collectors. Twenty-five years ago, it would have been nearly impossible for an aspiring Grueby collector to get a handle on what to acquire and how much to pay for it. Only a few books included Grueby, and just a few museums had a handful of pieces in their collections. Hardly any pieces appeared in dealers' galleries or at antique shows. There were no

▲ *$10,000–$15,000*
Red vase with folded top,
4¹/₂ in / 11.4cm, c.1900.
George Ohr.

▼ *$5,000–$7,500*
Schizophrenic vase, one side
spotted, the other fully
glazed, 5in / 12.7cm, c.1900.
George Ohr.

specialty auctions making efforts to present intelligent offerings of the ware, providing expertise or assurances to buyers. There was no Internet, no backlog of auction catalogs, and very few collectors to talk to.

Exactly the opposite is true now. In addition to all the resources above, collectors at every level can attend conferences across the country that focus on specific periods, including specialty lectures and workshops centered on individual art pottery makers. The Grove Park Inn Conference, held annually in Asheville, N.C. *(see "Where to See and Buy Art Pottery" at the back of this book),* is one such event and a favorite among new collectors because of its scope. You can learn as much about art pottery as quickly as you want, which is the upside of all this interest. The downside is that prices are considerably higher, restoration to damage more difficult than ever to obtain, and the proliferation of fakes more of a problem than at any time in our past. In short, not only is there more information available than ever before, but you have more need to absorb it.

These things we know to be true:

Robineau is rare. Perhaps 50 pieces, most of them boring, have been on the market in the last 30 years.

Roseville is not. More than 50,000 pieces have been on that market in the last 30 years (though some of the hand-decorated ware, and even some production ware, is less than common).

Grueby is usually green, and better for it.

And Artus and Anne Van Briggle created some heat between them.

No single book can teach you even most of what you need to know to determine how good a pot is or how much you should pay for it. This book, more than most, makes clear what has and has not traditionally been valued by pottery collectors, and it augments its illustration-directed format with insights gathered over the years.

Much of the pricing information this book provides on the pottery market reflects the authors' personal biases. I like Grueby more than Wheatley, for example, and I like Weller less than Roseville.

◀ ***$4,000–$6,000***
Reticulated vase with floral design in green, 7in/17.8cm, c.1910.
Tiffany Pottery.

▼ ***$4,000–$6,000***
Buttressed vase with reticulated throat, 14in/35.6cm, c.1910.
Fulper Pottery.

The best you can do is to learn enough about pottery to form your own biases. Once you decide what you like, use this book, along with the wealth of other information available, to help determine what it's worth. Buy auction catalogs and study the pricings. They represent the easiest and surest way not only to determine current values but to understand pricing trends, as well.

The Internet is a pottery collector's new best friend. Check out e-Bay and all the auction sites. Ragoarts.com, our own site, has actual online auction pricing for more than 3,000 objects sold through the virtual auction venue. Further, most major auction sites, including our own, post sales results that are searchable within the site's own system for free.

To understand the market for art pottery, you'll have to become a student of it. If you enjoy the craft, learn to appreciate the beauty of the objects, and integrate the history that fueled the fire of the kilns, you'll acquire the understanding of value as you go along.

Historically, socially, aesthetically, and maybe even financially, few hobbies have as much to offer.

▲ *$4,000–$6,000*
Exterior lantern with inset
leaded glass, 13in/33cm,
c.1910.
Fulper Pottery.

▲ *$50,000–$70,000*
Bottle vase with whiplash
leaves, 18in/45.7cm, c.1908.
Teco Pottery.

Caring for Pottery

Art pottery comes to mean many things to the many people who invest in it and collect it. But common to nearly everyone with an interest in art pottery is a fundamental understanding of its value. It carries monetary value, to be sure. For many, though, it also carries representative value—of an era, an aesthetic, a lineage, or an artist. As such, it invites the special attention and care that will not only make the most of it now but will preserve it for the future.

Most of the issues having to do with the care of pottery fall squarely within the realm of common sense. A single piece can range in cost from under $100 to well into six-figures. Obviously, pottery cracks, crazes, and breaks. Accidents happen with the best of precautions, and collecting breakable art carries that risk. Storing or displaying art pottery in a high-traffic site, however, or without adequate protection from extremes of temperature and air movement, is asking for trouble. (Attics and basements tend not to be good choices for reasons of moisture and temperature.) Using a pot as a planter or server at table puts it at regular risk of damage and may expose it to conditions for which it was never intended. So, too, does outdoor display. Consider what you value about your art pottery and plan its care accordingly. A small amount of forethought can prevent the loss of an irreplaceable treasure.

Less obvious is the issue of bringing out the best in your pottery. Many a fine piece of art pottery has endured years of poor storage and collected more than its share of grit and grime. Unless your art pottery is excessively fragile or already damaged to a high-risk degree, you may be able to restore it to a state that showcases its original beauty. If you have any question about the advisability of cleaning a pot yourself, contact a reputable local antique dealer or conservationist, and ask for advice.

▲ *$3,000–$4,000*
Matte Glazed Vessel, 6in/15.2cm, c.1905.
W.J. Walley.

How to Clean a Pot

Our secret formula for bringing a ceramic piece to its kiln state is to soak it for at least 24 hours in a bucket full of very hot tap water to which is added a cup of sudsing ammonia and at least a half-cup of liquid Spic and Span™. After the soak, remove the pot and soak it for at least another 24 hours in clean, hot tap water. Dry it in a soft towel.

If the piece is iridescent glazed, first clean *only* with Ivory™ liquid soap and very hot water. As the pot is just beginning to dry, rub it very briskly with a large, fluffy towel. You will literally see the nacreous colors emerge, then deepen. Finish with a light buffing with silver-mitted hands. Step back and admire your work.

If the piece is high glazed, just towel it off and buff it to a clear finish.

After Cleaning

If the piece is matte glazed, rub it deeply with finger-applied oil (we prefer double virgin olive oil). Towel off any excess. Do this over a table, cradling the piece in a large towel; oiled pots are slick.

▲ *$8,000–$12,000*
Sicardo Embossed Vase, 20in/5cm, c.1905.
Weller Pottery.

▲ *$30,000–$40,000*
Double-Gourd Handled Vase, 9in/22.9cm, c.1900.
George Ohr.

Displaying Art Pottery

One of the great pleasures that collecting art pottery yields is the opportunity to give the art you collect new life by displaying and enjoying it. Whether you create a gallery effect or incorporate a lovely piece into the general décor of a space, you offer yourself and others the joy of revisiting the past, honoring the artist, and adding visual interest and beauty to your environment. Options of how and where to display pottery are as varied as the pots themselves. The choice ultimately rests with you, the collector, according to the space you have available and what you hope to achieve.

Art pottery often stands up well to solo performances. A single piece can be given the spotlight (literally or in spirit) to offset unwanted distraction from competing elements around it. Carefully chosen color accents, light, or a textured background may be used to draw the eye to the piece. On the other hand, there may be a "natural" spot for a particular piece that requires only a simple placement in an otherwise unadorned setting.

Art pottery works well in multiples, too. A good selection of pieces may include combinations of color, form, style, and treatment that enhance the visual interest

▲ *Selection of Zanesville, Ohio, art pottery. Art ware from a single region can make an intriguing display. This grouping includes Roseville art and production lines and Weller art and production lines.*

▶ *Grouping of Newcomb College pottery. A variety of styles from a single pottery creates a portrait of the producer. In this case, the grouping includes early high-glaze, matte floral, and matte landscapes.*

of each piece. Groupings may include pieces that contrast with or complement one another. You may choose to create a thematic setting of pottery that focuses on ware from a single artist, pottery, year, or geographical region. You may look for a combination that revolves around color, aiming for a variety of forms in tones of a single hue or creating symphony of colors. Some groupings depend on similar subject matter; others on texture, proportion, or glaze. Grouping various pieces together offers the potential of finding new visions of familiar ware. It also carries an aesthetic risk—not all groupings work well—but it's one risk that costs nothing and is easily remedied by changing the arrangement.

In creating a setting for your art pottery, pay attention to lighting. Before you install a special light fixture or fixtures, consider the angle of the light source, which will affect which features of a piece are emphasized. Consider as well the type of light you use; certain types of artificial light distort the colors they illuminate.

A note of caution: displaying pottery will inevitably involve the risk of damage. You can minimize that risk by placing your pieces out of the flow of traffic and away from the attention of curious children and domestic animals. A glass case minimizes the need for handling and cleaning, but may also diminish the visual impact of a piece. For the most part, safety considerations simply call for common sense. In truth, art pottery is breakable and sometimes does not survive display. If you want to avoid the risk altogether, you might have to resort to a vault (and hope that fire and earthquake do not strike). If you collect art pottery because you enjoy it, however, weigh the risks and take a chance. It will repay you in pleasure.

▲ *Collection of Ohr bisque vases, c.1903. Potteries known for handcrafted, one-of-a-kind pieces invite a selection that shows off the originality of each vessel.*

▼ *Three early Van Briggle pieces, c.1903. It's possible to focus on a particular era in a pottery's history to create a grouping. These Van Briggles exhibit diversity of color, form, and subject.*

Assorted Teco Pottery. While green is the most common and popular color, the matte texture of other pieces allows for engaging combinations.

Varied grouping of Rookwood art ware, including Iris, Vellum, and Matte. Pieces should be grouped to complement one another in style, form, and color.

▶ *Brouwer (right) and Redlands (left). Although by two different producers on two different coasts, the harmony of Arts and Crafts pottery allows for compatible displays.*

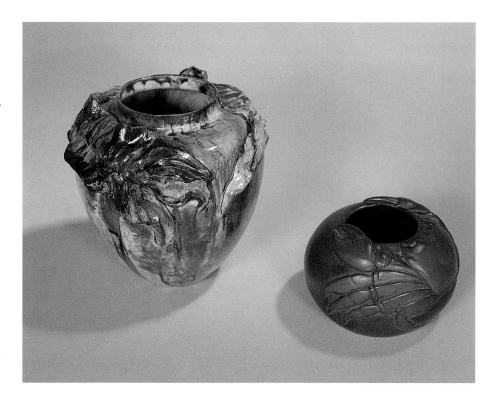

◀ *Rookwood pottery landscapes. Even similar subjects, if different in color and form, can work well together.*

An American Art Potteries Primer

One instructive way to understand art pottery producers and their respective styles is to consider where these companies operated. The Ohio Valley, for example, was home primarily to companies that, at the turn of century, hand-painted designs onto pottery in the Victorian tradition. Famous companies such as Zanesville's Roseville and Weller Potteries, and their Cincinnati rival, Rookwood, treated the ceramic surface as a canvas on which to render their subjects. This separation of design and vessel form was not unique to the Ohio Valley, but distinctly enough a part of its art ware that it has become synonymous with that potting center.

On the other hand, the New England style, espoused by Massachusetts pottery producers such as W.J. Walley,

William Grueby, and the Merrimac Company, was defined by hand-thrown ware with sculpted floral and leaf designs under rich matte glazes in garden hues, green being the color of choice.

And the California potters, although only slightly more diverse in style and technique than their East Coast predecessors, maintained a sensitivity of form and execution difficult to confuse with their peers. Their contribution to American ceramics, a decade later and more mature than the rest, took the best from their eastern forebears to produce something more sublime.

While this divergence of styles has provided fodder for hundreds of books and thousands of articles, it is rarely considered as a factor in evaluating pottery. Is one region's

▲ *Rozane Della Robbia vase with excised floral decoration, 13in/33cm tall, c.1906. Designed by Frederick Rhead. Roseville Pottery, Zanesville, Ohio.*

▶ *Hudson ware, with underglaze slip decoration, 24in/61cm tall, c.1905. Weller Pottery, Zanesville, Ohio.*

▼ *Early bisque-glazed ware in heavy slip-relief, 13in/33cm tall, c.1885. Designed by Albert Valentien. Rookwood Pottery, Cincinnati, Ohio.*

approach to ceramic design more desirable (and more valuable) than another's? If so, how does desirability and value vary within a region from maker to maker, and why? Does damage affect each style of ware to the same degree? What collecting criteria apply to different kinds of ware? Are collectors of Victorian pottery more or less forgiving than those who buy Arts and Crafts ware, and why? And does the market for one type of ware offer more promise in the future than another?

While a great deal of historical and collector-related information is contained in this book, its real distinction is the way in which these facts are employed to provide a basis for determining the value and collectibility of works by specific makers. It is important that you read this section before moving on to the two-page comparisons that follow. Here, you will first explore the major regions of ceramic production and be introduced to some of the makers and their styles and decorative techniques. You will also become acquainted with the prevailing attitudes of other collectors, information that can prove invaluable to your own success and satisfaction.

The Ohio Valley

Large-scale ceramic production in the United States began in Cincinnati, Ohio, about 3 years after Philadelphia's Centennial Exposition in 1876. A few of the city's leading ladies, with more energy than money, although blessed with sufficient amounts of both, returned from visits to the City of Brotherly Love determined to make Cincinnati the city of sisterly china painting.

European women had already laid the groundwork for this new American passion—decorating cool porcelain blanks with mostly amateurish paintings of flowers, birds, and the occasional naked lady. Importing shiploads of the finest china from factories in Limoges, Bavaria, Silesia, Austria, and beyond, these artistically inclined young women met weekly in the clubby confines of china-painting classes over "toast points" and elderberry wine, totally unaware that they were the incubator for American art pottery.

The most ambitious of Cincinnati's lady potters, women like Maria Longworth Nichols, Mary Louise

▲ *Squat, bulbous vase with tooled leaves in yellow matte and modeled trefoils in white, 6in/15.2cm tall, c.1905. Grueby Pottery, Boston, Massachusetts.*

▼ *A selection of undecorated Marblehead ware showing variations of form and glaze. Pieces range from 2 ¹/₂ in/6.4cm to 10in/25.4cm in height. Marblehead Pottery, Marblehead, Massachusetts.*

McLaughlin, and Clara Chipman Newton, refused to relegate their newfound passion to a mere diversion. Had a misunderstanding not caused a rift between Nichols and McLaughlin, we might never have benefited from the resulting enmity and the sublime art ware each produced.

Nichols, not an accomplished artist, soon became better known as a pottery mogul than a china decorator. Her Rookwood Pottery, perhaps the most famous and influential in the United States, defined the Ohio school's style. In 1880, Rookwood was only one of a number of Cincinnati's finest art pottery producers. Other seminal producers (which were, one must add, run by men) included Matt Morgan, Rettig and Valentien, T.J. Wheatley, and the Cincinnati Art Pottery. Yet by 1884, these companies were history, for the most part, and Rookwood was just beginning to hit its stride. Martin Rettig, Albert Valentien, and artists from some of these erstwhile competitors soon began decorating for Rookwood, making the company's victory complete.

This early work served as little more than the kindergarten of decorative ceramics in the United States.

During the first decade of American art pottery, American potters and their companies learned to play well with others, dabbled in the rudiments of the arts and crafts, and engaged in primitive versions of designs seen elsewhere. In fact, most American ceramic designs through the 1880s, at least in Ohio, were flimsy interpretations of somewhat more weighty European interpretations of sublime and meaty Japanese and Chinese art.

Nevertheless, while the quality and ingenuity of ceramic decoration would be vastly changed in a blink, the essence of the Ohio style was firmly established. The ceramic vessel was the canvas, and the potter was going to paint something on it. In the best of circumstances, a harmony would develop between the two. A masterful artist such as Rookwood's Kataro Shirayamadani would distinguish himself by his capacity to engage the surface of the pot, commanding every turn and shoulder with his wraparound designs. Yet objects from this period fell far short of a fusion between the material and the ethereal.

Rookwood survived until 1967 for many reasons. The firm had the money and the vision to hire the best

▲ *China-painted bowl,
8in/20.3cm, c.1900.
During the last quarter of the
19th century, china painting
was a favored pastime of
American women. They decorated blanks—porcelain and
sometimes earthenware—at
china-painting clubs across
the country.*

ceramic artists, chemists, and technicians in the United States. The factory, high on one of the Queen City's hills, provided a state-of-the-art facility, with access to the busy Ohio River for distribution of goods. Rookwood's marketing was equal to the task of establishing national sales outlets in the finest stores of the day. Better-heeled Americans commonly received pottery by Rookwood, in customary pearl-gray boxes, as wedding gifts. And the pottery's celebrated ware found its way into museum collections across the world—an accolade rarely bestowed on American companies in a world predisposed to think even less of American art pottery then than now.

But Rookwood did not just survive—it flourished. Through most of its tenure as the premier U.S. factory, the firm strove to expand its potters' knowledge of the ceramic art. No other American pottery sent its artists to study in Paris at the feet of the masters of the New Art. Rookwood enrolled its finest in this noble pursuit. Few American companies even bothered to compete at the Paris Exposition in 1900, understandably daunted by the Old World competition. Rookwood won a gold medal.

Rookwood's first major innovation was the development of hand-painted designs in slip-relief on darkly shaded ground colors, mostly browns with bursts of yellow, orange, and gold. This was a very Victorian pursuit, the equivalent of a child not wandering far from home. But the quality of this work was world-class and boded well for what was soon to follow.

Rookwood idled during the period between 1885 and about 1895. There was a bisque-glazed ware with painted flowers on lighter, mostly unshaded grounds. Very Oriental in feel, and clearly showing the influence of the English Aesthetic movement, this was only slightly more interesting than the Standard Brown ware (as it became known), although it echoed the former's standards of quality.

This would all change with the introduction of three new lines: Iris, Sea Green, and Aerial Blue in 1894. In retrospect, Rookwood seems to have been eerily prescient in anticipating the Art Nouveau style, many years before that trend penetrated to the American mainstream. These new Rookwood lines incorporated a rainbow of colors

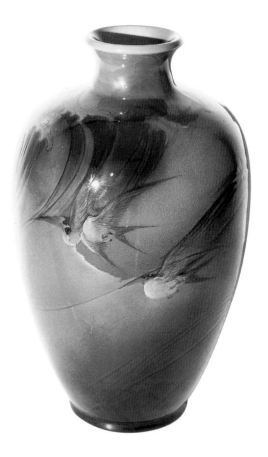

◀ *Vase, with applied seaweed, shells, and a crayfish, among Thomas Wheatley's best, 14in/35.6cm tall, c.1880. Thomas Wheatley opened his first pottery in Cincinnati, Ohio, working in the style made famous in Limoges, France.*
T.J. Wheatley Company, Cincinnati, Ohio.

◀ *Standard Brown vase, 10in/25.4cm, c.1898. Kataro Shirayamadani decorated this vase. While the technique and style were Victorian in derivation, Shirayamadani's treatment of the subject displays the flowing lines of the Art Nouveau period, and is typical of later Standard ware.*
Rookwood Pottery, Cincinnati, Ohio.

and brought with them a host of new subjects and perspectives.

For example, Aerial Blue work not only featured marine scenes, replete with sailboats and cresting waves, but provided a bird's-eye view of the subject matter. Sea Green pieces explored aquatic studies that didn't just mimic the Japanese-influenced designs of the 1880s, but represented a more naturalistic Art Nouveau realism. And the Iris Glaze floral renderings remain among the most vibrant and striking of Rookwood's work. These botanical studies, at their best, combined precise images of rare blossoms with bold assertions of the possibilities this nascent art form held.

Consequently, with so much emphasis on photorealistic representation, standards were set that would influence collectors well into the next century. The success of such a piece depended on how perfectly it captured its subject; the success of its technical aspects included how perfectly it fired (affecting glazing, evenness of surface, crispness of artistry, and so forth). It is hardly surprising

that modern-day collectors place emphasis on the same standards that brought success in the first place.

In fact, no other pottery is rewarded with such high prices for perfection nor is penalized so greatly for the lack thereof. A Rookwood vase with a single chip will lose nearly half its value and at least as many prospective buyers. Crazing, which occurs naturally in the kiln as the glasslike surface expands less than the body it covers, will similarly reduce the value and market for an otherwise flawless piece. Even a hole drilled neatly through the center of the *underside* will restrain the passion needed to pay more than two-thirds of what an otherwise whole example will realize.

Rookwood's importance is expressed most dramatically in the eventual number of its competitors. While its Cincinnati rivals soon fell by the wayside, their offspring flourished on the banks of the Muskingum River in another famous Ohio town 150 miles away, Zanesville. By 1900, with the novelty of art pottery gone and the desire for it on the rise, three major producers there were

▼ *Decorated vase with purple iris blossoms under a clear Iris Glaze, 13in/33cm tall, c.1900. Designed by Albert Valentien. Rookwood Pottery, Cincinnati, Ohio.*

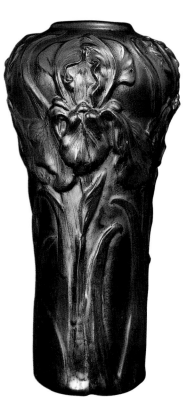

▲ *Vase with embossed iris under rich iridescent glazing, 12in/30.5cm tall, c.1905. Designed by Jacques Sicard. Weller Pottery, Zanesville, Ohio.*

stoking kilns of their own. The Roseville, Weller, and Owens Potteries, united in the edgy competitiveness one might expect from proximity to make this burgeoning city the ceramic capital of the world.

At first, however, Zanesville's potteries capitalized on the fame and style of their Cincinnati progenitor. While Rookwood continued producing Standard Brown ware, Roseville, Weller, and Owens offered Royal Dark, Louwelsa, and Utopian in response. When Rookwood became innovative with colorful Iris ware, the other three countered with Royal Light, Eocean, and Lotus.

Rookwood had a lock on nearly all the best ceramic painters and technicians and maintained a superior product in nearly every way for some time. Rookwood glazes were hard and clear, almost limpid in comparison to others. The artwork was crisper and more realistic, and the pottery was of a consistently higher standard. All the others could do was offer a similar product for less money.

But Zanesville's big three had a learning curve as well, and while they may not have been able to lure

Rookwood's great designers into their folds, they brought fine artists from around the globe to work magic of their own. Jacques Sicard, from the Massier Pottery in Golfe St. Juan in the south of France, made the unlikely voyage to the New World at Samuel Weller's behest. The innovative Englishman Frederick Rhead, a potter with a list of references second to none, also settled for a while in Zanesville, working for both Roseville and Weller.

The influx of new talent signaled the next round of competition in the Buckeye State. There was unexplored territory this new blood could master with alacrity. The potteries may not have been able to produce a better Standard Glaze, but that was old school anyway. Rhead introduced instead a series of new and exciting styles and techniques for Roseville, culminating with his Della Robbia line in 1906. Sicard, leaving France with the secret formula for a sublime iridescent glazing, more than paid his dues with his now-famous Sicardo line for Weller.

Clearly, the great entrepreneurs in Zanesville proved that the American penchant for innovation was alive and

▼ *Unusual Hudson vase with a shoreline scene in heavy slip relief, 13in/33cm tall, c.1905. Weller Pottery, Zanesville, Ohio.*

▲ *Fudji twisted vase with squeezebag enameled decoration on a bisque ground, 10in/25.4cm tall, c.1906. Developed by Gazio Fudji. Roseville Pottery, Zanesville, Ohio.*

▼ *Unusual woodland vase with an enameled decoration of an Art Nouveau woman on a bisque ground, 15in/38.1cm tall, c.1906. Roseville Pottery, Zanesville, Ohio.*

well in the ceramics industry. This would benefit modern ceramics lovers, with masterful works by a score of Ohio companies providing fertile ground for collectors to develop a personal expression of the ceramic arts.

Pricing standards were similarly established by the growing differences of style and expression. An 8in/20.3cm Standard Rookwood vase, for example, will always be worth more than a similar 8in/20.3cm Louwelsa or Utopian example. The ratio between the two has remained about two-and-a-half to one in Rookwood's favor. The gap is even larger when determining values between the lighter colored Iris ware and the Royal Light and Eocean lines—about four to one.

However, because the standards of excellence maintained by Rookwood were never expected of their competition, the impact of damage on the latter has remained less. While a Standard vase might lose half its value with a single rim chip, a Louwelsa vase might decrease in price by only 35%. Just as collectors of

Zanesville pottery are more accepting of human frailty, so too will they more comfortably accept a vase with a flaw.

New England

Little could be more different from the Ohio ideal than the New England interpretation of the ceramic art. In fact, the only common ground these two major American centers shared was the use of clay to build their wares. But while the Ohio firms seemed to tolerate the lowly material, the Arts and Crafts companies all but celebrated it.

The Arts and Crafts movement was, at its heart, a revisiting of simple and honest values. We are all, they reasoned, nothing more than the dust of the ground. Only through the hands of our Creator, or whatever one chose to believe in, can we rise and take form to flourish and prosper in our own right. Since Biblical times, the image of God crafting our bodies from the dirt of the earth has

◀ *A selection of matte glazed Rookwood ware showing the progression in the pottery's work from Victorian to Art Nouveau to Arts and Crafts—all within a 25-year period.*
Left: *carved matte;* **middle:** *painted matte;* **right:** *carved matte. Tallest: 10in/25.4cm, c.1905.*
Rookwood Pottery, Cincinnati, Ohio.

◀ *A selection of later porcelain pieces, illustrating Rookwood's commitment to developing new styles in response to worldwide trends. Tallest: 9in/22.9cm, c.1920. Rookwood Pottery, Cincinnati, Ohio.*

captured the nature of our being. And so, it was contended, did the potter, by raising plastic earth on his or her wheel and turning the meanest into the most revered.

The premier potter, George Ohr, of Biloxi, Miss., was very clear about this in stating that his objective as a potter was to get out of the way and "let God pot through" him. This was the manifesto of a democratic pursuit—the Arts and Crafts goal—that allowed the humblest of expressions alongside the majestic creations of our most important and innovative potters. Massachusetts visionaries such as William Grueby and W.J. Walley heeded the call and produced, with each vase, arguments in support of the fine arts.

Grueby, schooled in the Victorian aesthetic by the Low Art Tile Works of Chelsea, Mass., soon abandoned the relatively ancient production of art tile in favor of a more revolutionary and compelling style. Eschewing clear high glazes for opaque mattes of his own concoction, he championed the move toward "organic naturalism," in which his pottery became the decorative and philosophical cornerstone of the Arts and Crafts movement in the U.S.

While the pottery of the Ohio Valley was almost exclusively slip cast, or molded, the Arts and Crafts masters recognized the importance of wheel-throwing their ware. Their goal was to create handmade pieces that captured and defined moments in time. Much as the Japanese tea ceremony explored the cultural imperative of "one meeting, one chance," the turning of a pot also represented the confluence of time and space into the creation of a single work of art.

This was only one way the Arts and Crafts movement attempted to redefine the applied arts, to be sure, but it was an essential part of that philosophy. The Victorian approach was more sympathetic to maintaining consistent quality and appeal. Grueby's approach was to explore the subtlety of perfecting something, again and again.

Grueby covered his hollowware with glazes that replicated the textures and colors of vegetables. The best of these were smooth and rich, with matte crystalline veining and/or thick and complex mottling. A glossy Rookwood finish was beautiful to behold and just as uninviting to

◀ *Plastic sketch,*
7 x 12in/17.8 x 30.5cm,
c.1881.
J. & J.G. Low Art Tiles,
Chelsea, Massachusetts.

▶ *Selection of* **cuenca**
decorated tiles, 6in/15.2cm
square, c.1902–1910.
Grueby Pottery, Boston,
Massachussetts.

touch because of the smudges fingertips impart. A Grueby vase needed to be held in order to fully understand it, and it was intended to bring one back to earth in a very literal way.

For the same reason, the Arts and Crafts potters didn't paint their designs on the surfaces of their pots, but chose to sculpt or apply the decorations into the bodies of the vessels, thus integrating form and design. The very nature of this technique stylized the decoration so that instead of a perfect, photographic interpretation of a leaf or a blossom, one was left with a less obvious impression of an organic entity. Instead of admiring a piece's beauty from across the room, one would have to pick up the pot, turn it, and get in touch with it before it would yield its meaning—philosophically heavy stuff that did not play well to the masses then or now. And because Grueby was a one-trick pony (however great the trick), his business was as fleeting as the desire for the Arts and Crafts. Rookwood and the Ohio potteries changed with the shifting sands of style—the major reason for their

longevity. Grueby, true to his philosophy, only survived as a potter until about 1907 and as a tile manufacturer for another decade.

As you might imagine, the criteria for pricing Grueby are as different from Rookwood as his ware was. While a chip is a chip, its impact on value is relatively nominal on Grueby's progeny. That same small chip on that same 8in/20.3cm form might reduce the cost, these days, by a mere 10–20%. Some even joke that minor damage on a Grueby pot might *increase* its value. While Rookwood was in pursuit of a perfection of appearance, Grueby was more interested in the perfection of soul.

Such a perspective was aided by the fact that Grueby pieces are truly one-of-a-kind expressions of a single idea. An argument can be made that even though a Rookwood or Weller pot is molded, the artistry that adorns it is never exactly the same on any two pieces, no matter how similar. Yet ware such as Grueby (and that of his nearby contemporaries at the Walley and Merrimac studios) takes uniqueness to a new height. Put 20 examples of the "same"

▲ *Ware typical of Marblehead's earlier designs, with darker colors and incised geometric designs. Tallest: 10in/25.4cm, c.1908. Marblehead Pottery, Marblehead, Massachusetts.*

▶ *Delicate-handled pitcher in a frothy pink flambé, 7in/17.8cm, c.1900. George Ohr, Biloxi, Mississippi.*

piece of Grueby side by side—for he did repeat forms—and the differences, however subtle, will undeniably distinguish each vessel from its fellow. This is extremely important when valuing a piece, because if you happen to like the expression of a wholly handcrafted pot, you need to understand that you will not find another like it.

South

Only two major producers of art pottery flourished in the South, both integral expressions of Arts and Crafts in the United States. And both are as different from Grueby as Grueby is from Rookwood. Although they share bodies of clay and were wheel-thrown, all comparisons stop there.

George Ohr, from Biloxi, Mississippi, is a fly in anyone's ointment. He is probably one of America's most important artists, and luckily for American pottery, he happened to choose clay as his medium. Ohr worked at

his Biloxi pottery from 1884 to around 1907, during which time he created about 10,000 "unique" pieces. A true art potter, he built his studio with his own hands, stoked his kilns by himself, mixed his own glazes, and even dug his own clay. He was said to have walked through town, pushing wheelbarrows full of raw material from the Tchoutacabouffa River.

Ohr felt that since God didn't create any two souls alike, he shouldn't make any two pots alike. Excepting some of his press-molded fair trinkets, he honored this self-imposed restriction. He found it nearly impossible to market his art ware and was said to have resisted selling his "mud babies" on the rare occasions someone actually showed interest in them.

While this left him short on cash, he was perhaps the only artist of the period whose efforts remained almost entirely in his possession. This 10,000-piece legacy was sold almost in its entirety to a New Jersey barber/antique dealer in 1970, who drove it north in a tractor-trailer one snowy winter weekend.

▼ *Selection of bisque fired pieces, c.1905.*
George Ohr, Biloxi, Mississippi.

▶ *Ohr vase, 9in/22.9cm tall, c.1900.*
George Ohr, Biloxi, Mississippi.

Ohr began with a more traditionally based ware, derivative in style if not execution. Similar to the English and Pennsylvania pottery of the day, Ohr produced relatively thin-walled vessels showing both his deftness at the wheel and his capacity to mimic what had been done for centuries by others. During the 1890s, he slowly came into his own; pots from the earlier part of that decade occasionally provided glimpses of what was to come.

His odd studio was burned to the ground by the great Biloxi fire in 1893, wiping out not only the structure and his home but much of his treasured work. A disaster in many ways, the event proved to be a defining moment in his career. Liberated from his past, Ohr worked after the fire with an increasingly freer hand. Simple twists became magnificent and dramatic design elements. His range of glaze colors exploded into improbable flambeaus of reds, greens, blues, purple, and gunmetal gray.

His last work, from about 1901 until he closed his shop, was mostly bereft of glazing. He declared that since

God put no color in souls, he'd put none on his pots. This bisque-fired work, long thought to be "incomplete," was eventually recognized as the most mature expression of his craft. In the true Arts and Crafts style, he allowed the material to become the decoration, the raw clays fired in his crude kilns finished as naturally as the heat would occasion. He sometimes mixed, or scroddled, different clays, creating other opportunities to add color without the use of glaze. And these later pieces bore the wildest manipulations of his adept hands.

Transcending the vessel form, his hollowware was neither pot nor pitcher but some of each. He never intended that the pieces be used, in the final analysis. They were simply meant to command space in a new way. His work was outstanding. Sadly, at the height of his creative genius, Ohr up and quit his work in art pottery.

Ohr's work is less affected by damage than perhaps any other American maker because, by its nature, nearly every piece is unique. This means, in simple terms, that if you

▶ *Unusual circular charger with incised landscape under a glossy finish, 8in/20.3cm diameter, c.1900. Newcomb College Pottery, New Orleans, Louisiana.*

like what a piece is saying, you have to either buy it in whatever condition it's in or not acquire it at all. You won't find another copy of it elsewhere.

Ohr's earliest work, good as it is, attracts the least interest, because it speaks little of where he was headed, focusing instead on where he came from. Accordingly, damage can reduce the this ware's value by as much as 50%.

On the other hand, his masterpieces are worth the same in nearly any condition, and most of them have some kind of flaw or another. Pieces with multiple chips have sold for $50,000, and others with damage, were they to reach market, would bring in excess of $100,000.

His bisque pieces, by virtue of their lack of glazing, don't scale the same heights of price that the aggressively covered ones do. The best of them, with few exceptions, top out at about $10,000, with most under $3,000. They are probably less hurt by minor damage than are glazed examples, since a chip off a bisque piece leaves matching bisque behind.

In nearby New Orleans, La., thrived yet another of the U.S.'s most important potteries. As different from Ohr as Ohr was from Grueby (and as Grueby was from Rookwood), the ware produced by young women in training at the Sophie Newcomb Memorial College—simply known as Newcomb College, and now an adjunct of Tulane University—followed in the tradition of Rookwood's Ms. Nichols.

Newcomb College's mission was made more acute by the decimation of the male population during the Civil War. Women, it was thought, needed to get out of their Victorian parlors and into the work force. While toying with the applied arts—such as those taught at Newcomb—might seem an innocent start, ventures such as this helped clear the path toward women's rights.

Newcomb's earliest work, dating to about 1893, was interesting at best, although the learning curve was less steep than at other potteries. By 1900, the Newcomb women were producing some of the sweetest art pottery

▲ *Selection of glossy and matte pieces showing Newcomb College's artistic range. Tallest: 11in/28cm. Newcomb College Pottery, New Orleans, Louisiana.*

in the United States. Soft, feminine, and covered with local flowers, bayou scenes, and, rarely, birds and animals, Newcomb's ware quickly became an American favorite.

Its ware had changed considerably by about 1910, with designs fully carved into the vessel's surface, and now covered with rich matte finishes. The quality of craftsmanship was still quite high, although the number of student decorators decreased greatly, as did the diversity of the designs employed.

California

Some of the finest art pottery in the United States was produced in California, arriving about a decade later than that of the rest of the country after its slow migration westward. The Golden State was blessed with raw material—fabled vistas, exotic (by Eastern standards) flowers and animals, and some of the richest clay deposits in the country.

Most of the important California potteries were headed by masters who had earlier plied their craft in the East. Frederick Rhead for example, established his reputation at a number of potteries in Ohio (Roseville, Weller), and farther east in New York at the Jervis Pottery. He left for California to oversee two of the state's premier studios, Arequipa in Fairfax, and Rhead Santa Barbara, in the town of that name.

Albert and Anna Valentien, of Rookwood fame, were seduced by the state's natural beauty while summering there, painting wildflowers for the Scripp's commission in 1907. And Alexander Robertson, of the Chelsea, Mass., Chelsea Keramic Art Works, teamed with his West Coast love interest, Linna Irelan, to form the Roblin Pottery in San Francisco in 1898.

The first major potteries to open shop in California were Robertson's Roblin and the Valentien Art Pottery, in San Diego in 1910. Unlike their East Coast forebears, most of the California producers opened small studios with labor-intensive, handmade ceramics. These two were no

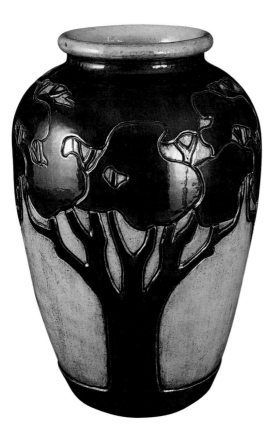

▼ *Fine, large excised vase with a stylized landscape, 13in/40.6cm tall, c.1900. Newcomb College Pottery, New Orleans, Louisiana.*

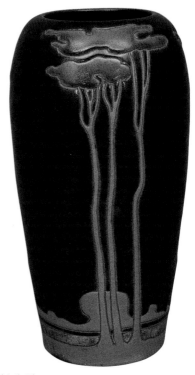

▲ *Exceptional inlaid landscape vase showing the influence California had on Frederick Rhead's later work, 12in/30.5cm tall. From the collection of James Carter. Rhead Pottery, Santa Barbara, California.*

exception. Their wares would set the pace for what was to follow; art pottery that was minimally decorated, finely crafted, and hard to find. Roblin's work was mostly destroyed in the great San Francisco earthquake of 1906, making its best work even scarcer.

Albert Valentien was one of Rookwood's most famous decorators. Painting on a clay body was no simple task for many reasons, not the least of which was the effect the heat of the kiln would have on the finished product. Not only would colors change once fired, but the entire decorative surface would move and shift based on the amount of heat and a pot's placement in the kiln. Albert understood the process well, producing some of the crispest and most lifelike painted pottery decoration in the United States, if not the world.

Anna's brushwork, by comparison, was restrained and relatively unimaginative until she, along with her husband, studied at the feet of Rodin in Paris, at Rookwood's behest. There the Valentiens were encouraged to sculpt, or model, decoration into the bodies of their ware. Their last

work at Rookwood clearly displays this new direction, and these material-sensitive techniques were to be the cornerstone of their pursuits in San Diego.

Much of what they fired in California did not replicate the figural work of their later Rookwood period. However, most of it showed the sculpted floral work that their Cincinnati colleague, Artus Van Briggle, was making famous at his factory in Colorado Springs, Colo. (He also studied under Rodin.)

Additionally, the Valentiens explored the use of matte finishes and matte glaze painting, bringing their experiments to a most beautiful and technically superior climax. Not much of their San Diego work remains, probably again because of limited production, limited market, and the occasional tremors that periodically increase the value of pottery by reducing supply. But those that survived offer solid proof that the Valentiens reached their creative peak while in California.

Alexander Robertson's work in San Francisco at Roblin, and later "on the fly" in other California locations,

▲ *Selection of decorated Arequipa vases. Tallest: 6in/15.2cm, c.1911. Arequipa Pottery, Fairfax, California.*

was as understated as American pottery from the period ever got. It is impossible to completely understand this ware, since much was destroyed in the San Francisco earthquake. But we can determine from what remains that, like his contemporaries, he was in search of simplifying his craft.

In a collection of 500 pieces of this elusive ware, soon after it left the care of the family estate in the 1970s, perhaps 400 were unglazed, exhibiting the marvelous clays for which California was known. Those that bore a finish were usually covered with one of a selection of perhaps five different glazes. Rarely did a piece have more than one.

Moreover, perhaps 475 of these pieces were under 5in/12.7cm tall, and about two dozen were decorated with slip-relief, modeling, or excising. Mostly, design elements were restricted to the finely tooled beading Robertson and Irelan imparted by hand, or the natural qualities of the clay they chose. It is worth noting that two of the pillars of Arts and Crafts methodology are

allowing the raw material to become decoration and emphasizing handiwork.

Robertson's work continued after Roblin, and there was some modification of his style. One piece, marked "on the" followed by a hand-incised fly, was covered with a richly sponged glazing of soft orange, yellow, and black. Also from the Robertson estate were a few pieces from his Halcyon Pottery, in Halcyon, Calif. (1910–13) and his Alberhill studio in Alberhill, California (1912–14). Such pieces were occasionally larger (with some 10in/25.4cm or more in height), and/or more decorative. One example was covered in an unusual, brick-red high gloss, decorated with a mint green salamander crawling up its side. Whatever its manifestation, Robertson's work on the West Coast was considerably more restrained than his output in Massachusetts.

Rhead's progress as an artist in the United States can be traced as he moved from one company to another. His earliest work in this country was characterized by a heavy decorative style. His famous Della Robbia ware, for

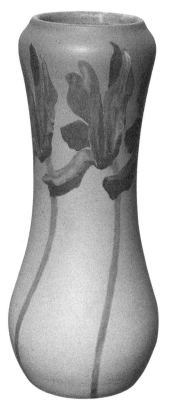

▶ *Exceptional matte painted vase, 12in/30.5cm tall, c.1910. Designed by Albert Valentien. Valentien Pottery, San Diego, California.*

▲ *Fine squeezebag-decorated vase with a stylized floral design, 5in/12.7cm tall, c.1911. Designed by Frederick Rhead. Arequipa Pottery, Fairfax, California.*

example, displayed excised, enameled, and incised work from top to bottom. The Jap Birdimal line he introduced at the Weller Pottery was similarly covered with his trademark squeezebag, or slip-trail decoration, displaying marvelously overdone scenes of kimono-clad women.

By the time Rhead settled in California, however, he was able to describe more with less. Rather than overwhelm the vessel surface with fully articulated designs, he reduced his expression to simple gestures. Where at Roseville he would display a leaf, attempting to "fool the eye" with veining, crisp edges, and enamel colors, his work at Fairfax would trace the merest outline in slip trail, leaving the background glaze to provide color. These remain some of the finest, most subtle, and most intelligently decorated pots produced prior to World War I.

As stated earlier, much of this work is handmade and fairly unique. Further, output was small, and relatively little of it remains. While the market for California pottery is among the smallest in the country, collector interest is strong and prices are high. Prices for all pieces of Arequipa

pottery bearing squeezebag decoration begin at $2,500–$3,500, and can cost in excess of $10,000. While an average piece might lose 35% of its value because of a visible rim chip, a rare one could bring exactly as much as a perfect example.

Roblin pieces are unique but fairly repetitious, so damage does have considerable impact on value. However, as with Arequipa, rarer works with flaws show little loss in value.

There are more California potters of note, just as there are important makers from across the country who have not been included in this short history. In the pages that follow, prime examples of these potteries work will go some distance toward filling in the story begun here. The more exposure you have to individual examples of a wide variety of potteries, the stronger your instincts will become and the better informed your aesthetic choices. Allow the works of these great potteries to enter your life and delight your soul, and you will join the ranks of many who have collected this art form with great satisfaction.

▲ *Selection of Grand Feu ware, typical in quality and style of this elusive work. Tallest: 7in/17.8cm, c.1915. Grand Feu Pottery, Los Angeles, California.*

American Art
Pottery

American Encaustic Tiling Company

The American Encaustic Tiling Company, also known as AETCO or AE, in all of its incarnations was the largest producer of decorated tiles in the United States before the building boom of the 1950s, and perhaps even since. One of the earliest potteries to capitalize on the demand for art tiles in the 1870s, it explored many different styles and techniques and remains a cornerstone of American tile production.

This ware also represents a foundation for most tile collectors, whether novice or advanced. As the company's prolific output spanned many decades, its tiles appear frequently on the tables of antique dealers, making a basic collection easy to build. AE used many approaches, creating something for everyone's taste: encaustic (inlaid floor tiles of unglazed colored clays); molded; stove tiles (mostly circular, molded); architectural faience; and fountain spouts; transfer-printed with designs by such established illustrators as Englishman Walter Crane; photographic (carved in intaglio); Arts and Crafts (matte glazed); Art Deco; hand-painted; *cuerda seca*; based on nursery rhymes; and more. However, the firm was and still is best known for its Victorian molded tiles and panels.

Most in demand are the large panels, which were usually designed for fireplace surrounds or hearths. While AE horizontal or vertical three- to five-tile friezes are quite collectible, a premium must be paid for the same image on a single tile panel, for obvious reasons. Also very much in demand are the best of the company's Arts and Crafts, or 1920s, faience tiles—thicker pieces covered in matte micro-crystalline glazes; similarly, rare tiles with fine designs of any period are desirable: Victorian, Arts and Crafts, or Art Deco. Examples of AE tiles can be seen in their town of Zanesville, Ohio, at the Muskingham County Court House and the Zanesville Art Center.

Practically every tile found today was once permanently affixed to a wall or floor, removal of which may have incurred damage more severe than that attributable to normal wear and tear. The mere fact that some remain in good condition is enough to make these examples valuable, especially in the case of a larger panel.

The Victorian aesthetic has not been as popular during the past decade as other decorative-arts periods, but some of AE's 19th-century designs—even those considered sentimental and derivative—are still lovely by any standard.

Seasonal Panel by Herman Mueller, *c.*1890

This is a large panel in good condition, although the crazing detracts from its value.

The light pink glaze color is unusual.

Note the attention to detail in the clothing, flowers, and feet, and the artistic rendering of the putti.

This was designed and signed by chief modeler Herman Mueller.

Size:12in/30.5cm tall
Value: $1,500–$2,000

Woman in Period Costume, *c.*1890

This is a good-size panel, more desirable than one made up from three separate tiles, but not as large, rare, or impressive as the example opposite.

The woman in period costume is not nearly as charming a topic as the Neoclassical goddess and putti.

The emerald-green glaze is strong Victorian color.

The panel is not signed.

Size: 18in/45.7cm tall
Value: $350–$450

• *While AE pressed a vast number of tiles over a long period, it is best remembered for those made before 1900, many of which remain.*
• *Dust-pressed tiles embossed with a patterns in relief were produced in the 1880s and 1890s.*
• *Many Elizabethan profile portraits appeared, as well as Colonial lads, banjo-playing frogs, and reclining Roman soldiers, all with Victorian monochromatic glossy glazes.*
• *Amber/caramel, olive-green, and burgundy colors predominated; red, blue, and yellow glazes are much more rare and desirable.*
• *In tune with the Arts and Crafts movement in the U.S., AE produced limited numbers of matte-glazed tiles by the* cuerda seca *process. Hard to find, these command a premium, as do the few fine panels done in an Arts and Crafts–Art Deco blend, using matte and glossy glazes.*

Key Facts

One of the earliest and longest-lived tile-producers in the United States, American Encaustic was founded in Zanesville, Ohio, in 1874 to produce encaustic floor tiles in the style of the medieval English tiles that pave major cathedrals and government buildings.

Within a few years, AE had extended its product range. As showrooms opened in New York, the demand for AE tiles grew rapidly. The Zanesville plant was insufficient, but the firm's plans to relocate to New Jersey were fiercely—and sucessfully—resisted by the citizens of Zanesville. This resulted in a new local tile factory —one of the world's largest—that

helped to establish Zanesville as a major U.S. pottery center, home to Roseville, Weller, and J.B. Owens, among others.

Before World War I, an additional plant was purchased in New Jersey; shortly after the war, the first of two California plants opened in Vernon. AE had to sell its Zanesville facilities during the Great Depression to the Franklin Pottery of Lansdale, Penn., which reorganized and later merged with AE and the Olean Tile Company, forming the American Olean Tile Company. American Olean merged in the mid-1990s with Dal-Tile, keeping a vestige of AE alive to this day.

Arequipa

It took Frederick Rhead nearly a decade of travel in the United States before he landed in Fairfax, Calif., in 1911. Once he established his small studio there, heading the Arequipa Pottery, it all seemed to come together for him. Much can be learned by tracing not only Rhead's travels in this country, but by evaluating his artistic progress along the way.

In California, it seems, seduced by the lush vegetation, striking sunsets, and the loud quietude of the desert, Rhead hit his stride, understanding how to express most what he rendered least. Earlier Geisha girl designs disappeared, and simple leaves and berries remained. The working of an entire vessel surface was out, and a mere gesture of slip trail at the rim was definitely in.

It would be years before most modern collectors figured out this sublime and subtle aesthetic. In most eyes, after all, more is usually more. But the meditative beauty of the California ceramics school kept hammering away at the public consciousness until finally, more than 25 years

into the revival of interest in the movement, collectors have caught up with Rhead's work.

It is important to distinguish between the master's work at Arequipa, and that of the students who potted there during and after Rhead's tenure. Much of what remains of Arequipa's production is lumpy and unexciting. Even some of Rhead's work is repetitive and uninspired.

He successfully experimented with black Chinese glazes, but collectors most admire vases with slip-trail, or squeezebag, decoration. More colors are better, and collectors prefer an enamel-like gloss to the interior negative space of Rhead's designs. While little of his work actually "covers" the surface of Arequipa's vessels, some of the best incorporates the background glazing into the overall design.

This work is extremely rare, and minor damage on a well-decorated piece will reduce value by no more than 25%. It is likely that serious collectors of this work will accept fine examples in nearly any condition.

Multicolor Squeezebag Vase, c.1912

The vase's border design falls against a typical matte ground.

The work exhibits an unusual multicolor squeezebag decoration.

The interior color (not shown) is "enameled."

This is a typical cabinet-size vase.

The potter gave this vase a thrown ovoid form.

The ware's mark (not shown) establishes this from the Rhead period, prior to 1913.

Size: 3in/7.6cm
Value: $5,000–$7,000

Large Gourd Vessel, *c.*1912

The "enameled" interior design color adds to the vessel's value.

Like the example opposite, it displays an unusual multicolor squeezebag decoration.

This piece is larger than most decorated Arequipa.

The body design is exceptionally full.

This hand-thrown vessel is in a typical gourd form.

Size: 7in/17.8cm
Value: $13,000–$17,000

• *Most Arequipa ware is undecorated, adorned only with a single glaze color, usually with a matte finish.*
• *Rhead and his wife, Agnes, were at Arequipa for only a few years. The operation survived their departure by several more, but only work done during their tenure is considered highly valuable.*
• *All company marks during the Rhead period are either hand-painted in blue on a white ground or incised into the raw clay.*
• *Nearly all Arequipa vessels are small, with those 8in/20.3cm or taller considered large.*
• *Damage has little impact on value, especially on exceptional pieces.*
• *While later pieces of Arequipa may have decoration that is either carved or embossed in the mold, the Rheads' work almost always focused on squeezebag applied.*

Key Facts

In 1911, Dr. Philip K. Brown, director of the Arequipa sanatorium for tuberculosis in Fairfax, Calif., hired the well-known English ceramist Frederick H. Rhead and his wife, Agnes. He charged them with establishing a pottery that would train the young women patients to decorate, and hopefully throw, vessels.

From a family of ceramists, Rhead had already been employed at several potteries: Vance/Avon, in Tiltonville, Ohio; Weller, in Zanesville, Ohio; Roseville, in Roseville and Zanesville, Ohio; Jervis, Oyster Bay, N.Y.; and University City, St. Louis, Mo. Rhead's talents lay in design and decoration.

In an attempt to separate the pottery from the sanatorium, the Arequipa Pottery was incorporated in 1913. The Rheads left during the summer, and Frederick joined the Steiger Pottery of San Francisco, then founded the Rhead Pottery in nearby

Santa Barbara. In 1917, he moved back to Zanesville to became artistic director for the American Encaustic Tiling Company. After a decade, he left to join the Homer Laughlin China Company, and is credited for designing the wildly popular Fiesta Ware line.

Meanwhile, Albert Solon, the son of the English ceramist Louis Marc Solon of Sevres and Minton's, arrived at Arequipa. The pottery's output greatly expanded, feeding a demand on the East Coast. Solon worked on several new glazes, including some Persian finishes in different colors.

The pottery won gold and bronze medals at the Pan-Pacific Exposition of 1915, the same year the corporation was dissolved. Solon left in 1916 and was replaced by Englishman Frederick H. Wilde. He introduced hand-pressed Hispano-Moorish tiles to the curriculum, which soon became the popular mainstay of the business.

Batchelder Tiles

Eastern artisans such as Gustav Stickley, Elbert Hubbard, William Grueby, and countless others had drawn inspiration from Englishmen John Ruskin and William Morris, whose 19th-century socialist philosophy celebrated the work and spirit of the craftsman. By the time the movement reached California, around 1910, the movement had shifted in emphasis, and its aesthetic had matured. The lines had grown more sophisticated and softer. Tiles made in California in the 20th century reflected the beauty of the open countryside and the sunny climate, with brighter colors, idealized landscapes, Mayan-inspired designs, and stylized flowers.

The faience tiles of Ernest Batchelder exemplify the pottery style of the California Arts and Crafts movement.

Done in the style used at the Moravian Pottery and Tile Works—mainly molded, with impressed designs, they feature local flora, Western landscapes, or Mayan motifs.

Practically anything from the Arts and Crafts era has been steadily increasing in popularity and value for the last several decades. Batchelder tiles have a strong, hand-pressed look and a quiet, uncomplicated aesthetic that is warm and illustrative. Mounted in broad, dark-stained oak frames, they are available in many sizes, from 1in/2.5cm-square tiles to large panels measuring in feet/meters. Despite the relatively large number of examples in circulation, prices have climbed steadily. While a tile measuring 1in/2.5cm can sell for about $50, a picture panel will sell for as much as several thousand dollars.

St. George Slaying the Dragon I, c.1915

Because this remarkable example of a single large panel was never actually mounted, it remains as pristine as on the day it was made.

This finely modeled piece, with single-color engobe, looks almost like stone.

The illustrative design is stylized and well rendered.

Notice the chain-link border that adds texture by framing the main picture.

Size: 14in/35.6cm tall
Value: $2,000–$2,500

St. George Slaying the Dragon II, c.1920

The bright colors of this panel give it more of an Art Deco note than the relatively subdued Arts and Crafts version. The later date will also lower its price.

The fact that this work was made in six pieces instead of a single panel reduces its value. It will need grout between the tiles, which will add to the Arts and Crafts effect but also break up the design's continuity.

Because there are more edges, the chances of damage are much greater. In fact, several small chips appear along the sides of most of these tiles.

Size: 13½in/34.3cm tall
Value: $1,500–$2,000

• A single large tile panel is a fairly rare occurence since so many have suffered damage during removal.
• Most Batchelder tiles were dipped in engobe, or colored slip, and their surfaces were then wiped clean, leaving engobe in the crevices.
• Less common tiles were covered in a soft semi-matte glaze. Most rare are those done in polychrome.
• Production included multi-tile friezes, moldings, fireplace surrounds, and some stunning (and rare) large hearth panels, often depicting lyrical fairy tales and nursery rhymes.
• Art Deco/Hispano-Moresque cuenca tiles, attractive with overall patterns of brightly colored flowers, typified a portion of Batchelder's output, as well.

Key Facts

Ernest Batchelder taught crafts at the Minneapolis Handicraft Guild and at the Throop Polytechnic Institute in Pasadena, Calif. In 1909, he started making tiles in a small workshop next to his Pasadena home, where he also taught and produced small quantities of other crafts.

In 1912, he formed a partnership with Frederick Brown in order to expand, and the company name changed to Batchelder and Brown. When, in 1920, Lucien H. Wilson became a partner, the name changed again to Batchelder-Wilson and the business moved to Los Angeles. These changes in identity were not reflected on the tile markings, which appeared only as Batchelder-Pasadena (early and rare) or Batchelder-Los Angeles (most

often found today). In 1932, the business closed, and Batchelder and Wilson sold their inventory to Pomona Tile Manufacturing and Bauer Pottery. Ernest Batchelder returned to making pottery in 1936.

The best of Batchelder is not determined by a particular line or artist, but is rather a function of size. More work and better design generally went into the larger tiles, which are also rarer and therefore more desirable. The larger works display more descriptive pictorial schemes, showing such scenes as pioneer caravans crossing the desert of California, or medieval landscapes with castles, stone walls, and figures. The large pieces also display more color and detail than the smaller, more stylized tiles.

Brouwer Pottery

Of the most important U.S. potters, two stand out as artists who marched to the beat of their own drummers. One was George Ohr. The other was Theophilus Brouwer, from Long Island, N.Y.

The pottery Brouwer created does not appeal to everyone. But like many offshoots of the Arts and Crafts movement, his work can be an acquired taste. What may appear as confusion to the unfamiliar viewer becomes beauty to the more informed. More and more, collectors have come to understand Brouwer's peculiar aesthetic.

His primary contribution to art pottery was his invention and development of open-kiln glazing. In this process, a potter gripped the vessel with a pair of long metal tongs and inserted the piece directly into a blazing kiln. As the flames licked over the vase's surface, they literally "painted" brilliant nacreous colors of orange, red, and yellow onto the surface in a pattern that mimicked the shape of the fire—a method called "fire painting."

Many Brouwer pieces look similar and, in recent years, have become harder to sell. The best pieces are distinguished by rich, vibrant color over most of the surface. His work was relatively small in scale, with a 12in/30.5cm example considered large. Occasionally, Brouwer added applied decoration such as leaves and flowering plants to the surfaces of his pieces. Rarer still were vessels to which he added textures or colors different from those already on the surface.

Damage hardly depreciates very good pieces. Because the biscuit was not fired to great hardness, pieces tended to chip at the edges. As with any pottery, the more important the piece, the less value reduction occurs due to damage.

New collectors should take heart in knowing that Brouwer ware is still obscure enough and distribution wide enough that pieces new to the market regularly turn up across the United States.

Tall Lamp Base, c. 1910

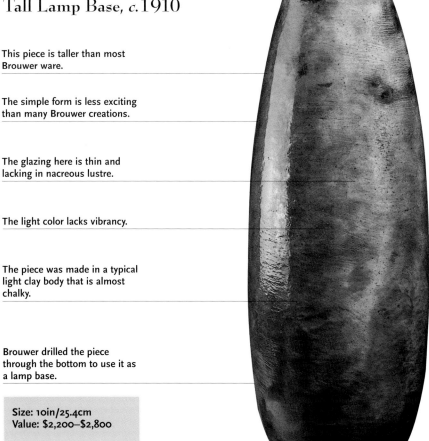

This piece is taller than most Brouwer ware.

The simple form is less exciting than many Brouwer creations.

The glazing here is thin and lacking in nacreous lustre.

The light color lacks vibrancy.

The piece was made in a typical light clay body that is almost chalky.

Brouwer drilled the piece through the bottom to use it as a lamp base.

Size: 10in/25.4cm
Value: $2,200–$2,800

Baluster Lamp Base, *c.*1910

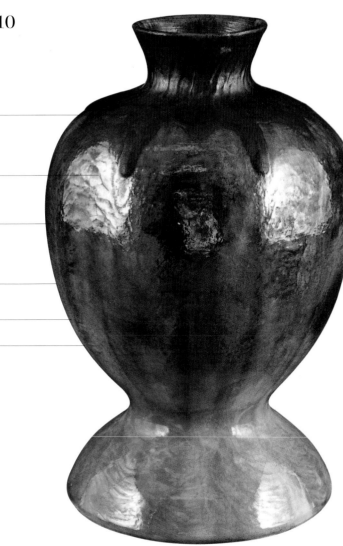

The textured flambé dripping from the top of the piece is unusual and adds considerable value.

The rare and beautiful two-color flambé enhances both appearance and value.

The body is slightly heavier than usual for Brouwer's work.

Like the example opposite, Brouwer intended this as a lamp base.

The expressive baluster form adds value to the piece.

This is a large piece by Brouwer.

Size: 12in/30.5cm
Value: $10,200–$13,200

- *Brouwer pottery is undervalued today due, in part, to its uneven quality and lack of variety, which has caused it to be misunderstood and underappreciated.*
- *His ware was potted of light clay and not highly fired, causing more than average damage on surviving pieces.*
- *Despite running a one-man operation, Brouwer's output produced hundreds of pieces that have survived him.*
- *Damage, if minor, is more acceptable on Brouwer's work than on that of most of his contemporaries.*
- *Most Brouwer ware can be purchased for under $1,500, though his best pieces can sell for more than $10,000.*
- *While a variety of Brouwer's decorative techniques have been noted over the last few decades, his most popular work is still his fire-painted ware.*

Key Facts

Theophilus Anthony Brouwer, Jr., a talented artist with scant knowledge of ceramics, opened a small pottery on Middle Lane in East Hampton, N.Y., in 1894. He had been experimenting with unusual glazes for about a year at the time. Like his colleague George Ohr in Mississippi, Brouwer made his own molds and did his own casting, throwing, glazing, and selling. A tall whale jawbone marked the entrance to his property, an image he repeated in his pottery mark to frame an "M."

Brouwer sold the pottery in 1902. Largely on his own, he erected a new plant in the neighboring town of Westhampton in 1903, apparently known as the Brouwer Pottery.

Brouwer branched out in around 1911, concentrating new efforts on sculpture. Most notably, he carved figures out of concrete and then fired or treated them to transform them into a material similar to stone. Several of these graced local school lawns.

In 1925, Brouwer incorporated as the Ceramic Flame Company and patented his "Fire Painted Brouwer Pottery." It is unclear whether he was still producing ceramics by then.

California Faience Tiles

Chauncey Thomas and William Bragdon founded the Tile Shop in Berkeley, Calif., in 1916 to produce vases, tiles, and architectural faience, which they labeled "California Faience." Not until 1924 did they officially rename the pottery to reflect their label.

The California Faience style combined elements of the Arts and Crafts movement with Art Deco and Hispano-Moresque styles. This blend manifested itself in symmetrical abstract designs executed in matte and glossy *cuenca*; and for pottery as classically shaped cast vessels covered in either fine matte or glossy glaze. Both reflected the partners' high aesthetic and quality standards.

The majority of tiles produced at California Faience found today were trivets of circular or square shape with rounded corners, hand-pressed with red faience clay into finely carved molds, and sometimes designed by local artists. California Faience rejected the popular notion of irregularity or "distress" in manufacture, producing tiles in small quantities that appeared perfect enough to pass for machine-pressed work. The firm also cast vessels of simple, elegant shapes. These recall Marblehead pottery and are similarly covered in monochromatic glazes. In the market, they often bring $400 and up.

Today, the West Coast market for California Faience ware is very strong, especially for the earliest and rarest items. By and large, the trivets range in value from $400 to $550. More unusual items will be valued in the thousands. Their appeal is found in the high quality of handmade art tiles; the strong California aesthetic; and the mix of Arts and Crafts, Art Deco, and Hispano-Moresque styles. Tiles were produced and have survived in quantities large enough to create a broad collector's market.

Circular Trivet in Hammered Copper Mount, *c.*1920s

The rare copper mount by master craftsman Dirk Van Erp of San Francisco adds significant value to this piece.

The trivet features an often-imitated design of a basket with fruit and flowers.

The stylized Art Deco design is executed in polychrome *cuenca*.

Matte and glossy glazes lend the piece a transitional Arts and Crafts touch.

Size: 5in/12.7cm diameter
Value: $1,500–$2,000

Circular Trivet with Stylized Flowers, c.1920s

This beautifully designed pattern of stylized flowers is also executed in *cuenca*.

The matte and glossy glazes are in three colors.

Slight wear around the rim from use will decrease value.

The design is better than that of the example opposite, but the piece is worth significantly less because it has fewer colors and lacks the copper mount.

Size: 5in/12.7cm diameter
Value: $400–$500

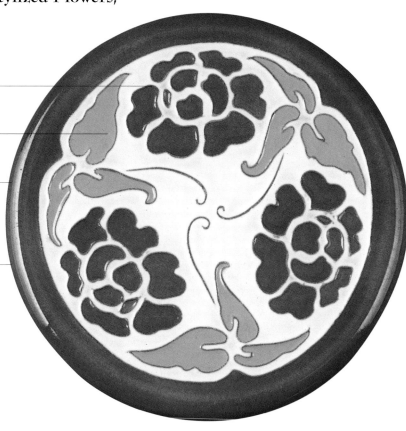

- *California Faience products were often decorated in* **cuenca** *with gargoyles, desert landscapes, and baskets of fruit in California hues of blue, red, yellow, and green. Artists used black as accent on these pieces and mixed glossy and matte glazes.*
- *Designs were influenced by the late Arts and Crafts period and early Art Deco, as well as the faience and Hispano-Moresque decorations popular in California during the 1920s.*
- *Some molded tiles were produced with patterns in high relief (worth $500–$1,000), as were* **cuenca**-*decorated tiles (valued at $200–$650), moldings, friezes, and three-dimensional architectural faience (valued in the thousands of dollars).*
- *During the 1920s, the firm produced a line of high-fire vessels for the West Coast Porcelain Manufacturers of Millbrae. Glazes were adapted (some might say upgraded) to high-fire capacity, with fine micro-crystalline and mottled effects ($400–$1,500).*

Key Facts

The Tile Shop founders Chauncey Rapelje Thomas and William Victor Bragdon met while studying under Charles Fergus Binns at the New York School of Clayworking and Ceramics in Alfred, N.Y. Both later taught ceramics at the University of Chicago and at the California School of Arts & Crafts. Between teaching assignments, Bragdon assisted the great Taxile Doat at the University City Pottery (1912–14), where he learned a great deal about high-fire grés.

Along with producing tiles, the Tile Shop manufactured fine pottery in the tradition of Binns and Doat. All of its wares were stamped "California Faience," which officially became the pottery's name in 1924. The following year, Bragdon and Thomas developed a line of commercial art ware for the West Coast Porcelain Manufacturers, in

Millbrae, Calif. The line bore high-fired micro-crystalline glazes in a style similar to that of Danish pottery and was marked "California Porcelain." Architect Julia Morgan commissioned California Faience to produce tiles according to her design for La Cuesta Encantada, William Randolph Hearst's castle in San Simeon, California, a contract the firm fulfilled in 1927. These tiles can be viewed on-site at the mansion today.

The Great Depression brought production to a halt, although California Faience made some tiles for the 1932 Chicago World's Fair. Bragdon bought out Thomas in the late 1930s. He then turned to teaching, making molds, selling clay, and firing local potters' works. He continued in this line until his death in 1959, when the pottery closed.

Chelsea Keramic Art Works

One of the earliest and finest of American art potteries was the Chelsea Keramic Art Works, in Chelsea, Mass. Steeped in the English tradition of high-end, Victorian decorated ware, the Robertson family developed and sustained an amazing array of work at this pottery, incorporating several existing styles and developing new ones.

Their innovations included a red clay of Classical influence; cold-painted ware; high-fired, semivolcanic, and orange-peel textured glazes; hand-carved work; and "hammered" Oriental forms. These creations are all the more interesting because they drew little from American precedent, relying instead on the craft of ancient potters and the Robertsons' ingenuity to develop the work.

The Robertson family enjoyed success in nearly every undertaking, and one of the sons, Hugh, is credited with rediscovering the long-lost process for turning a simple celadon green into a scintillating oxblood red. Among Chelsea's most enduring work are its hand-carved designs, modeled into the plastic surface of hollowware vessels. Occasionally, the Chelsea factory produced floral designs that were achieved by pressing flower and plant forms into the still-wet clay.

Collectors are reconsidering these early masterworks, along with many of the best products of the Victorian era in American ceramics—including pieces the Low Tile Works, Faience Manufacturing Company, and the Bennett Pottery. Of these, Chelsea Keramic pieces remain underpriced, with current values still considerably less than those of decades ago. Such bargains are not likely to continue for long because quality and scarcity eventually bring the prices up.

Good early examples are clearly decorated with floral designs and covered with the crisp, fine, transparent glazing that endures as one of this company's hallmarks. Some are artist-signed, usually by one of the Robertsons' workers rather than a family member. A transparent glaze envelops the best pieces—usually heavily modeled with scenes of animals and/or people and often designed by Hugh Robertson himself.

Condition is critically important in a market so bereft of buyers. Yet, especially for the best work, minor damage in the form of a base chip or rim nick simply creates a greater buying opportunity. As of this writing, modeled Chelsea Keramic ware in good to excellent condition is considered a "best buy."

Pilgrim Flask, *c.*1880

This example is a molded form of typical size for Chelsea Keramic ware.

The simple floral decoration was both pressed and incised into the surface.

A factory-hired artist executed the flask and signed the surface of the piece (not shown).

Notice the crisp, transparent glazing.

While decoration was usually heavy on the front side of a flask, the rear was either minimally decorated or bare.

Size: 8in/20.3cm
Value: $900–$1,100

Covered Pillow Vase, *c.*1880

A covered piece such as this is extremely rare and is usually damaged.

Like the example opposite, this vase is a molded form, but it is slightly larger than most Chelsea Keramic ware.

The figural subject matter in the heavily modeled decoration makes the piece more desirable.

The vase is signed by the artist Hugh Robertson (not shown).

Notice the fine, transparent glazing.

Size: 7 x 10in/
17.8 x 25.4cm
Value: $1,700–$2,300

• *Chelsea employed a small cadre of decorators, but the best work was usually executed by a family member, and most often by Hugh C. Robertson. These pieces have always been the most valuable.*

• *Production standards of Chelsea's hand-modeled work were among the highest in the country. Such pieces seldom exhibit firing flaws, typical elsewhere, such as kiln cracks or surface blemishes.*

• *Hand-modeled pieces were meticulously marked with one of the pottery's block stamp designations.*

• *Artist signatures were usually incised into vases' surfaces, though they were occasionally incised into the bottoms of the pots.*

• *Pilgrim flasks—footed, flat-walled, ovoid vessels—were a Victorian standard and are among Chelsea Keramic's most common forms.*

Key Facts

Alexander Robertson established the A.W. Robertson Pottery to produce brown ware in Chelsea, Mass., in 1865. Joined in 1868 by his brother, Hugh Cornwall, he replaced brown ware with flowerpots and changed the pottery's name to A.W. & H.C. Robertson.

The Robertsons' father, James—a fourth-generation potter from Scotland—and their brother, George W. of the East Boston Pottery, joined the company in 1872. The company became James Robertson & Sons, while the factory became the Chelsea Keramic Art Works. By 1875, they had refined production once again, this time for creating copies of Greek urns and bronzes. Among the potters they employed during the period were John Low, later of the Low Art Tile Works, and the artist George W. Fenety.

In 1876, the Robertsons developed a white clay body that allowed the full richness of clear tinted glazes. These transparent finishes would be produced in light and spinach greens, soft and dark browns, and light and deep blues.

In 1879, George left to join the Low Art Tile Works. In 1880, James died. Alexander left for California in 1884 and there established the Roblin Art Pottery.

Meanwhile, in 1888, after four years of experimenting on a Chinese oxblood glaze, Hugh Robertson fired two stoneware vases that he considered perfect and named the "Twin Stars of Chelsea." The glaze—"Robertson's blood" or "Sang de Chelsea"—is the brilliant red color of fresh blood, with golden lustre and some color mottling.

Chelsea Keramic Art Works ran out of money and had to close in 1889. Two years later, backed by wealthy collectors of Asian ceramics, a new pottery called Chelsea Pottery U.S. opened. When it moved to Dedham in 1896, it became the Dedham Pottery.

Claycraft Potteries Company

The Claycraft Potteries Company is part of a continuum of faience tile makers who came from Scotland and England on their way to California by way of the East Coast. Once in the West, the craftsmen founded or joined such tileries as California Art Tile, Muresque, Calco, Acme, and Claycraft and produced tiles that reflected the West Coast vernacular or looked back to the English countryside.

Ernest Batchelder probably led this trend of "California Faience" tile making when, in 1910, he began to follow the medieval style of Henry Mercer. Claycraft's Fred Robertson and Gus Larson picked up on the idea about a decade later, adapting the style to something lighter, sweeter, and more colorful than the abstract patterns of the Arts and Crafts movement. Soon after, other companies opened their doors and imitated the new Southern California standard.

The most collectible of these wares have thick, slightly uneven bodies and feature quaint landscapes or cozy, English, thatched-roof cottages in a storybook style.

Molded with soft outlines and using appealing colors with matte or vellum finish, Claycraft tiles appeared in a variety of sizes, from a charming 3in/7.6cm square series (valued at $200–$300) to large horizontal hearth panels (worth over $1,000).

Among the most desirable is a series that features National Park sites on rectangles measuring 12 x 8in/ 30.5 x 20.3cm. While not high art by any means, these tiles, worth between $1,500 and $2,000, offer a quaint depictions and contribute warmth to their surroundings—especially when framed in broad Arts and Crafts moldings.

Claycraft, like other companies of its kind, needed to please many different clienteles. In the interest of reaching markets beyond that for the muted landscape tiles, they produced a line of Art Deco panels with hard-edged, raised-line designs of birds and flowers, as well as Hispano-Moresque patterns in bright, glossy glazes. These bring considerably less than the matte-glazed tiles of comparable size, as long as the market for the Arts and Crafts aesthetic prevails.

English Garden Tile, c.1920s

The crosshatched sky on this hand-pressed, molded piece, is typical Claycraft.

The molded form is traditional Arts and Crafts style.

This is a typical California faience subject. Behind a stone wall stands a cozy English thatched cottage with wooden door and wisteria blossoms.

The soft, muted vellum glazes are very desirable and rarer than the dead-matte engobes.

The self-framing feature is typical of Claycraft.

Size: 6in/15.2cm square
Value: $650–$750

Spanish Doorway Tile, *c.*1920s

Hand-pressed in a mold, this tile has a sky similar to that of the example opposite.

With its soft vellum finish and dead-matte glaze—which create a "drier" feel and a brighter tone—this tile is less rare and therefore more desirable than the example opposite.

The small size of this tile is charming.

It bears the usual Claycraft self-framing.

This typically California Faience scene features an old mission wall with a glimpse at a desert landscape. Notice the fallen jug.

Size: 4in/10.2cm square
Value: $200–$300

- *Claycraft designs used an illustrative style, raised, recessed, and usually covered in dead-matte polychrome glazes.*
- *Most were self-framed and often made in unusual sizes, including large panels of rectangular or square tiles.*
- *Art Deco inserts made of cuenca, or raised-line designs, are typical of tiles in the California or Southern vernacular, showing birds and flowers in bright, glossy colors.*
- *Claycraft's many lines of machine-made tiles include "Faience" tiles created with controlled irregularities that added visual interest; single-fired "Claycraft" tiles distressed for an antiqued look; and "Handmade" tiles with uneven surfaces and rounded edges.*
- *Architectural faience included grates, brackets, fountains, pilasters, and fireplace surrounds. Garden pottery and lamp bases were also produced.*

Key Facts

The Claycraft Potteries Company was incorporated in 1921 with the goal of producing tiles, garden pottery, and chemical stoneware. The company employed Gus Larson and Fred Robertson, both formerly with the Los Angeles Pressed Brick Company.

Fred Robertson had pottery in his veins. His uncle Hugh had been a principal at the Chelsea Keramic Art Works and the Dedham Pottery. His father, Alexander, also formerly at Chelsea Keramic, moved to California and founded the Roblin Pottery, where Fred worked from 1903 to 1906. Fred then went to L.A. Pressed Brick, working with new clay mixtures and winning medals for his lustred and crystalline glazes. He stayed until joining Gus Larson at Claycraft in 1921. There he acted as general superintendent, focusing on the development of bodies and glazes.

Fred's son George worked at Claycraft as assistant superintendent and designer starting in 1925.

An unusual category of Claycraft tiles depicted scenes from American National Parks. All these tiles are self-framed, molded faience tiles impressed with the landscapes and covered in dead-matte polychromatic glazes. They stand apart as among the few large single-tile landscape panels and the only ones depicting (and naming) actual sites. The price of these has risen rapidly in the past 5 years.

Claycraft produced a large variety of plain bread-and-butter tiles, as well as decorated architectural faience, fountains, garden pottery, and lamp bases. When George Robertson left Claycraft to found the Robertson Pottery in 1934, Fred joined him. Claycraft closed in 1939.

Clifton Pottery

The originator of the Clifton Pottery, William Long, had already founded three potteries and worked at two others by the time he came to Clifton, N.J., in 1905 to develop a new line of pottery. He brought with him at least one other ceramic luminary, decorator Albert Haubrich, whose slip-relief work ranks among the best in the United States.

What Long also delivered to the Garden State was the diversity of design and experimentation he had learned elsewhere. This resulted in a rather impressive range of art pottery, especially considering that the company was relatively small and lasted only a few years.

Collectors of Clifton ware seem most to favor the prized "Crystal Patina" finish, a micro-crystalline glaze (sometimes static and occasionally flowing) in tones of soft green, silvery brown, and cream. This glaze sparkles with life, providing an attractive finish for the quirky selection of forms chosen by Long. It is best utilized on forms with raised decoration, including flowers, plant life, and, occasionally, heavily embossed fish. Such work is also found with silver deposit decoration in the florid Art Nouveau style, though the addition of such decoration seems at odds with the relatively sedate glazing.

Other lines include a robin's-egg blue glaze, a Native-American style ware called "Indian," and a slip-decorated line called, for whatever reason, "Tirrube." This last usually featured relief flowers in matte glazes on a brick red bisque ground.

The general quality of Clifton's production was consistently high, although the robin's-egg blue work often lacked visual interest. On the other hand, the Crystal Patina line was usually at least good, with exceptional examples appearing that used flambés of orange-brown and dripping green.

Because Clifton Crystal Patina pottery is molded, damage significantly decreases a piece's value. A single chip can reduce worth by as much as 50%. Nearly all pieces have been clearly marked with Clifton's CAP cipher. Teapots, a common form, are occasionally found with a single, die-stamped, shape number instead of a mark.

Robin's-Egg Blue Vase, *c.*1906

The glaze is robin's-egg blue, the least interesting of Clifton's lines, and certainly of less interest than that of the example opposite.

This molded body has a typically quirky two-handled form.

Clifton molded this line from hard, white Jersey clay.

This example is smaller than most pieces.

Size: 3in/7.6cm
Value: $130–$170

Crystal Patina Vase, *c.*1906

The molded body of this piece has a quirky form that is typical of and unique to this company.

The glaze is augmented by introduction of brown streaking.

The vase displays an excellent Crystal Patina Glaze, Clifton's most successful glazed line.

Like the example opposite, this vase was molded from hard, white Jersey clay.

The piece is typical in size for Clifton.

Size: 8in/20.3cm
Value: $350–$450

• *Clifton ware was molded.*
• *Nearly all examples bear at least the "CAP" cipher, which has a hand-incised look to it, but is probably die-stamped. The mark is often paired with a date.*
• *In descending order of collector interest, Clifton art lines included Crystal Patina, Tirrube, Indian, and robin's-egg blue.*
• *Clifton worked on a fairly small scale, with Crystal Patina pieces usually measuring under 8in/20.3cm in height.*
• *The best of the Crystal Patina line were decorated with embossed flowers and, on rare occasions, fish.*
• *The Crystal Patina Glaze is usually found with a sparkling micro-crystalline finish of beige, soft yellow, and light brown. Better examples incorporate drippy flambés of darker brown, green, and, at best, a shimmering gold.*

Key Facts

A famous contemporary studio potter once suggested that one of the reasons the New Jersey area was so rich in ceramic history had to do with its mother lode of natural clay deposits left behind by glaciers. This seems a reasonable explanation for so many important companies working in so small a state. In fact, even Tiffany Pottery, which produced its ware in New York, went to the trouble of hauling its clay from New Jersey.

Perhaps that is what first enticed William Long to choose New Jersey when he left Denver, Colo., in 1905. There he founded the Clifton Pottery, one of the more popular of the New Jersey pottery companies, which boasts a history and production that speak tomes about both the ceramics industry in the Northeast and the migration of talent from one company to another.

William Long began his pottery career with the formation of the Lonhuda Pottery Company in 1892. In partnership with W.H. Hunter and Alfred Day, he produced underglaze pieces with slip decoration on a brown background. The pottery was exhibited at the Chicago World's Fair in 1893, where it caught the eye of Samuel A. Weller. Weller convinced Long to join him in Zanesville, Ohio, where they opened a new firm in 1895 known as the Lonhuda Faience Company. When a fire destroyed most of the plant, Long left to work for J.B. Owens Company in the same town.

Four years later, Long shifted again, this time to Denver, Colo., where he created the Denver China and Pottery Company. It was from this venture that he finally moved to New Jersey and yet another firm. Although the company operated only until 1908, it produced a diversified line of pottery that continues to attract collectors up to the present. Long would return to Zanesville to work for Weller again, then Roseville Pottery, and finally American Encaustic Tiling Company, before his death in 1918.

Dedham Pottery

The tale of the Dedham Pottery is one that resulted in work that attracts two totally different types of collectors. Originated by Hugh C. Robertson, one of the masters of American art pottery, Dedham ware began as handmade art ware of the highest order.

There is an immediacy to Robertson's earliest work at Dedham. The pots themselves seemed hurriedly thrown, offered as thick and often clumsy canvases for his masterful glazes. Much of his early work is unexceptional, with single compositions of brown and apple green bubbling, pooling, and otherwise flowing over the surfaces.

It was when Robertson mixed these glazes, especially his more colorful tones of red, blue, and enameled green, that his mastery became most evident. Better variations have a volcanic quality, where knuckles of gathered glaze stretch and pull across the vases. Occasionally, pieces appeared that expressed his painter's side, using flowers and landscapes covered with the clear crackled finish he is said to have discovered by accident.

Dedham crackleware is collected for different reasons. Its homespun appeal matches perfectly with early and traditional American interiors, where a dearth of dinnerware alternatives makes it a natural choice. Because it comes in scores of patterns, the more popular of which include cats, chicks, porpoises, turkeys, and various flower forms, it provides sufficient fodder for collectors. And any serious art pottery aficionado needs at least a token representative for a well-rounded portfolio.

Robertson's art ware, owing to its unique, handcrafted nature, maintains most of its value in spite of minor damage. In fact, it is difficult to find an example without some kiln-inflicted flaw. Robertson's rough throwing hands produced thick, lumpy vessels that pulled apart when fired and/or induced thin underglaze "hairlines" on any rim. As with any art pottery, the less damaging the damage, the better the example.

Dedham crackleware is a different animal when damaged. Because this is ware produced with a pattern, mostly oft repeated, minor flaws greatly compromise prices on all but the best of examples. In the eye of the Dedham collector, even the quality of the crackling is examined carefully to determine value.

Early Experimental Vase, c. 1900

This is a typical, easy-to-throw form.

Note the heavy, white, almost porcelainlike, clay body.

Vibrant glaze combinations, especially this red and blue, are among the most desirable.

Hand-thrown and signed by Robertson himself, this piece is smaller than most Robertson examples.

Size: 5in/12.7cm
Value: $1,000–$2,000

Dedham Crackleware, *c.1920*

This line was produced almost exclusively in molded, utilitarian forms, such as bowls and plates.

While this form is less common than the usual flatware, it bears the most common of decorations, the rabbit.

The work is always covered with a clear, crackled glaze.

Nearly 99.9% of all crackleware has blue painted design (probably through a stencil) on a white clay ground.

Size: 7in/17.8cm diameter
Value: $300–$500

• *Robertson's earliest work at the Dedham Pottery, with rich, thick glazing, is his most desirable and valuable.*
• *Early examples usually have thick, white clay bodies, bearing in-fire crevasses and underglaze lines. Robertson achieved more with glazing than potting.*
• *Robertson's rarest, most beautiful, and valuable creations are his red pots; he made many relatively dull brown and green ones.*
• *Most early Dedham pieces are under 10in/25.4cm tall, and the majority of these are about 8in/20.3cm tall.*
• *Robertson's hand-incised "HCR" cipher graces about 80% of what survives.*
• *In spite of the commercial nature of Dedham crackleware, it is extremely fine in quality and charming in its appeal.*
• *Rabbits proliferate in life, and so too on Robertson's dinnerware. The rarer the pattern (clovers, cats, owls, chicks), the greater the value of the piece.*

Key Facts

Hugh C. Robertson, formerly of the Chelsea Keramic Art Works, probably wasn't much of a husband or a father. He was said to sleep next to his kilns so he could better supervise the heat generated therein. But his glaze experiments became his second family, and with these, he raised many beautiful children. For one, he was credited with rediscovering the long-lost Chinese formula for Sang de Boeuf, or blood of ox, the best of which he claimed resembled the color of "fresh arterial blood."

Robertson founded Dedham Pottery in 1895. The pottery ran two kilns: one was used for the crackle-glazed dishes that brought the pottery notice; another was used for pieces that were fired ten to twelve times to produce "accidental glazes," or "volcanic ware."

The last two decades of the 19th century were a difficult time for studio potters, and Robertson's quirky aesthetic was as difficult to sell as it was to create. He eventually flirted with bankruptcy and was forced to

turn to businessmen to keep his venture afloat. Ironically, his crackle glaze became a life raft, and his ceramic production made an about-face from esoteric art ware to very fine, if somewhat cutesy, tableware.

The crackle-glazed dinner plates and serving pieces, adorned mostly with cobalt blue bunnies on a cream ground, have preserved Robertson's legacy. However, he probably would not find such a prospect appealing, considering his predilection for extreme glazing. But the financial success of the bunny ware enabled him to continue his kiln experiments for several decades, into the 20th century. Even for ceramic masters such as he, artistic life demanded compromise.

When Hugh died in 1908, after suffering for years from lead poisoning, his son, William A. Robertson succeeded him as head of the pottery. The firm flourished until William's death in 1929, but continued to operate under the leadership of William's son, J. Milton Robertson, until its closing in 1943.

Franklin Tile Company

The fact that Malcolm and Roy Schweiker, Franklin's founders, had worked at the Empire Floor and Wall Tile Company (formerly J.B. Owens) is apparent in several of Franklin's designs. Indeed, many of its tile patterns are derivative of such other tile makers as Rookwood, California Faience, Claycraft, and Mosaic, bridging the Arts and Crafts and Art Deco styles. Nonetheless, Franklin produced high-quality faience tiles in a variety of styles and techniques that enjoy a good following among collectors today.

During the late 1920s, Franklin introduced a series of silhouetted figures and landscapes evoking a wonderfully mysterious, Japanese feeling. The silhouettes were glazed in glossy black, raised against excised backgrounds with chiseled texture, and usually glazed in a dusky, glossy golden-yellow.

One of the best of these designs featured a young man swinging a lantern that emanated a warm, colorful glow ("Lantern Boy," 9in/22.9cm square, worth $450–$550). Other tiles showed a Spanish knight brandishing a spear on a rearing horse ("Lancer," 9in/22.9cm square, worth $350–$450); a flying horse ("Pegasus," 9in/22.9cm square, bringing $400–$500); a Northern wildlife scene ("Moose and Geese," 13 x 9in/33.0 x 22.9cm, valued at $850–$1,000) and a similar piece depicting a Native American ("Indian," $500–$750).

The rarity of these, combined with their strong graphic designs and warm tones, makes them highly collectible and relatively expensive for their sizes and vintages. (Watch for scratches and abrasions on the glossy black surface.) Franklin made other tiles with silhouetted animals, using different colors, mostly 6in/15.2cm square; these are also quite good, but not as striking or desirable.

The Schweiker brothers stated in one of their catalogues that "Our Hand-Made Tiles are not so lost in ultra-artistic thought as to be of passing mode in shape or design, or impractical in the long wearing qualities so rightfully expected of Tiles." Their decorated "Hand-Made Tiles," however, were probably not their biggest sellers. When purchasing the American Encaustic Tiling Company in 1935, Malcolm apparently decried AE's lack of plain, or "bread-and-butter," tiles.

"Spider Web" Tile, c.1932

This tile is unusually large for a Franklin Tiles piece.

The *cuenca* technique resulted in fine, even lines.

Cherry blossoms and spiders, both popular Japanese patterns during the Aesthetic and Arts and Crafts eras, are rendered here in an Art Deco style.

The glazes are matte polychrome (this glaze also came in black).

A frame of original Arts and Crafts molding would add value to the tile and elevate it to art.

Size: 9in/22.9cm square
Value: $600–$800

"Moose and Geese" Tile, c.1925–1930

This is an exceptional vertical tile panel with silhouetted moose and flying geese in black against a golden sky.

The tile is self-framed, a desirable feature.

The glossy and matte glazes are a late 1920s–early 1930s technique.

This very rare tile is among the best made at Franklin.

Size: 13 x 9in/
33.0 x 22.9cm
Value: $1,000–$1,500

• *Franklin's handmade tiles include four types of pavers, all pressed of plastic clay: Polychrome Flints, Colonial Reds, Faience, and Faience Mosaics.*
• *Some of the decorated tiles worked in conjunction with the floor tiles, using a glazed, impressed design against an unglazed surface. These included a full line of ecclesiastical patterns.*
• *The designs on other tiles were either incised, outlined, or done in cloisonné or* cuenca *(with raised lines of clay used to separate the different glaze colors).*
• *Special tiles ranged from Arts and Crafts to Art Deco, covering a very broad range of topics popular at that time, from airplanes to zodiac signs.*
• *One of the firm's series featured excised, silhouetted figures and animals, in glossy black against a textured ground of contrasting color.*
• *Franklin also offered a full line of such bread-and-butter items as dust-pressed wall tiles, bathroom accessories, lighting fixtures, and heaters.*

Key Facts

Malcolm Schweiker and his brother Roy founded the Franklin Pottery in Lansdale, Penn., in 1923. By 1925, they were producing machine-made, hand-decorated tiles, and changed the name to Franklin Tile Company. The firm manufactured plain and art tile in several different techniques. It also created single-fire, craze-proof, self-spacing, and cushion-edge tiles.

The Schweikers' motto, "You May Delay But Time Will Not" (borrowed from Benjamin Franklin), provides insight into the their philosophy. They combined good business practices with charming design to create a company that stood out among its contemporaries as a survivor.

Over the years, Franklin acquired or merged with several other tile companies, including Domex, Olean Tile Co., National Gypsum, Murray Tile Co., and the venerable American Encaustic (AE), in 1935. Due to Malcolm's business savvy, Franklin was one of the only tile companies to survive the Great Depression. Its name changed to American Encaustic in the late 1930s, and then to American Olean Tile Co. It was purchased by Dal-Tile International in 1993.

Fulper Pottery

Work by the Fulper Pottery resides in the nether world between labor-intensive, hand-decorated pottery and mass-produced commercial ware. The company's work was almost exclusively slip cast, or molded, but a trained decorator individually glazed each piece. The glazes were rich and varied, with a broad selection of mattes, crystallines, and bright colors that were used individually or together, creating handsome glazing effects.

The best Fulper ware, and the most collectible today, is the Vasekraft line, produced prior to World War I. The forms were influenced by the German potter John Martin Stangl, reflecting a medieval European aesthetic. The glazing during this period was equally interesting, and the quality was consistently high. Pieces made during this time were usually marked with a vertical, rectangular ink stamp. Nowhere else is this curious European-American hybrid to be found. While too intense for some collectors, it is increasingly recognized for its quirky appeal—at once ancient and modern.

Fulper's second period, from about World War I to about 1925, saw the phasing out of its early Germanic ware and the introduction of softer, Oriental forms. Fulper's quality began to slip at this time, as the artists used fewer glazes and mixed them with less creativity. Pieces from this middle period are usually marked with a vertical designation that appears to be hand-incised but is probably die-stamped. One must be particularly discerning when buying middle-period pieces. The ratio of fine to below-average examples is about even, with less interesting shape selection and inconsistent glaze quality.

The pottery's last period, after about 1925 until it closed a decade later, took an Art Deco bent. Pieces made during this time are lighter in weight and often poorly glazed, showing less stringent production standards. These pieces usually bear a horizontal, die-stamped designation.

Be extremely careful in buying pieces from this final period. Some pieces show bold Art Deco design and occasionally sport the last of Fulper's interesting glazes. For the most part, however, the work that was produced during this era of Fulper's production is one step removed from flower-shop ware, the company mark often being the only element of merit.

Germanic Brown-Glazed Vase, *c.* 1910

The buttresses on this vase reinforce the vertical form and its overall visual strength.

This vase displays an angular Germanic form, Fulper's most important design contribution.

Notice the rich matte brown glazing.

The heavy clay body is of high-fired New Jersey clay.

The design is molded, not hand-modeled.

The piece bears a rectangular, ink-stamp mark on its base (not shown).

Size: 8½in/21.6cm
Value: $2,500–$3,500

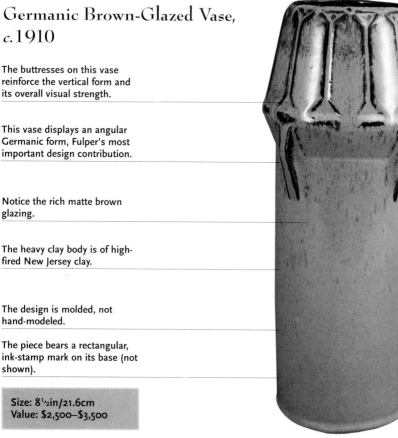

Art Deco Vase, *c.*1930

This piece shows the influence of the Art Deco movement.

The glazing is thinner on this piece than on the one opposite.

The lighter clay body of the vase denotes a later piece.

As with much molded decoration, this is more charming than interesting.

This piece bears a horizontal mark (not shown).

Size: 13in/33cm
Value: $600–$900

• *Fulper pottery is usually marked. Markings give some indication of date, but because the time period of certain marks overlapped, this is not an exact science.*

• *Fulper pottery is almost always molded. Nevertheless, through the company's 25 years of production, perhaps 1,000 different shapes and sizes were created.*

• *Early pieces were often Germanic in influence; middle-period were Oriental; later pieces showed the Art Deco style.*

• *Clay bodies grew lighter in weight from the 1910s into the 1930s. While heavier is not necessarily better, lighter almost always isn't.*

• *In 1920, Fulper introduced the first solid-colored, glazed dinnerware to be produced in the United States.*

Key Facts

Samuel Hill opened a pottery in 1815 in Flemington, N.J., for manufacturing drain tile. In 1847, Dutchman Abraham Fulper, an employee since the 1820s, became Hill's partner. When Hill died, Fulper purchased the company.

The name was changed to Fulper Brothers, then to G.W. Fulper & Bros. Upon Abraham's death in 1899, the firm was incorporated as the Fulper Pottery Company. Such utilitarian stoneware as pitcher and bowls sets and water coolers were its mainstay.

At the turn of the century, the founder's grandson, William Hill Fulper II, began experiments with colored glazes. In 1909, he introduced the Vasekraft line. Made of the same stoneware clay and fired at high temperatures in the same kilns as the commercial ware, it was inspired by Oriental, Greek, and Germanic forms, and covered in spectacular flambé, mirrored, matte, or crystalline glazes.

German potter J. Martin Stangl joined the company in 1910. By then, the company was already represented in the old Tiffany Studios building in New York. Stangl left Fulper in 1914, but returned four years later. After a fire destroyed the main Flemington pottery plant in 1929, most of the operation was transferred to Trenton. Stangl purchased the pottery in 1930. In 1955, it became the Stangl Pottery and offered commercial ware.

Fulper Lamps

Fulper Pottery production included vases of all shapes and sizes, urns, bowls, console sets, and various types of light fixtures. Fulper's best work, however, and the most expensive then and now, was its handsome table lamps. Each of them was richly glazed and created to strict quality-control standards. The lampshades were inset with leaded glass that had been arranged in stylized patterns. Occasionally, these patterns formed insects such as the dragonfly; rarely, lamps were produced with patterns of 1910 touring cars.

Fulper first offered lamps in 1910, in its earliest and best period of production. Some styles from among the pottery's table lamps had pottery shades, while others had glass. The glass shades often exhibited an intricate network of pieces that created rainbows of color when lit. The colors were applied by hand to each of the various sized and shaped glass sections.

At times, Fulper experimented with the lamps in ways that accepted a high level of risk. A lamp might combine glass and ceramic, for example, despite the disastrous possibilities of working in two materials with different cooling and heating temperatures.

Fulper's status in the world of Arts and Crafts was such that the pottery supplied ceramic lamp bases to the famous furniture manufacturer Gustav Stickley and won a Medal of Honor for their display in the 1915 Pan-Pacific Exposition. William Hill Fulper II was also designated Master Craftsman by the Society of Arts and Crafts in Boston, Mass.

These rare and lovely pieces are now highly valued by collectors. Exquisitely crafted and costly even when new, the lamps command a high price in the collector's market. Because they are so hard to locate and acquire, damage typically does not dramatically affect their value.

Toadstool Boudoir Lamp, *c.* 1910

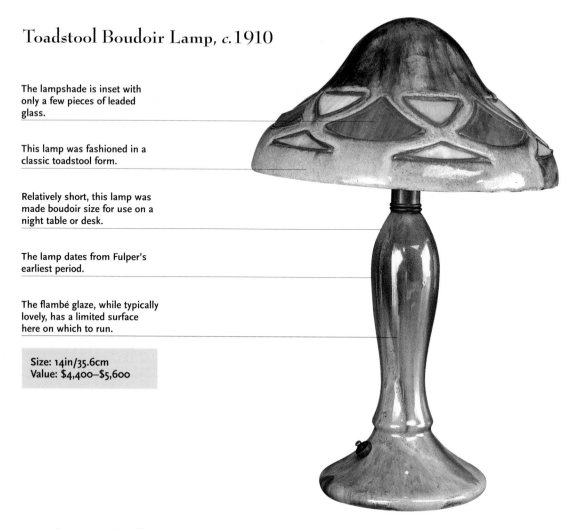

The lampshade is inset with only a few pieces of leaded glass.

This lamp was fashioned in a classic toadstool form.

Relatively short, this lamp was made boudoir size for use on a night table or desk.

The lamp dates from Fulper's earliest period.

The flambé glaze, while typically lovely, has a limited surface here on which to run.

Size: 14in/35.6cm
Value: $4,400–$5,600

Table Lamp, *c.*1910

The shade and the lit lamp are enhanced by the multiple pieces of leaded glass.

This example, unlike the one opposite, is a full-size table lamp.

Notice the great leopard-skin crystalline glaze.

The lamp was created in a Japanese-influenced form.

Size: 20in/50.8cm
Value: $22,000–$28,000

• *Fulper lamps were produced only during Fulper's earliest period, from about 1910 to 1915, which contributes to their rarity.*

• *Production standards were extremely high, a result of their stiff price and the flagship nature of their best product.*

• *Fulper lamps are seldom found without at least some damage, and imperfect examples have sold for more than $20,000.*

• *Some of Fulper's best glazes and glaze combinations are found on these pieces.*

• *These lamps are especially prized, even by art pottery and Arts and Crafts collectors who generally have little interest in Fulper pottery.*

◀ *A lamp such as this was expensive when made. The initial cost, the fragility of this remarkable shade, and its top-heavy design are part of what make it—like most Fulper Lamps—so rare.*

Grand Feu Pottery

Grand Feu is one of the finest U.S. art potteries. At the same time that this pottery maintained the California tradition of creating superior art ware, it reflected few of the naturalistic tendencies one usually sees in products from the Golden State. While most of Grand Feu's contemporaries, such as Rhead Santa Barbara and Valentien pottery, explored floral decoration, Grand Feu (French for "high fire") developed intense and sumptuous glazes on ceramic hard bodies baked at extremely high temperatures.

Like many other California studio ventures, Grand Feu's operation was short-lived with limited production. Its work has been among the scarcest of American art potteries. Perhaps because it does not bear representational decoration (such as painted flowers or landscapes), it does not enjoy the collecting base it deserves.

Dr. Paul Evans, author of *Art Pottery of the United States*, states that Grand Feu is one of America's best producers. While the glaze selection was not boundless, certainly a dozen different glazes, or varieties thereof, have appeared on existing examples in recent years. From the simplest matte brown to the most vibrantly shimmering metallic silver-green, the overall output has been universally exemplary, from foot ring to flared rim. Grand Feu produced memorable pieces, including ones with blue matte crystalline trails drizzled over white matte crystalline bodies, and those with a three-glaze flambé of eggshell, metallic pumpkin, and glossy metallic brown.

Most pieces have remained without damage, probably because of the density of the clay body achieved by the high temperatures used in the firing. In fact, on the few "damaged" pieces seen, nearly all defects occurred during the firing process itself. Virtually all Grand Feu is marked, either with "Grand Feu Pottery L.A., Cal." (about 1912–16), or "Brauckman Art Pottery" (about 1916–18). Some rare pieces are unmarked but identifiable.

As a rule, the more visually engaging the glaze, the more desirable such a piece is to modern collectors. Pieces average about 7in/17.8cm in height. A chip on the rim of an exceptional piece might reduce value by a third.

Vase in Metallic Flambé, c.1915

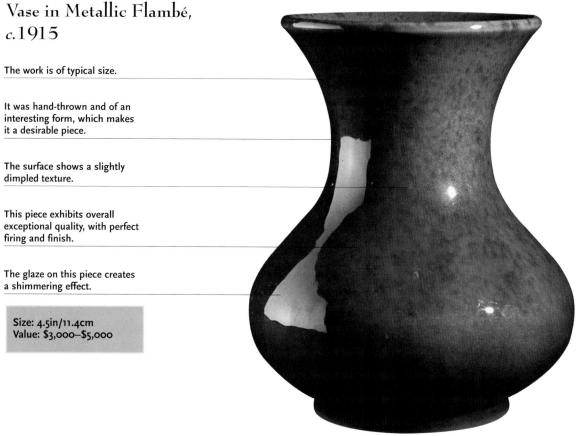

The work is of typical size.

It was hand-thrown and of an interesting form, which makes it a desirable piece.

The surface shows a slightly dimpled texture.

This piece exhibits overall exceptional quality, with perfect firing and finish.

The glaze on this piece creates a shimmering effect.

Size: 4.5in/11.4cm
Value: $3,000–$5,000

Vase of Earthenware, *c.*1915

This piece is slightly larger than most.

It has a form less noteworthy than the one opposite.

The work was hand-thrown of high-fire earthenware.

Notice the rich flowing Mission Matte brown finish.

While this is one of Grand Feu's more common glazes, an unusual amount of activity appears here.

Size: 6in/15.2cm
Value: $2,500–$3,500

* *Most Grand Feu is small in stature, and while the average height is about 7in/17.8cm, one is more likely to find pieces between 4in/10.2cm and 5in/12.7cm tall.*
* *While Grand Feu employed at least a dozen glazes and combinations, the pottery seemed to finish the majority of pieces in either a rich, flowing matte brown or a static (but fine) metallic green matte crystalline.*
* *A few later examples have surfaced that may not share the level of quality seen in the earlier ware. These can be identified by the mark "Brauckman Art Pottery," rather than "Grand Feu."*
* *Most pieces that have been located were found, not surprisingly, in California. More curious are the several prime examples that have surfaced in rural eastern Pennsylvania.*

Key Facts

Cornelius Brauckman of Missouri founded the Grand Feu Pottery around 1913 in Los Angeles, Calif., for the manufacture of high-fire ("grand feu") stoneware called gres–cerame. Similar to porcelain but duller in color and opaque, pieces of the gres technique were popular at the turn of the century with French potters, including Greber, Delaherche, Dalpayrat, and Taxile Doat of the Sevres Porcelain Manufacture (who wrote an influential text on the matter, *Grand Feu Ceramics*).

The Grand Feu Pottery had closed its doors by 1918, possibly earlier—it is unlisted by 1916. But before it did, its wares had won the Gold Medal at the Panama California Exposition in San Diego in 1915. It had also exhibited at the First Annual Arts & Crafts Salon in Los Angeles in 1916.

The Grand Feu Pottery managed to make a place for itself despite the pottery's short operating history and limited output. Production standards were among the highest in the United States. All but the latest pieces of Grand Feu were hand-thrown. And only the hand-thrown ware is worthy of merit. While the selection of glazes was limited, the overall quality was exceptionally interesting.

Grand Feu produced some larger pieces (over 7in/17.8cm), but they are rare. Rarer still are pieces with covers and/or handles. One reticulated (cut through) piece is known to exist, but most are simple, easily thrown vase forms. In all cases, identification is straightforward, because Grand Feu diligently marked its ware with one of two precise, die-stamped company designations.

Grueby Pottery

Grueby pottery has finally emerged as one of the favorite U.S. art potteries, although it took decades of benign neglect to reach this point. The subtlety that defined Grueby's aesthetic seems also to present a challenge to potential buyers in today's market.

In a sense, this could be considered the Arts and Crafts potter's art pottery and, in many ways, a manifestation of the American ideal. While not exactly "one artist, one piece" ware, it was vegetal, natural, fine, and original—clearly not the product of a large, Rookwood-type factory.

William Grueby made his most important contribution with his matte green glaze—the richest, subtlest, finest, micro-crystalline cucumber dead matte finish in the country. Next in importance was his sense of form (or at least his capacity to hire talented designers such as Addison LeBoutillier and George Kendrick). Grueby's best ware looked picked rather than potted.

Grueby also enjoyed an ideal position in Boston, Mass., at the center of the most important region in the United States for the Arts and Crafts movement. Grueby was, in many ways, the flagship decorative ceramic that made credible American art pottery and encouraged more than 100 admirers, competitors, and imitators in the United States alone.

Perhaps 40% of Grueby's pottery is bereft of any decoration, save the extraordinary glazes covering it. Pieces of this sort are less desirable to collectors and less valuable, but fine pots nonetheless. Second in command are vases in a single-color glaze with tooled and applied or simply tooled stylized leaf and floral designs. Next in line are multicolor examples *(see pages 68–69)*, with flowers in a dramatically contrasting color (such as yellow or red) on a matte ground (typically green). The very best Grueby pieces are usually single-color pots, but with extreme tooling, such as applied handles, deep ridges, and over-the-top leaf and floral designs.

More than 100 years after the pottery's inception, this ware still represents the *summum* in turn-of-the-century art pottery, commanding the highest prices from avid (and discerning) collectors.

Single-Color Vase, *c.*1905

Grueby produced a fine gourd-shaped vessel in this piece, but one that is still far less intriguing than the one opposite.

The vase is hand-thrown and, while not the only attempt at this form, still unique.

Notice the rich matte green finish.

The leaf decoration is tooled and applied.

The crisp edges of decoration here typify Grueby's handwork.

This piece is typical in size.

Size: 9in/22.9cm
Value: $4,300–$5,700

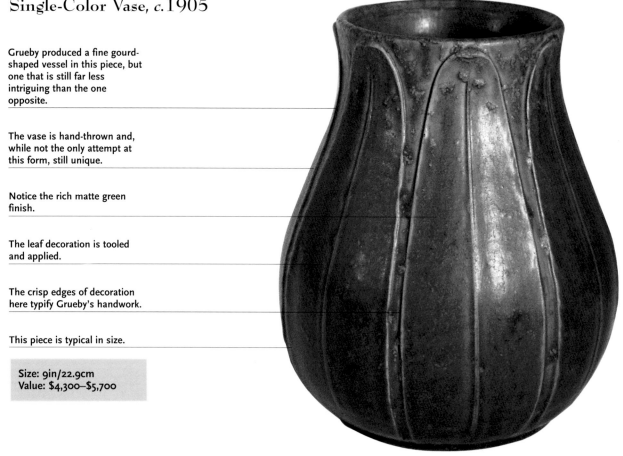

Ochre Vase with Handles, *c.*1900

This is organic Grueby at its best.

The leaves are tooled and applied, as are the handles.

The rich ochre matte finish distinguishes this piece, adding to its rarity.

The exceptional detailing can only be obtained through modeling rather than molding.

This piece is larger than most Grueby, adding to its value.

George P. Kendrick designed this vase.

Size: 13in/33cm
Value: $43,000–$57,000

- *Much of Grueby's single-color ware is simply glazed, usually in a green matte finish.*
- *Grueby pieces were also glazed in matte colors of light and dark blue, ochre, brown, oatmeal, and mauve.*
- *All Grueby vessels were hand-thrown.*
- *Decoration was either tooled off the vessel and applied and/or carved into the piece's surface.*
- *Most Grueby pottery was produced in the period between 1897 and 1907.*
- *Damage, especially minor chipping or nicking to edges of leaves, has little to no impact on value.*

Key Facts

Since their inception in the 1890s, Grueby pottery and tiles have been the most important clay products of the American Arts and Crafts movement. Surrounded by very talented designers, William Grueby of Boston created lyrical and stylish examples of art pottery following the strictest quality standards. The company's tiles, vases, and architectural faience were highly praised by contemporary critics, earning the factory many awards.

Among these were medals won at the Paris Exposition Universelle, 1900, which served to increase the company's visibility and contracts, and to place Grueby pieces in museum collections. Grueby also took the gold medal at the International Artistic and Industrial Exhibition of Ceramics and Glass in St. Petersburg, Russia, in 1901.

That same year, the pottery won the gold medal at the Pan-American Exposition in Buffalo, N.Y. Grueby also won the Grand Prix at the Louisiana Purchase Exposition in St. Louis, Mo., in 1904. Also in 1904, the pottery took the highest award at the International Exhibition in Turin, Italy.

Grueby may have absorbed the styles of coexhibitors such as French potters Ernest Chaplet and Auguste Delaherche at the World's Columbian Exposition, held in Chicago in 1893. The products of his company soon took on that organic quality that would become his hallmark.

By 1909, competitors were offering successful, cheaper versions of Grueby's wares. In that year, the firm went into receivership, at which point Grueby Faience and Tile Company emerged.

Grueby Pottery—Multicolor

L earning to love Grueby pottery is like acquiring a taste for avocados (which, coincidentally, are covered with a Grueby-esque rich, vegetal, matte green finish). A collector's first brush with this ware might be underwhelming, but the more he or she learns and pays attention, the more accessible the pottery's virtues become.

Just as Grueby was the lynchpin ceramic of the American Arts and Crafts movement, so, too, is it often a turning point in a collector's awareness. That person who can respond to the subtle rhythms of this sublime art ware is well on the way to establishing a strong addiction to things delicate and beautiful.

Damage does not seem to have the same negative impact on the value of Grueby ware that it does on most other American pottery, and damage has even less negative impact on multicolor Grueby than it does on single-color ware. There are several reasons for this. Grueby is a relatively low-fire ware, and the biscuit does not suffer the level of abuse that porcelain or denser earthenware does. Furthermore, the tooling and applied decoration found on Grueby is so finely detailed that collectors expect to find nicks and small chips on the edges of leaves and flowers. Sharpness of detailing is critical in determining the success of a piece and its current value. The more color run in the decoration, the less valuable the piece.

But more to the point, Grueby ware is one-of-a-kind artwork in which each piece expresses a moment in time captured by a talented artist. As such, collectors who appreciate that expression understand that there will never be another piece exactly like each and every piece they collect. This is a very Arts and Crafts approach to collecting Arts and Crafts. And this, after all, is the point.

Small Multicolor Vase, *c.*1907

This vase is hand-thrown.

The yellow seen here is the most typical second color in Grueby ware.

The multipetaled flowers are less usual than the simple bud forms.

Nearly all decorated pieces have a green matte ground.

This piece is slightly smaller than most decorated pieces.

The work shows excellent definition. The second color on Grueby pieces often runs.

Size: 6in/15.2cm
Value: $6,400–$8,600

Large Multicolor Vase, *c.*1907

The bud design is quintessential Grueby.

Crisp yellow glazing on the buds enhances the vase's value.

The leaves are hand-tooled and applied.

This piece is massive in size for Grueby ware.

The sensuous, hand-thrown form of this piece adds to its appeal.

Notice the fine matte green ground.

Size: 14in/35.6cm
Value: $60,000–$70,000

- *Less than 10% of all Grueby bore more than a single glaze color.*
- *Less than 1% of all Grueby had more than two glaze colors.*
- *One in a thousand pieces of Grueby are decorated in more than three or four colors.*
- *The vast majority of multicolor Grueby pieces have green grounds with yellow flowers or buds.*
- *Most decorated Grueby pieces bear applied buds. A small percentage have uncomplicated floral designs.*
- *On rare occasions, pieces were designed with unusual flowers such as calla lilies or jack-in-the-pulpits.*

◀ *The crisp edges of the leaves can be achieved only by modeling; molded edges are rounder and softer. The yellow color of the buds is unusually sharp, the product of a perfect firing.*

Grueby Pottery—Tiles

William Grueby apprenticed at the Low Art Tile Works in neighboring Chelsea, Mass., at the age of 13. He began making tiles and architectural faience with Low co-worker Eugene Atwood at Fiske, Coleman and Company under the name of Atwood & Grueby, c.1890–94. In 1894, he opened Grueby Faience Company with George Prentice Kendrick, a brilliant designer, and business manager William Graves. Grueby's strength would be glazes and enamels, between which the founder made a pointed distinction.

Initially known for architectural faience, Grueby created tiles that would soon be found in installations nationwide. Constant and vocal support by a popular industry journal, *The Brickbuilder*, as well as regular exhibitions in architectural leagues and Arts and Crafts societies, kept the firm's name on everyone's lips and kept contracts coming its way. Besides countless commercial and residential buildings, Grueby tiles covered the walls of large restaurants, hotels, railroad stations, and the original New York City subway system. Gustav Stickley, the most important manufacturer of quality Arts and Crafts furniture, used only Grueby tiles to line his tables and plant stands.

Those pieces of Stickley furniture today command tens of thousands of dollars. Ever since the early 1970s, when pieces from the Arts and Crafts movement started making a comeback as collectibles, Grueby's prices have been climbing steadily. A table lamp with a Grueby pottery base and simple Tiffany glass shade—purchased for $2,500 in 1972—sold in 1998 for $280,000. Single 6in/15.2cm *cuenca* tiles depicting animals, tulips, or trees now regularly bring $3,000 or more; 4in/10.2cm tiles sell for over $1,000.

This is not to discourage collectors from looking into Grueby as a potential investment—no sign exists that this market will slow down anytime soon. In addition, plenty of less expensive ways to collect Grueby are available. Plain floor tiles can still be purchased for $50 per square foot; molded tiles with ship, musician, or floral designs are available for under $1,000.

Pine Frieze Tile, *c.*1905

One of Grueby's blue-chip stock tiles, the Pines consistently perform well.

Attributed to Addison LeBoutillier, it might have been originally designed for Dreamwold and comes in two different versions that complement each other.

This tile exhibits fine *cuenca* technique; always crisp molds and well fired.

Complementary earth-tone glazes create a quiet, natural Arts and Crafts feel.

The piece uses Grueby's signature matte green enamel.

The "curdling" or "oatmealing" of glaze seen here is an effect difficult to achieve and part of Grueby's high-quality arsenal.

Size: 6in/15.2cm square
Value: $2,800–$3,300

Goose Tile, *c.*1920

This later tile was made with the C. Pardee Tile Works.

This tile is smaller in size than the example opposite.

This was not part of a frieze.

This small chip detracts value.

Rendered in an illustrative, stylized design, this work is more commercial and less ambitious than the piece opposite.

It was decorated in *cuerda seca* instead of *cuenca*, a technique used at a later time by Grueby's production.

Size: 4in/10.1cm square
Value: $900–$1,200

• *The finest Grueby Arts and Crafts faience tiles were made of wet clay, molded, or decorated in* cuenca.
• *The pottery became renowned for original matte glazes that Grueby referred to as "enamels."*
• *Grueby's signature dark green glaze resembles the skin of a cucumber, which is why Grueby enthusiasts claim that a fine piece of Grueby looks more picked than potted.*
• *Other glaze colors include brown, indigo, blue, blue-gray, mustard, burgundy, ivory, and a large palette of greens.*
• *Molded floor tiles inspired by Henry Chapman Mercer's work were made of bisque-fired clay, with glaze filling hollow areas, and the flat or embossed surface wiped clean.*
• *Tiles made in conjunction later with the C. Pardee Tile Works are often thinner, dust-pressed, and decorated in* cuerda seca *with flowers, ships, animals, or* Alice in Wonderland *characters.*

Major Tile Installations

Grueby vases and Moorish tiles were shown at the first exhibition of the Society of Arts & Crafts in 1897, which had a profound impact on Grueby's business. Kendrick, Graves, and Grueby all became members—apparently, among other reasons, to stay in touch with the society's several architects as potential business contacts. When the New York subway system opened, Grueby tiles (along with Rookwood and Hartford Faience) were chosen to cover the walls of several stations.

Grueby's (and the Arts and Crafts movement's) most important tile schemes graced the walls of Dreamwold, the Thomas Lawson mansion in Scituate, Mass. Created by the Boston architectural firm of Coolidge and Carlson (1902–04), the mansion's many bathrooms, fireplaces,

and a conservatory were outfitted with Grueby tiles. The overall project was a collaborative one among the architects, Boston potter Russell Crook, and graphic designer Addison LeBoutillier, who had drawn advertisements for Grueby since 1899.

LeBoutillier joined the firm as director of design in 1903, shortly after the pottery supplied the tiles for Dreamwold. Many of its installations are attributed to him, including a spectacular bathroom wall with water lilies, irises, and friezes of turtles and horses, all done in *cuenca*. The scope and quality of this project is unrivaled for the period. Most of the tiles were removed in the early 1980s, and they come up on the market from time to time, commanding some of the highest prices among Arts and Crafts tiles.

Hampshire Pottery

The Grueby Pottery's success can be measured in many ways, not the least of which is the more than 100 imitators bobbing in the firm's wake. Not all of Grueby's imitators were created equal, however, with some sharing only glaze color and others imitating everything but the Grueby name. Hampshire Pottery, of Keene, N.H., was arguably the most imitative, but the ware it produced was of sufficient style and charm to warrant individual attention here.

The producers at Hampshire Pottery made little secret of what they were doing. They copied Grueby's work while lowering production standards, enabling them to sell a similar look at lower prices. Economies were created by eliminating Grueby's noted handcrafting. While Grueby pots were always hand-thrown, Hampshire vessels were nearly always molded. Grueby's designs were either modeled into or applied onto the surface of a pot, while Hampshire pieces were decorated in-mold. The few exceptions were simple vase forms with no decoration, simply glazed and usually unmarked.

Nevertheless, Hampshire produced a body of work that approximated the Grueby style with enough quality and diversity to create its own market niche, then and now. As prices for Grueby ware have risen steadily in the last decade, the value of Hampshire pottery has increased accordingly.

About half of Hampshire ware was simply glazed; the rest was decorated with some sort of embossed work. The most popular designs are Grueby-influenced, with leaves and/or simple flower buds. Less successful designs include full-stemmed flowers, swastikas, and overall organic designs that are often made less appealing because they compete with the basic vessel form.

The vast majority of Hampshire pottery is covered with a medium matte green glaze. Better examples have a rich butterfat texture. Hampshire also produced a good quality matte blue finish, as well as a textured light ochre, a textured mauve, and a nacreous black.

Because Hampshire was molded and often repeated, minor damage can decrease value by as much as 50%.

Blue Matte Vessel, c.1910

This is a typical vase form for Hampshire.

The design includes no embossed decoration, which makes the vessel less valuable than the example opposite.

The molded body is of buff clay.

Notice the unusual blue matte finish with rose highlights.

The piece is typical in size.

Size: 6in/15.2cm
Value: $300–$400

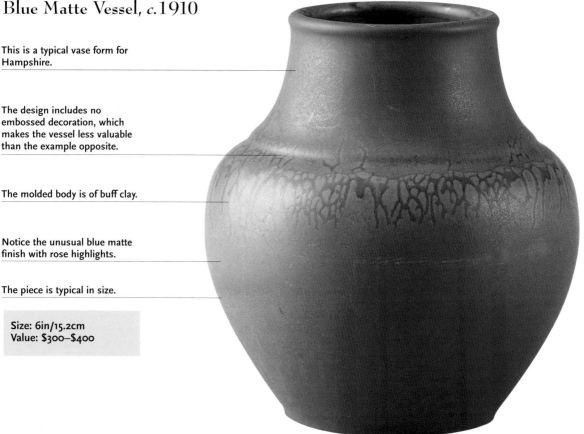

Embossed Leaf Vessel, *c.*1910

This piece exhibits a typical Arts and Crafts form.

Such an unusual feathered mauve matte finish will bring a higher price.

The embossed leaf decoration increases the value of the vessel.

The molded body, like the one opposite, is of buff clay.

This piece is also typical in size for Hampshire ware.

Size: 5½in/14cm
Value: $600–$800

Key Facts

- *Most Hampshire ware was covered in a good, medium green matte glaze. Other popular colors include matte blues and ochres. Hampshire also produced a fine nacreous satin matte black.*
- *Typical decoration includes embossed leaves and buds in the style of Grueby.*
- *Hampshire employed a buff clay but covered the bottoms of its ware in a stark, white semi-gloss.*
- *Pieces were almost always marked on the bottom with the die-stamped designation "Hampshire Pottery" and the letter M in a circle.*
- *The average size of Hampshire ware was about 6–7in/15.2–17.8cm.*
- *Forms include assorted vases, mugs, tea sets, lamp bases, pitchers, and bowls.*

James S. Taft was born in Nelson, N.H., in 1844. In 1871, along with his uncle James Burnap, he purchased the Mile Stone Mill on the Ashuelot River in Keene, on the southwestern corner of New Hampshire. After having been outfitted, but before any wares could be produced, the place burned down. It was quickly rebuilt, and the company started in earnest in 1872 with the manufacture of redware, soon to be followed by utilitarian stoneware.

Taft and Burnap moved the flowerpot and other redware work to a building they acquired in 1874, while keeping the stoneware production in the original plant. Englishman Thomas Stanley arrived as superintendent at the company in 1879. He introduced the dark majolica glazes for which the Keene pottery became known.

Hampshire decorated pottery production began in 1882, including an underglaze, slip-painted line, as well as a series of commemorative ware designed by Wallace King, featuring transfer-printed images of various locations in the United States and historical events.

The Hampshire Pottery joined the Arts and Crafts movement in 1904 with the addition of Cadmon Robertson, Taft's brother-in-law and a resourceful chemist. Promoted to superintendent, Robertson introduced matte glazes to the production and added over 900 glaze recipes in all.

Wallace King retired in 1908. Cadmon Robertson died in 1914. Taft closed the pottery before the end of the year. George Morton of the Grueby Pottery bought the company in 1916, complete with equipment and glaze formulae. For a year, Morton reproduced Hampshire art pottery, before returning to Grueby. He started production at Hampshire once again after the war, manufacturing hotel china and mosaic tiles until forced to close in 1923, the year of Taft's death.

Jervis Pottery

The Jervis Pottery of Corona, N.Y., is one of those esoteric producers whose influence is as important as the decorative ware it created. In business for just a few years, Jervis was a significant outlet, not least because it brought together William P. Jervis and the famous Frederick H. Rhead.

The pottery created by Jervis was quirky and crude, with forms either hand-built or haphazardly crafted. All but a small percentage of objects were simply glazed. The artwork on the rest was often amateurish. It takes a sampling of perhaps 50 pieces to understand what Jervis accomplished. This can be a daunting task because so little Jervis ware of any quality is available.

Nevertheless, sufficient examples of its work have appeared over the years for studious collectors and dealers to assemble a fair picture of Jervis production. About 35% of the work appears to have been adorned with one or two glazes only. About 50% of the pieces seem to bear simple decoration, line, and squiggles of some sort, applied in squeezebag, incised, and/or modeled. A relatively small number, about 15%, comprises the finer Jervis ware, which shows more technique and design elements. These are the pieces collectors most want and will pay well to obtain.

The best Jervis ware is not necessarily large in size, with 6in/15.2cm seeming the average height. But whatever the dimensions, standout pieces combine various decorative techniques to create memorable ware from what was, by all appearances, a fairly ill-equipped studio. The most impressive techniques include squeezebag, sgraffito, enameling, inlay, and incised designs.

Peacock Vase, c.1909

Unlike the example opposite, this is larger than most Jervis ware.

The design was rendered in squeezebag, enameling, and inlay.

The figural nature of this design, a peacock, is quite rare and greatly increases the value.

Notice that the design covers entire surface.

While not signed by Frederick Rhead, this is almost certainly by his hand.

The colors are typical of Jervis ware.

Size: 10in/25.4cm
Value: $4,500–$5,500

Stylized Landscape Vessel, c.1909

This is smaller than most Jervis pieces.

The artist rendered this design in squeezebag and sgraffito.

The design covers most of the surface.

The stylized landscape design was a Rhead favorite.

Color choice on this piece is unique to Jervis ware.

Size: 3in/7.6cm
Value: $1,700–$2,300

• *Much of the ware produced by the Jervis Pottery is modestly crafted, at best.*
• *Only about 15% of Jervis ware bears more than the simplest decoration.*
• *While Rhead was responsible for decorating much of the Jervis ware that bears any design, only one example signed by him has been located.*
• *Jervis's crude, studiolike conditions made for a relatively low-fire ware that was prone to nicking and chipping.*
• *Most decorated pieces show only traces of slip-trail designs. More interesting and valuable are those with incised and inlaid decoration.*
• *Exceptional pieces of Jervis pottery lose little value in the case of minor damage.*

Key Facts

The author of *Rough Notes on Pottery* (Newark, N.J., 1896), William Percival Jervis of Stoke-on-Trent, England, first worked in the United States as a graphic artist. In 1902, he wrote the *Encyclopedia of Ceramics*, the most important text on art pottery since E.A. Barber's *The Pottery and Porcelain of the United States*.

Jervis managed the Vance Faience Company from 1902—the year its name changed to the Avon Faience Company—until 1903. While there, along with Frederick Hurten Rhead, he introduced the squeezebag, or slip-trail, decorating technique to the United States, while continuing his research in matte glazes.

Jervis left Vance/Avon to open a studio at Anton Benkert's Corona Pottery in Corona, N.Y. When a fire ravaged the pottery in December 1903, destroying its entire inventory, Jervis joined the Rose Valley Association. At this Arts and Crafts community in Media, a suburb of Philadelphia, he continued his experiments on matte glazes of different colors. In 1905, his pieces were exhibited at the New York Society of Keramic Arts.

In mid-1905, Jervis left Rose Valley for the Midwest, and secured a position at the Craven Art Pottery in East Liverpool, Ohio. Under Jervis's leadership, Craven produced pieces decorated in squeezebag, incised, or covered in polychromatic matte glazes. Poor economic conditions led Jervis to leave in 1908 for Long Island, N.Y. Later that year, Craven closed its pottery for good

Jervis then established the Jervis Pottery in Oyster Bay, on the north shore of Long Island, N.Y. Frederick Rhead, his comrade from Vance/Avon, joined him for a few months after leaving Roseville Pottery, and before going to University City. Jervis designed simple forms to be molded, as well as most of the pottery's decoration, done in enameling, squeezebag, and/or sgraffito. He went on to publish *A Pottery Primer* in 1911. Jervis Pottery closed around 1912.

Losanti Ware

Mary Louise McLaughlin was among the most important figures in American decorative ceramics. Like her Cincinnati, Ohio, contemporaries—Maria Longworth Nichols and Clara Chipman Newton—she was inspired by the Centennial Exposition in Philadelphia, Penn., in 1876. Back in Cincinnati, she began experimenting with and developing the Limoges style ware that marked this country's entry into high-styled decorative arts.

Offended by Nichols, who claimed as well to have "discovered" the Limoges technique, McLaughlin chose to chart her own course. While this may have alienated her socially, it fueled her innate genius, which resulted in her becoming one of our earliest art pottery pioneers. Her underglaze slip work, with floral design in a thick impasto application, displayed the surest hand in this nascent style. She was among the few (along with Matt Morgan) to employ rich, red local clays, whose interaction with the surface pigments yielded an excellent ware.

But McLaughlin's best work came around the turn of the century, when she began to develop one of the first modeled art porcelains in the United States. Deeply influenced by Asian precedents, McLaughlin's work was hand-formed, thin-walled porcelain ware meticulously carved with floral designs and covered with rich, colorful glazes. Most glazes tended toward celadon and soft hues of blue and cream, although she occasionally stepped out, choosing bright reds and vibrant blues and green.

She also developed "grain of rice" decoration, in which designs were reticulated through the vessel surface and grains of rice were inserted into the holes. She then glazed them with her patented finishes and, as the rice burned away during the firing, the reticules remained with only the glasslike glazing as a covering.

Extremely rare, McLaughlin's work is eagerly sought by advanced collectors and museums alike. Each piece was initialed by McLaughlin, numbered by hand, and incised with the Losanti designation. Damage has little negative impact on the value of these pieces. While a broken piece by any maker is of minimal value, minor flaws such as chips and short cracks will reduce value by only 20%. It is worth noting that McLaughlin's work was extremely experimental and is often marred by in-fire flaws such as underglaze firing lines and blistered glazes.

Silver-Collared Jar, *c.*1900

The silver collar is unusual for this ware and suggests that this jar needed a cover.

The porcelain body may have been molded, the only such known example.

Decoration is hand-carved into the vessel surface.

The decoration and surface were both painted with relatively high-fire pigments in contrasting hues.

The jar is large by Losanti standards.

Size: 6in/15.2cm
Value: $6,000–$7,000

Celadon-Glazed Vessel, *c.*1900

This is a hand-formed porcelain body.

Notice the soft, celadon glazing, typical of Losanti.

The piece exhibits a curvilinear floral decoration.

The decoration is carved into and from the vessel surface.

This is typical in size for Losanti ware.

Size: 4¹⁄₂in/11.4cm
Value: $10,000–$12,000

- *Nearly all Losanti ware is of hand-formed porcelain.*
- *About 80% of these pieces bear hand-carved designs and are extremely valuable.*
- *Undecorated examples are of some interest but are relatively inexpensive.*
- *As a rule, the more Art Nouveau the influence and curvilinear the design, the more valuable the piece.*
- *McLaughlin's most successful glazes are the rich, soft, transparent finishes of Asian influence.*
- *She appears to have used only floral designs on the more valuable pieces.*
- *Her decorative techniques also included enameling and "grain of rice."*
- *McLaughlin worked on a very small scale, with the average piece being under 6in/15.2cm in height.*
- *Losanti pieces were diligently marked, and nearly all extant pieces bear at least one of her trademark designations: "L M^c L", Losanti, and/or a number.*

Key Facts

Mary Louise McLaughlin studied drawing, woodcarving, and china painting in Cincinnati. In 1876, she exhibited china-painted ware and a carved wood cabinet at the Centennial Exposition in Philadelphia. There, she conceived a desire to emulate the Limoges wares exhibited by Haviland.

By the end of 1877, she produced a successful version of Limoges by painting moist, "green" ware with colored slips, or liquid clays. Her first perfected example, a pilgrim vase painted with roses, was fired in January of 1878. Bickering soon broke out between McLaughlin and other potters, including Maria Longworth Nichols, all of whom claimed to have discovered the secret to the Cincinnati faience. In fact, McLaughlin was first.

After earning an honorable mention from the Paris Exposition

Universelle of 1879, McLaughlin organized the Cincinnati Pottery Club, operating first out of the Dallas Pottery, then out of the Rookwood Pottery, until eviction in 1882.

McLaughlin went on to win the Silver Medal for her decorative metalwork at the Paris Exposition of 1889. Starting in 1894, she worked on a type of inlaid ware that she named "American faience." She experimented with Chinese carved porcelain bodies and glazes. She named her wares "Losanti," after the early name for Cincinnati, "Losantiville."

In 1901, she perfected a single-fire technique for body and glaze. She won a bronze medal from the Pan-American Exposition in Buffalo, N.Y. By 1906, McLaughlin had put pottery aside to concentrate on metalwork. She died in 1939 at the age of 91.

J. & J.G. Low Art Tiles

Low tiles' collectibility derives from their relative rarity, their beauty and unusualness, and their rich glazes. Like most of the tiles produced in this country at that time, they were American versions of the Aesthetic movement's molded tiles made at Maw or Minton's in England. Produced after the 1876 Philadelphia Exposition, they embodied the end of the Victorian era, featuring Japanese asymmetry and themes in dark earth tones, but also distinctive renderings of uncommon subjects.

Their greatest contribution to the period was the "plastic sketch," an oversized tile panel made of wet, or plastic, clay. Time-consuming and difficult to create, these plaques by English modeler Arthur Osborne were sold as fine art, in frames, meant to be hung on walls. The quality of the tiles was exceptional in technique, as well as in design and glaze. Any tile that has survived installation, removal, and the passage of a hundred years is technically rare and therefore desirable.

The plastic sketches were expensive when originally produced in small numbers and continue to be a unique art form. The delicate carving of the molds, and the offbeat beauty and originality of such themes as weathered faces, monks in their monasteries, or herds of animals (often depicted from the back), place them in a category of their own. While they represent the best of American tiles at the time and have a good collector following to this day, Low tiles are not currently as popular as tiles covered in matte enamels made during the Arts and Crafts movement. This is purely a question of changing fashions and has no objective bearing on their aesthetic value.

"The Milky Way" Plastic Sketch, c.1881

This plastic sketch represents the very best of the Low production. It is one of the largest made.

This piece is probably from an early pressing of the mold (subsequent pressings lose sharpness).

An unusual view of a bucolic subject, these grazing cows are seen from a low angle.

Note the original frame, covered in (frayed) velvet. This adds value and should be left intact.

The "AO" signature stands for Arthur Osborne.

Size: 10³⁄₄ x 10³⁄₄in/ 27.3 x 47.6cm
Value: $2,500–$3,000

First Love Tile, c.1892

The title of the piece can barely be made out: *First Love.*

While still a very good quality tile, this does not represent top-of-the-line for Low. Nevertheless, it is a warm and unusual portrayal of this old couple, with a sweet title.

The mold is very soft.

The lines of the faces are muddy.

The glaze pools excessively, making the effect too dark.

A small chip to the corner will affect salability.

Size: 6½ in/16.5cm square
Value: $225–$275

- *The majority of tiles produced at Low were dust-pressed in relief molds.*
- *Low's tiles generally followed the style prevailing in England at the time.*
- *Tiles usually featured profile portraits, Japanese-inspired landscapes, animals, and floral or stylized motifs.*
- *Low tiles were covered in rich, monochromatic glossy (majolica) glazes.*
- *One of the qualities that set Low apart was the depth of the studio's glazes, which were apparently applied twice—once covering only the relief decoration, and again to cover the entire surface.*

Key Facts

The firm of J. & J.G. Low (1877–1902) was founded by the Hon. John Low and his son John Gardner Low, in Chelsea, Mass. John the younger, a scenic painter, had gained ceramics experience as an employee of the Chelsea Keramic Art Works. Just a year after its official startup in 1879, the Low Art Tile Works won the first prize in an international ceramic competition held in Crewe, England. This unlikely victory made trade news in the U.S. and abroad and firmly established the new American company.

By 1879, Low had hired English artist Arthur Osborne, who designed plastic sketches and most of their tiles, sculpting the molds with usual views of various subjects. While often not beautiful in the classical sense, Osborne's tiles offered charm, humor, and a hand-made quality that came to be valued as fine art.

Marblehead Pottery— Decorated

The New England contribution to art pottery was important for both the overall quality of the product and its diversity. Among the many types of work coming from there at the time, Marblehead pottery is, and has been, one of the most popular.

Two distinctly different types of Marblehead ware appeared, although both are essentially the same product. The first, and by far the more common, are hand-thrown forms covered with Marblehead's trademark enameled glazes. Far from pure dead mattes, with the slightest gloss to the finish, they come in an interesting range of colors that includes green, dark blue, pink, mustard, and gray. These were mostly produced in vessel forms, although utilitarian pieces and plates appear occasionally.

The second of Marblehead's two products—by far the rarest—are decorated pieces with one or more additional colors surface painted, or surface painted and modeled, into the vessel wall. These run small and have stylized, geometric designs with no modeling. Some early examples are modeled, with no additional colors. These pieces, while rare, are not particularly valuable.

The best decorated Marblehead pieces—extremely rare—are usually in excess of 6in/15.2cm tall, bearing more than a few colors, with modeled designs that cover a good deal of the surface. Most Marblehead is small, averaging about 5in/12.7cm tall, made of a fairly durable biscuit, and relatively resistant to a century of abuse.

Marblehead's best contribution was this geometric decoration on tiles or pottery, of which only small quantities were produced. Many more decorated vases were produced than tiles, but both ranged from fairly ordinary to exceptional.

Geometric Decorated Vessel, c.1910

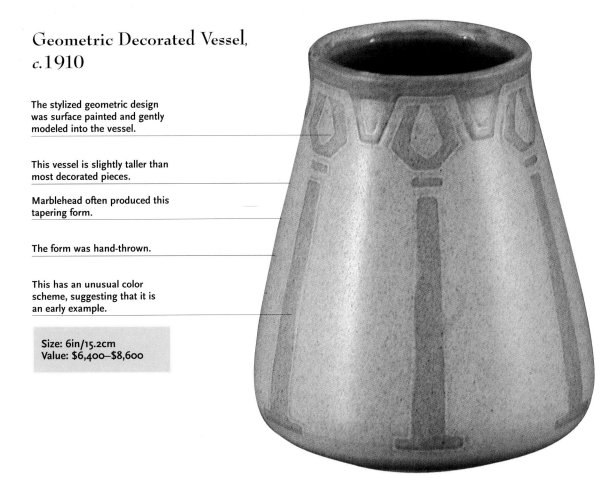

The stylized geometric design was surface painted and gently modeled into the vessel.

This vessel is slightly taller than most decorated pieces.

Marblehead often produced this tapering form.

The form was hand-thrown.

This has an unusual color scheme, suggesting that it is an early example.

Size: 6in/15.2cm
Value: $6,400–$8,600

Floral Decorated Vessel, *c.*1910

This is taller than most decorated pieces.

The vessel exhibits an extremely rare decorative motif, with stylized flowers.

The artist modeled the decoration into the vessel's surface.

The multicolor decoration makes the piece both rarer and more valuable.

The typical bulging form was hand-thrown.

This vase holds the price record for Arts and Crafts pottery sold at auction.

Size: 7in/17.8cm
Value: $102,000–$138,000

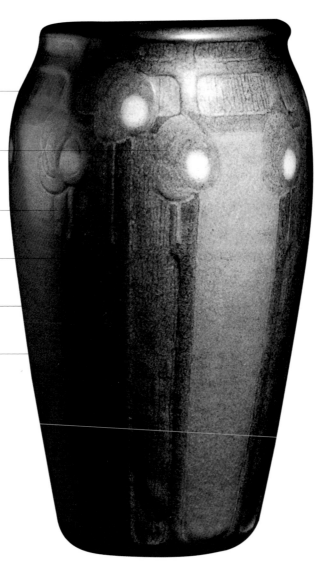

• *Better geometric examples have designs that are both modeled and surface painted.*
• *Generally speaking, the more of the surface covered by the decoration, the better.*
• *At least 90% of work by Marblehead uses only a single glaze.*
• *About 90% of their decorated pieces are small with simple designs, probably stenciled and painted onto the vessel surfaces.*
• *While most decorated pieces have designs of stylized flowers, rarer ones show stylized birds, rabbits, jungle cats, and sea creatures.*
• *The pottery's latest work often comes with a misty, glossy finish. Designs on these pieces are more stylized and less representational, often just squiggly lines.*

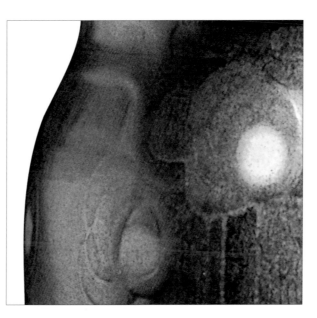

◀ *Most Marblehead pieces are simply surface painted. This close-up shows the gentle modeling, or tooling, that characterizes Marblehead's best work.*

Marblehead Pottery— Undecorated

Marblehead pottery is collectible for several reasons. As a category, it is neither common nor rare, so enough of it has surfaced over the years to keep collector interest well-stoked. Undecorated examples usually sell for under $500, so they have remained within the reach of most collectors. Because decorated pieces often sell for less than $2,000, even these are affordable. First and foremost, however, Marblehead is a handsome, quality product that has endured three decades of collector and academic scrutiny. As such, it is one of the blue chip art potteries in the United States.

Like decorated ware, Marblehead's undecorated pieces do not damage easily, so the vast majority of them are found in perfect condition. A good deal of the damage that is found on this ware occurs in the form of small, broken glaze blisters and flat nicks around the neatly shaved foot rings. Minor damage does not reduce value much, although it can hamper salability.

This work is found in a pleasing array of shapes and colors, all of which blend well together, allowing for the handsome accessorizing of the Arts and Crafts interior. While Marblehead's array of colors—including green, brown, yellow, blue, pink, and gray—is distinctive, it is compatible rather than competitive. This is typical of the Arts and Crafts aesthetic, sometimes called the "team player of the decorative arts."

Simple Undecorated Vase, c. 1915

This simple form is typical of Marblehead undecorated ware.

The enameled glazing is smooth and finely grained.

Note the hand-thrown form.

This piece is typically small in stature.

Size: 4in/10.2cm
Value: $255–$345

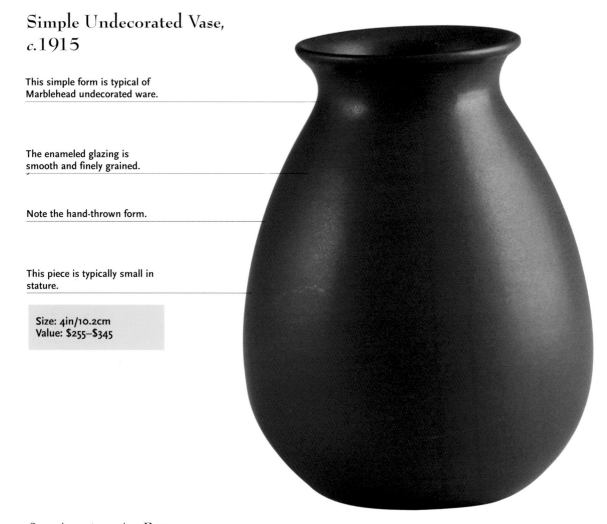

Semi-gloss Undecorated Vase, *c.*1915

This is considered an easy-to-throw, or unforced, form.

The smooth, semi-gloss enameled glaze is of a better color than the example opposite.

The hand-thrown form is larger than most examples, increasing its value.

This shape is typical of Marblehead ware, simple and pleasing to the eye, but distinctive and bold in its way.

Size: 7in/17.8cm
Value: $500–$700

• *Marblehead is almost always hand-thrown. Exceptions include solid objects such as tiles and bookends. A few later pottery pieces have decoration embossed in the mold.*

• *Marblehead is almost always marked with the die-stamped ship/"MP" cipher used by the company, allowing for easy identification.*

• *The pottery used almost exclusively a medium-dark red clay, which aids in identifying pieces with unclear marks. It is worth noting, though, that early examples occasionally are found in a buff clay.*

• *While Marblehead offered a variety of glazes, these are as identifiable as a fingerprint. The exception to this rule is the less common piece with flambé or multiglazing, probably resulting from either glaze experiments or kiln failures.*

Key Facts

For a long time, undecorated Marblehead pottery was not well regarded as a collectible, resting as it did in the shadow of its decorated Marblehead brothers, as well as those of Grueby, Van Briggle, and Newcomb College. In the past few years, however, undecorated Marblehead work has come into its own. Its high quality and elegant lines have earned it the respect of collectors facing an ever-growing dearth of good merchandise.

Once prices for first-tier Arts and Crafts pottery reached the stratosphere, making the best and earliest pots nearly impossible to find and even harder to afford, collectors had no choice but to start "making do" with pieces they might once have snubbed.

Ware from companies such as Hampshire, for example, or Wheatley or Weller quickly gained popularity as the "next best thing." If one could not afford hand-tooled flowers on a vase, one could always obtain a molded piece covered in matte glaze, which yielded a similar effect.

For much the same reason, less extravagant examples from first-tier companies have become very desirable. Hand-thrown, well designed, and covered in the world's finest enamels, undecorated Grueby, Marblehead, and Van Briggle offer affordable and elegant alternatives to the scene-stealing decorated vessels these companies produce, especially when displayed within a similar grouping.

Marblehead Tiles

Located just north of Boston in the picturesque seaport of Marblehead, Mass., the Marblehead Pottery evolved from an arts and crafts activity to a world-renowned enterprise. In 1904, Dr. Herbert Hall founded the pottery as part of the Handcraft Shops, an arts and crafts center for recovering patients from a nearby sanatorium. Headed by Arthur Baggs, a talented young potter, the pottery's work proved too taxing for the patients, and it soon became a business in its own right.

Over the following 30 years, Marblehead produced about five different lines of wares: hand-thrown vases in smooth, speckled monochromatic matte glazes; similar ware that was incised or painted with decoration from Arts and Crafts to Art Deco; tin-glazed dishes; incised or matte-painted tiles; and molded commercial tiles. It should be noted that artist Arthur Wesley Dow, known for his soft, minimalist paintings and wood-block prints, taught in nearby Ipswitch, Mass., for several summers. His presence had to be known to Mr. Baggs, and they may very well have had a teaching or working relationship that influenced Marblehead designs.

Today, as the Arts and Crafts market strengthens, virtually all of Marblehead's wares command attention. The tiles are no exception. While the pottery produced the commercial-grade molded tiles in abundance, it also was responsible for tiles that were hand-decorated and of the highest quality.

Marblehead's decorators created some tiles of great beauty, matte painted or incised in soft, earthen tones on perfectly fired bodies. Some feature misty landscapes in tones of blue or in polychrome, birds, or ships (one of the most popular motifs of the Arts and Crafts period that is not as much in demand today). The 6in/15.2cm landscape tiles—rare and desirable—easily bring $3,000 on the auction market.

The most common tiles, dating from the 1920s and 1930s, feature molded ships covered in a white vellum glaze against a blue background, or brown on yellow. These usually measure less than 5in/12.7cm square and are not by any means strong Arts and Crafts statements, but probably were produced for the tourist trade. They can be had for a few hundred dollars.

Tree Tile, *c.*1910

This is a rare example of a matte-painted, 6in/15.2cm, Marblehead tile.

The tile features a stylized oak tree, a popular motif during the Arts and Crafts period.

This tree is depicted among other, taller trees (three on each side), creating narrow vertical lines around the central mass.

Quiet green glazes complement one another and make a strong Arts and Crafts statement.

The third glaze color, the pink center, adds a warm touch and third dimension—it also adds a few hundred dollars to its price.

"Self-framed" with glaze running along the edges, this tile was probably meant to be used as a tea tile or trivet.

Size: 6in/15.2cm square
Value: $2,500–$3,500

Tall Ship Tile, *c.*1920s

This tile was produced at a later date than the one opposite.

Molded rather than matte-painted or incised, it was commercially produced in great quantity.

Marblehead covered these tiles in blue and white vellum glaze.

The tile is self-framed.

The design is rather banal, lacking the strong stylization of the tree tile.

Size: 4 ³/₄in/12.1cm square
Value: $450–$550

• *Marblehead produced a limited number of tiles molded of wet clay (faience), made as souvenirs for tourists (tea tiles or trivets) or for architecture.*
• *Glazes appeared generally in speckled matte, very smooth and even, and in indigo, gray, brown, or yellow.*
• *Better tiles, quite rare, were matte-painted with simplified landscapes in the style of artist Arthur Wesley Dow.*
• *Thousands of 4 ³/₄in/12.1cm tiles molded with ships were produced during the 1920s and 1930s, in a style very different from the rest of Marblehead's wares. The tall ships were embossed in white vellum glaze on a blue background.*

Key Facts

The Marblehead Pottery was initially set up in 1904 as a therapeutic activity for Dr. Herbert Hall's sanatorium patients, as part of the Handcraft Shops. At the recommendation of Charles Binns, Hall hired a promising young graduate, Arthur Baggs, to run the pottery.

When Dr. Hall pulled the pottery from the sanatorium in 1908, he established it as a commercial outfit, with profits to benefit the hospital.

Baggs introduced a line of tin-glazed faience dishes in 1912, of which few pieces remain. He bought out the company when Dr. Hall moved his

sanatorium to Devereaux, Mass., in 1915. He was subsequently awarded several prizes, including the Charles F. Binns Medal, as well as one from the Society of Arts and Crafts in Boston.

Having set up an autonomous staff, Baggs spent less and less time in Marblehead, involving himself instead in teaching at the Ethical Culture School (N.Y.), the School of Design and Liberal Arts (N.Y.), and Ohio State University, and working at the Cowan Pottery in Ohio.

The Marblehead Pottery remained a small operation, with only a half-dozen workers. It closed in 1936.

Merrimac Pottery

Work by this important New England pottery is not easy to find and is often stylistically clumsy, which probably explains why it does not fully enjoy the collecting base it deserves. Nevertheless, even Merrimac's average product is among the best ware of the Arts and Crafts potteries; it seems only a matter of time before collectors recognize its true value.

Merrimac's biggest contribution to the whole of art pottery is its striking matte and semi-gloss glazes, the best of which founder T.S. Nickerson himself developed. Although the range was limited, using mainly tones of green, these showed an uncommon depth and richness, as well as a curious color range from the deepest spinach-black to the softest lime. Other colors included a feathered orange, a dense and lifeless matte white, and gunmetal.

Most of the work was hand-thrown, though some was slip cast. While the decoration on numerous pieces seems to have been imparted by mold, there also exists evidence of hand-tooling after the fact. The shape selection ranges from languid to bulky.

For every elegantly modeled and glazed piece of Merrimac, there are several thick-walled vessels with either hastily tooled leaf decoration or none at all. Merrimac seems to have straddled the line between handcrafted and mass-produced ware regularly here, resulting in a body of work that ranges from striking to just good.

Nevertheless, even Merrimac's average ware is worthy of merit. In addition, its pottery will never glut the market because production remained limited for the reason, among others, that the firm operated for only 6 years.

Vase with Leaf Design, c.1905

The vessel is thick-walled.

The vase size is typical of Merrimac.

The feathered, dark green matte finish is excellent.

The stylized leaf design is hand-modeled.

Nicking at the rim and edges of the decoration has little negative impact on value.

The simple form is crudely potted.

Size: 8in/20.3cm
Value: $3,400–$4,600

Vase with Metallic Glaze, *c.*1905

The form is interesting, but thick and molded.

The metallic, dark-green glaze is extremely good.

The size is typical for this maker.

There is no modeled decoration.

The ware is unmarked.

Size: 8in/20.3cm
Value: $675–$875

• *Most Merrimac is handmade, although possibly 25% of the ware was molded. This strikes an odd note among Arts and Crafts makers, who usually chose to throw their ware.*
• *The majority of Merrimac pottery is adorned only with Nickerson's fine glazing; perhaps 20% is hand-modeled.*
• *About 90% of Merrimac ware is glazed with one of the maker's matte or semi-gloss green finishes.*
• *Most Merrimac pottery is under 10in/25.4cm tall; rarely do pieces exceed 12in/30.5cm in height.*
• *Merrimac is often unmarked. Earlier pieces bore a large black and white label that was often lost. Later pieces bear a large, die-stamped sturgeon over the company name. (The Native American word* merrimac, *meaning "sturgeon," is the name of the river that runs through Newburyport.)*
• *This ware tends to be heavy, due to the thick-walled vessels of red clay.*

Key Facts

Merrimac pottery was made in Newburyport, Mass., from about 1902 to about 1908. Founded by T.S. Nickerson in 1897 as the Merrimac Ceramic Company, the pottery produced inexpensive house ware and tiles, and reorganized 5 years later as the Merrimac Pottery Company.

Nickerson had studied in London with the English chemist and physicist Sir William Crookes and later spent considerable time experimenting with colors and glazing techniques on his own before launching his art pottery enterprise. While some resist any comparison between Merrimac's output and that of the nearby Grueby Pottery, no one denies that Grueby got there first and did a better job of it.

Nevertheless, Merrimac certainly ranks among the best of this country's Arts and Crafts producers. It distinguished itself in its exemplary selection of matte green finishes—a selection which is, in some regards, more interesting than Grueby's. The best of Merrimac's hand-decorated pottery is second to none.

Merrimac ware was heavily influenced by Roman antiquity, and much of its production centered on re-creating Classical forms and ideas. This preoccupation may ultimately have diverted the pottery from creating a more singular Arts and Crafts ware. Even so, Merrimac pottery was featured in Gustav Stickley's national magazine *The Craftsman*.

It remains a mystery why the company ceased production during the height of the Arts and Crafts period. It was sold to Frank A. Bray in 1908. Later that year, the pottery building and much of Merrimac's work was destroyed in a fire, making it difficult to determine whether the pottery had begun to focus on a more consistent Arts and Crafts style at this time.

Moravian Pottery and Tile Works

The Arts and Crafts products of the Moravian Pottery and Tile Works stand apart from anything else being fired at the turn of the century in the United States. The high-quality wares—handcrafted by laborers trained by founder Henry Chapman Mercer himself—exhibit the Arts and Crafts movement well.

While many of the designs were borrowed, as was typical, from medieval floor tiles, cast-iron stove panels, and architectural elements, the process with which they were manufactured was not. Mercer, a well-traveled archeologist and antiquities collector, sought to bring back the medieval craft of tile making. This required that wet clay be thickly pressed by a single craftsman into a hand-carved mold, fired in a small kiln, then painted with different-colored glazes, and fired once more. This time-consuming method contributed to Mercer's growing reputation as a serious proponent of the Arts and Crafts

movement. He proved to be an inspiration to many of this country's tile makers, including William Grueby, Ernest Batchelder, and Mary Chase Perry.

For elaborate installations, the Tile Works produced cookie-cutter-shaped "brocades" as paving tiles, on which the decorative elements were incised or impressed and glazed, leaving the hard-wearing surface in its biscuit state. It also created mosaic panels that looked like stained-glass windows, thematic fireplace surrounds, odd-sized large tiles, crockery, inkwells, and candle sconces. Collectors of tiles or Arts and Crafts items aggressively seek out the rarer and larger items.

The pottery also produced several lines of 4-inch molded tiles representing tall ships, zodiac signs, and farming through the seasons, among other subjects. These are fairly common, making them a good starting point for someone wishing to collect tiles (under $100).

Green Tree Tile, c.1915

This is a fine, rare, and large tile for Moravian.

Notice the unusual oval shape.

The stylized tree was a popular motif during the Arts and Crafts movement. This particular one was designed from an early 19th century Philadelphia cast-iron fire mark.

The entire tile is dipped in buff slip (liquid clay), and then a transparent green glaze is added, topped by a clear overglaze.

This one fired beautifully. The large panels often have firing lines where the clay split during firing.

Size: 12in x 8in/
30.5cm x 20.3cm
Value: $1,000–$1,300

Steamboat Tile, *c.*1915

This tile is extremely rare.

Large by Moravian standards, this example is one of relatively few 6in/15.2cm tiles that were produced.

Both the firing line and the chips to the edges will decrease this tile's value.

The pottery covered this tile in a fine green and ivory semi-matte glaze.

The piece is self-framed.

Size: 6in/15.2cm square
Value: $4000–$600

• *The brocade wall tiles were pressed in molds. These feature such topics as historical depictions, flowers ($35–$50), and musicians ($200–$250).*
• *The pottery produced a limited number of molded drinking cups, bowls, and plates—rare and worth from $500 to $1,000 or more.*
• *The pottery also built items from 4-inch tiles. These included cube-shaped inkwells and boxes (rare, especially with lids, worth $500–$700), candle sconces ($250–$500), planters ($3,000 and up in good condition), and side tables set with 4-inch tiles.*
• *Aside from his most popular glazes, Mercer painted his brocades in polychromatic matte and glossy colors. He also produced a line of 4-inch-tall ships in dead-matte Wedgwood blue and white.*
• *Most original tiles are not signed. A few were stamped "MP" or "Moravian HCM." Tiles done since 1974 are stamped "MP" on the back and dated.*

Key Facts

Concerned that the ancient method of tile making was being lost and forgotten, the archeologist and artefact collector Henry Chapman Mercer founded the Moravian Pottery and Tile Works on his family's estate in Doylestown, Penn., in 1898. The name "Moravian" came from the German immigrants who brought the tile-making process to Pennsylvania in the 18th century.

Mercer trained a crew of men to produce tiles by pressing wet local clay into handcarved molds. He designed all the tiles, mostly using patterns borrowed from other sources, such as European and Middle Eastern tiles, Mexican pictographs, and Moravian (German) stove plates.

In 1904, Mercer won the grand prize for tiles at the Louisiana Purchase Exposition. He built himself a larger pottery building made of concrete in the style of a Spanish mission in 1912. He also built a state-of-the-art concrete castle, Fonthill, on the same property. This served not only as his home but as a showcase for his extensive collection of tiles. The Mercer Museum, another imposing concrete building, was erected in Doylestown from 1913 to 1916, to house Mercer's collection of early tools and implements, which he donated to the Historical Society.

The tile works enjoyed steady success for several decades until Mercer passed away in 1930. It was subsequently owned and operated by several people, starting with his assistant, Frank Swain. The pottery closed in 1964 and was reopened as a museum in 1969 by the Bucks County Department of Parks and Recreation. The reproduction of tiles began in 1974 and has continued ever since.

Mosaic Tile Company

The Mosaic Tile Company of Zanesville, Ohio, bridged the era between Victorian dust-pressed majolica tiles and the faience tiles of the 1920s and 1930s. Managed by astute businessmen, its early products appear to have been such bread-and-butter items as plain, dust-pressed floor and wall tiling. However, Herman C. Mueller went on to launch a line of mass-produced, dust-pressed encaustic floor tile that brought the firm a new level of success.

Used mainly for flooring, indoor and out, the mosaic was inlaid and matte, or bisque-fired, like encaustic tiles. Because of its texture and small, square design, it resembled petit-point embroidery or Southwestern Native-American textile patterns (the tiles' inspiration). The mosaics were also available in Classical patterns or in a German-American vernacular popular in the Midwest, featuring mounted elk heads or beer-drinking scenes. Both artistic and practical, the new line proved sufficiently successful for the company to open a lavish eight-story office building and showroom in New York City at the turn of the century.

The Mosaic tiles most sought after today were produced only after 1918. Made of plastic clay, these faience tiles had a thicker body and a charming irregularity that was missing in the machine-made, dust-pressed tiles. Some of the sheer, matte-finish glazes also recalled tile work of the Arts and Crafts movement. Produced in 4in/10.2cm and 6in/15.2cm squares, the larger-size examples seldom appear on the market. Several of the firm's most successful designs—including a galleon and an elephant standing on a ball inscribed with the company's initials—have subsequently been reproduced. The reproductions are much more common today than the originals.

Some of the panels produced in the 1940s and 1950s, while not of faience bodies, have collectible value. Made of thin commercial tile, these have hard-edged decorations in *cuerda seca*, a wax-resist process that creates a black outline around the different glazes. They feature popular subjects, such as fishing boats or flamingoes, which are stylized so as to resemble children's illustrations or run-of-the-mill commercial art.

Faience Tile with Camel and Rider, *c.*1920

This thick, irregular, red-clay faience tile dates from Mosaic's most sought after period, post-1918.

The matte micro-crystalline glaze, slightly sheer, allows the clay to show through.

The stylized design adds interest, as does the unusual subject matter.

The tile is self-framed.

Size: 4in/10.2cm square
Value: $225–$275

Encausstic Mosaic Tile Floor, c.1895

This installation of encaustic mosaic tiles from Zanesville, Ohio, shows a four-tile snowflake pattern.

Made of poured clay with a high-fired body, the tiles' decoration was produced from colored clays within a grid of very small squares.

Because of its "inlaid" and unglazed construction, the pattern is hard-wearing and the tiles used mostly as flooring.

The Florentine arabesque and snowflake pattern, while attractive, is not as desirable as a landscape or animals.

Soft, natural clay colors that lack punch make these tiles an acquired taste.

Most tiles have sustained considerable damage over the last century, and therefore do not come up for sale often.

Several chips and cracks affect the value of these tiles.

Size: Four 6in/15.2cm square tiles
Value: $150–$200

- *Encausstic Mosaic tiles are not highly collectible today. A 16-tile panel, in good shape, brings less than $1,000.*
- *Mosaic produced fine tiles in 6in/15.2cm red-clay faience beginning in 1918, decorated with galleons, cars, children, and balancing elephants.*
- *Well-crafted 4in/10.2cm tiles had unusual subjects—a child riding a lamb or goat, or an egret with what seemed to be a human head in its beak.*
- *"Hispania" tiles, transfer-printed on faience bodies, used two-dimensional polychrome.*
- *A single 4in/10.2cm, dust-pressed tile in cuerda seca, c.1940s, of a frog might bring $50; a panel of nine to twelve tiles could bring $350–$550.*

Key Facts

The Mosaic Tile Company was founded in Zanesville, Ohio, in 1894 as a floor-tile plant, with modeler Herman C. Mueller and chemist Karl Langenbeck as superintendents. The creation and patent of the encaustic mosaic tile proved a great success.

The hard-wearing, vitreous floor tile was dust-pressed from up to about a dozen colored clays into very small squares (2,601 per 6in/15.2cm tile, to be exact). Borrowing from many different styles and techniques, Mueller took the concept of the old encaustic tile further by making it cheaper to produce in a greater range of designs. While his innovation won him the John Scott Medal from the Franklin Institute of Philadelphia in 1898 and was a commercial success, the tiles were not produced after 1900.

In addition to the Zanesville plant, the company opened an eight-story showroom, with an extravagantly tiled façade, in New York City in 1901 (demolished in 1954). Two years later, Mueller left, eventually to open the Mueller Mosaic Tile Company in Trenton, N.J. *(see pages 92–93).*

In about 1918, Mosaic added the production of faience tile to its output, supervised from 1920 to 1923 by Englishman Harry Rhead (brother of Frederick Hurten Rhead), formerly with the Roseville Pottery. By that time, Mosaic had showrooms in the major metropolitan centers of the U.S. Its business actually thrived through the Great Depression, primarily by diversifying. Mosaic outlasted its rival, the American Encaustic Tiling Co., purchasing other tile companies along the way before it closed in 1967.

Mueller Mosaic Tile Company

Herman Carl Mueller opened the Mueller Mosaic Tile Company in Trenton, N.J., in 1909. He located his new company on the former site of the Artistic Porcelain Company at Chambers Street and Cedar Lane. There, he designed and produced high-quality, handmade faience tiles of thick red clay. Available in different sizes, often in friezes or mosaics, these Arts and Crafts tiles were covered in superior matte glazes textured with "oatmealing" or subtle speckling.

The Mueller Tile Co. also produced mosaic tiles for walls, floors, bathrooms, mantels, and swimming pools. The company catalog of 1909 identifies these tiles under such categories as "Florentine Mosaic," "Oriental," "Roman Faience Mosaic," and "Modern." The firm produced plain pavers, borders, moldings, and numbers and letters like those made at Moravian Pottery and Tile Works.

Mueller had trained as a sculptor and, once on his own, did a fair amount of three-dimensional architectural faience. Buildings all over the country used his faience in their ornamentation, including the Crescent Temple in his local town of Trenton. Mueller's tiles also adorned several stations of the New York City subway system, as well as the Garden Pier in Atlantic City, N.J. In addition, his tiles were chosen for the American embassy in Tokyo.

Since then, the Mueller Mosaic tile panels have become quite collectible. While usually unmarked, they are easily recognizable after a little study of Mueller's techniques and glazes. The red plastic clay body, molded or incised technique, Arts and Crafts style, and distinctive glazes may be similar to some produced by his former company, the Mosaic Tile Company, but they can usually be ascribed to his hand after examination.

Six-Tile Peacock, c. 1925

This large and elaborate panel uses many colors and a complicated design to make a single image.

The peacock—originally a Persian motif—was used often during the Aesthetic and Arts and Crafts movements and during the Art Deco period.

While unsigned, this piece can be found in the Mueller Mosaic catalog.

The incised, red clay shows through.

This work was glazed using the "enameling" technique.

The work is mounted in an old frame (not shown).

Size: 18 x 12in/ 45.7 x 30.5cm
Value: $1,800–$2,500

Pair of Birds, *c.*1915

This is another example of panels made up of tiles that create a single design.

While not marked, these pieces were pictured in the original Mueller Mosaic catalog.

Typical of Mueller's speckled matte glazes, these are earlier and more in the Arts and Crafts style than the peacock panel opposite.

While a little folksy, they have a pleasing, handmade quality to them.

Although mounted or grouted on board, this work is not framed.

Small chips to the corners lower the work's value.

Size: 16 x 4in/
40.6 x 10.2cm
Value: $1,500–$2,000

• *Mueller Mosaic tiles are handsome, high-quality tiles and panels of thick red plastic clay (faience), molded or incised with designs in the Arts and Crafts style and covered in fine matte enamels.*
• *Mueller produced faience tiles in 6in/15.2cm and 8in/20.3cm sizes molded with a variety of designs, including the arts, zodiac signs, Dutch scenes, ecclesiastic symbols, flora, fauna, medieval characters and castles, nursery rhymes, ships, and trees.*
• *Mueller also made large rondelles with more elaborate designs, such as European towns, faux-mosaic nursery rhyme motifs, ships, and peasants in national costumes.*
• *Mueller's large, single-tile or frieze panels depicted similar patterns and were incised and glazed with polychromatic matte enamels.*

Key Facts

After having studied in Nuremberg and Munich, Germany, Herman C. Mueller arrived in Cincinnati, Ohio, in 1879. During the 1880s and 1890s, he worked in several important American tile factories, including the Matt Morgan Art Pottery (Cincinnati, *c.*1883–84); Kensington Art Tile Company (Newport, Ky., 1885); and American Encaustic Tiling Company (Zanesville, Ohio, 1887–94). In 1894, Mueller founded the Mosaic Tile Company in Zanesville, Ohio, with Karl Langenbeck.

Mueller left Mosaic and moved to Trenton, a major pottery center by then, to work at the Robertson Art Branch of the National Tile Company in 1903.

Finally, in 1909, he founded his own Mueller Mosaic Tile Company in Trenton. While Mueller Mosaic produced tiles and architectural faience for buildings all over the country, one project stands out for its originality and scope.

A cutting-edge dairy farm in Plainsboro, N.J., had become renowned for its experimental "Rotolactor process." It opened its doors to visitors by adding an observation room situated just above the milking room. It was for the interior of this area that Mueller Mosaic produced 15 large murals depicting the history of the dairy industry through the ages. The dairy operation ceased on June 18, 1971, and the building was eventually demolished.

Mueller Mosaic Tile Co. continued to operate until shortly after Mueller's death in 1941.

Newcomb College Pottery

The pottery produced at Newcomb College in New Orleans, La., has been a collector favorite for three decades. Soft, attractive, and feminine, the ware was usually glazed in shades of blue, covering natural designs of indigenous flowers, nightscapes, and occasionally, creatures of the bayou.

One of our true Arts and Crafts potteries, Newcomb College was founded by Ellsworth Woodward to introduce Victorian women to the applied arts. While its curriculum included bookbinding, metalwork, and needlework, it is best remembered for its decorative and highly popular works in clay, each of which was a one-of-a-kind example.

Newcomb pottery was always hand-thrown (in the case of tiles, hand-built). Early pieces were decorated with surface painting. Gentle incising was later added, making the design stronger. Eventually, decoration was modeled into the raw clay, providing more depth and detail.

Early pieces from Newcomb—those most sought by modern-day collectors—are covered in mirrorlike glossy finishes. Colors on these early pieces are usually blues and creams. Pieces with yellow decoration command the highest prices. Such pieces are distinctive and unique, with themes varying greatly from one piece to the next.

The biscuit used was fairly dense, and most pieces have remained intact. Minor damage is acceptable.

Large Lily Pitcher, c. 1905

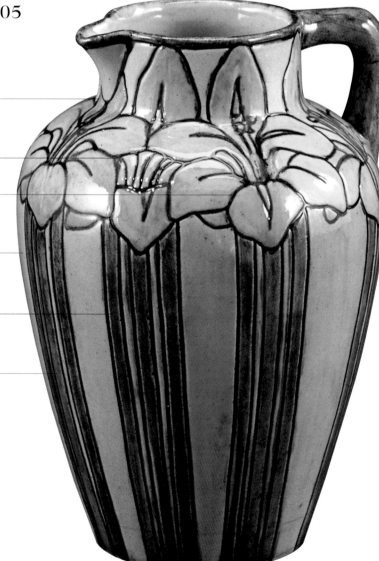

Vivid color contributes to the effect.

The strong design is distinctly Arts and Crafts, which is very desirable.

The design is deeply incised and boldly drawn.

The graceful curves of this pitcher enhance the attractiveness of the piece.

The work is not delineated in a band but is carried throughout the surface.

For a Newcomb pitcher, this is larger than usual and therefore more valuable.

Size: 8½ in/21.6cm
Value: $14,000–$16,000

Flower Band Pitcher, *c.*1905

The curving form is less graceful than that of some of Newcomb's comparable work.

The piece is smaller than Newcomb's average size of 8in/20.3cm.

The flowers are tightly drawn, but not lush and large.

This design is restricted to a band.

The decoration is crisp though not brightly colored.

This high-glazed finish is typical of Newcomb's early work and is very desirable

Size: 6½ in/16.5cm
Value: $5,000–$6,000

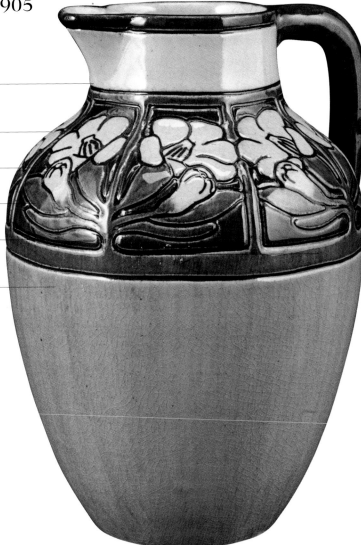

• *All Newcomb College ware was made by hand, most of it thrown by Joseph Meyer. Even the tiles were hand-built, as seen by the "HB" cipher.*
• *Newcomb is a soft and feminine ware, with curving forms covered with tones of blue and green. The forms are unforced, or easily thrown on a potter's wheel.*
• *Most pieces of Newcomb pottery are under 8in/20.3cm tall. Taller examples, some over 20in/50.8cm, are known to exist; pieces taller than 10in/25.4cm are "large."*
• *Newcomb is one of the only potteries the value of which has never decreased over the last 30 years.*
• *Some damage is acceptable to modern-day collectors, partly because of the uniqueness of each piece.*
• *Flowers are the most common decoration, followed by native landscape and bayou scenes. Insects, quadrupeds, and birds are the rarest of Newcomb subjects and always sell for a premium.*

Key Facts

Newcomb College Pottery was the brainchild of Ellsworth Woodward, an important New Orleans artist and an excellent teacher. Founded in 1896, the college's mission was to give students "practical information as to a method of earning a living through the curriculum." Other skilled teachers joined the staff, including Paul Cox, Mary Sheerer, Leona Nicholson, and Frederick Walrath.

During the early period, many of the pottery decorators were undergraduate female students. They were able to sell some of their pieces in the campus store and could keep a percentage of the profit generated. The pottery's early high-glazed work was phased out by about 1910. A transitional period was characterized by soft, "waxy" finishes, mainly in blues and soft greens. By about 1914, nearly all Newcomb's work was covered in the soft matte finishes for which the studio is now best known. Later work, from about 1935 until the mid-1940s, was again finished in high glaze. This, however, has little of the quality and charm of earlier efforts, which is reflected in its value.

Newcomb College—
Early Incised Ware

These pieces come from what is considered Newcomb's most successful period. Designs are bold, colorful, and lushly drawn, combining the best of European and American influences. As with any pottery, vase forms command the highest prices.

Numerous artists worked as teachers during this early period, including several whose work is eagerly sought. These include Harriet Joor, Leona Nicholson, and Henrietta Bailey. The earliest art ware from the time was surface-painted, and the lack of modeled or incised decoration limited definition, depth, and value. Works like those seen here, c.1902–1909, show how Newcomb College ware evolved more sophisticated forms and decorative techniques during this most flourishing period.

Surface modeling can range from the simple incised outlining of the design to deep modeling and the gentle excising of the negative space. In general, the more tooling of the surface, the more valuable the piece.

Blue Thistle Vase, c.1905

This piece has an early, high-glazed finish.

The thistle is a strong Arts and Crafts design and is rarely used by Newcomb College.

Decoration is both modeled and surface-painted.

The design extends the length of the vase.

Color is limited but well used.

The cylindrical form is not a collector favorite.

Size: 9in/22.9cm
Value: $15,000–$20,000

Lilies Vase, *c.*1905

This is a classic Newcomb form.

The large, fleshy blossom is soft, feminine, and beautiful.

The vase is both modeled and hand-painted.

Decoration commands the surface of this piece, which is larger than most Newcomb ware.

This vase is everything Newcomb collectors are looking for.

Size: 12in/30.5cm
Value: $25,500–$34,500

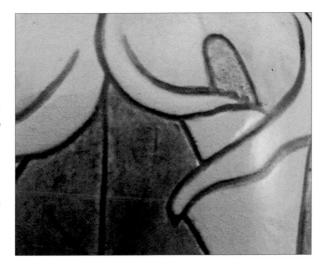

• *Height, as always, matters in terms of value: 8in/20.3cm is average, 12in/30.5 is considered large, and 15in/38cm or more is unusual.*

• *Colors from this early period are mostly in tones of blue, green, and cream, though yellow appears more at this time than at any other. Rarely, violet is also used.*

• *During this time, Newcomb experimented with a* **Sang de Boeuf** *finish—a rich, glossy red that ultimately competed with the decoration and was discontinued.*

• *Nearly all work done at this time is modeled and/or incised, as well as surface decorated.*

◀ *This close-up shows how the design on the vase above was delineated by incising the border and coloring the outline with dark (usually cobalt) glazing. Note the gentle modeling of the surface, creating depth and greater detail.*

Newcomb College— Matte Floral Ware

Newcomb College ware evolved from high-gloss finishes to soft matte glazes around 1910. Though these pieces seldom command prices as high as the pottery's earlier ware, they have always been collector favorites because they display much of the same quality and charm. Such middle-period work is almost entirely floral or scenic and almost always expressed in tones of blue and cream. Even though each piece is handmade, and therefore unique, the range of the work is relatively limited, and the pieces tend to be similar in appearance. Such pieces always have designs that are hand-modeled, although the depth and detail of the cut differ from piece to piece, varying the impact. They tend to have designs that are restricted to the upper portion of the pot; those with all-over designs command a premium.

Colors tend toward the blues and greens. The addition of yellow and cream creates a more visually interesting and valuable piece.

Tall Vase with Flowers, c.1920

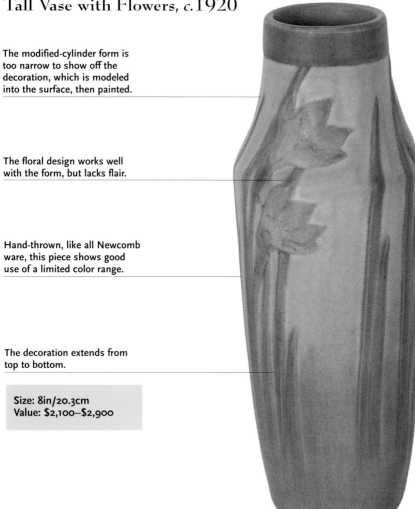

The modified-cylinder form is too narrow to show off the decoration, which is modeled into the surface, then painted.

The floral design works well with the form, but lacks flair.

Hand-thrown, like all Newcomb ware, this piece shows good use of a limited color range.

The decoration extends from top to bottom.

Size: 8in/20.3cm
Value: $2,100–$2,900

Squat Vase with Daffodils, *c.*1915

The vase form is large and bulbous.

These alternating leaves and flowers are beautifully designed.

The modeled decoration is crisply drawn.

This broad shape is a collector favorite, pleasing and well-suited to displaying decoration.

The use of color is good.

Artwork covers almost the entire surface.

Size: 8in/20.3cm
Value: $8,500–$11,500

• *Many of the criteria that pertain to early glossy ware are the same for matte-glazed pieces produced later.*
• *Sharper carving delineates the decoration, adding strength and value. Not all work from this period is crisp, however: look for depth and detail.*
• *Additional colors that were used occasionally, including yellow, mint green, and pink, will always add value.*
• *Fewer artists worked at this time: 90% of middle-period ware is from the hands of Sadie Irvine, Henrietta Bailey, and Anna F. Simpson.*
• *Such pieces often show decoration only near the top of the vase. All-over designs make a piece more valuable and salable.*

◀ *Note the carved detailing tooled into the surface of the pot, sharpening the design and giving it a strong sense of dimension.*

Newcomb College—
Bayou Scenes

Flowers are the most common of Newcomb designs. However, the pottery's languid bayou scenes, often with views of a full moon seen through live oaks, are its most popular. Like the flower motifs, these scenes can appear repetitive because the same theme is so often used. Yet each piece was individually crafted, and subtle differences between examples abound, apparent to the careful observor. Better—and more valuable—examples have deeper modeling, stronger color, and bolder design.

Occasionally, landscape scenes depict houses, fences, and, on rare pieces, church steeples.

Other factors that determine value are size and shape. These bayou scenes are best when designed so that viewing a piece from a single vantage point still allows the viewer to see most of the scene. As such, squat, bulbous forms showing sweeping vistas seem best suited. Taller vases with long, modeled oak trees offer another attractive variation that fits form and subject.

Vase with Blue Tree, c.1915

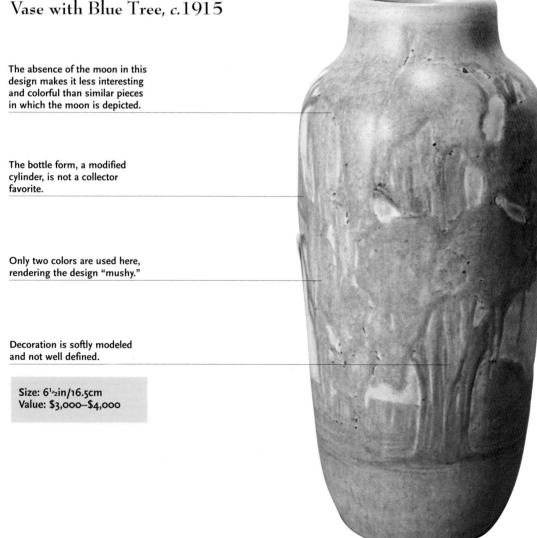

The absence of the moon in this design makes it less interesting and colorful than similar pieces in which the moon is depicted.

The bottle form, a modified cylinder, is not a collector favorite.

Only two colors are used here, rendering the design "mushy."

Decoration is softly modeled and not well defined.

Size: 6½in/16.5cm
Value: $3,000–$4,000

Vase with Drooping Tree, *c.*1915

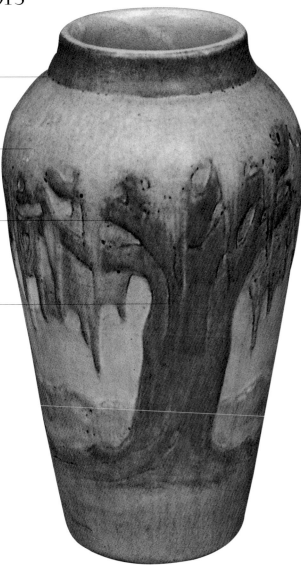

This vase is taller than average and has a classic Newcomb form.

The mottling of the glaze occurred during the firing and resulted in an unusual effect.

Crisper modeling helps make it distinctive.

Deeper colors and a greater range of colors add visual appeal.

Size: 9in/22.9cm
Value: $7,000–$9,000

- *All Newcomb vases were hand-thrown, including these bayou scenes.*
- *While most landscapes are variations on the same theme, some are augmented by the addition of buildings, fences, and a full moon.*
- *Colors tend toward shades of blue and green. Rarer and more valuable are those with yellow or pink horizons.*
- *The majority of Newcomb College's bayou pieces stand about 6in/15.2cm in height, although a handful have surfaced measuring over 18in/45.7cm tall. The latter are extremely valuable.*
- *The depth of cut, or modeling, varies greatly. The deeper the cut and the sharper the detailing, the more valuable the piece.*
- *Collectors prefer the foreground hues that were designed in the deeper, darker colors, especially dark blue.*

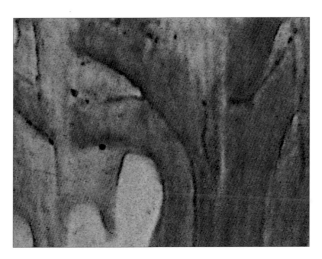

◀ *The surface of this vase was carved in degrees, providing the appearance of depth. This example was more intricately carved than most.*

George Ohr Pottery

George Ohr was arguably the best potter this country produced. His eccentric personality extended to his pottery, and he created a body of work that is unlike that of any other American artist.

While Ohr's early work was fairly traditional, reflecting the somewhat primitive country pottery of the day, his hand grew freer as he matured. He usually glazed his early pieces in tones of yellow, green, and brown. Their forms were also typical of the times and limited to such utilitarian uses as pitchers. These pieces are the least valuable from a collector's point of view.

During the 1890s, almost certainly motivated by the fire that destroyed his building, kiln, and stock of pottery, Ohr explored deeply an unconventional style he had earlier only toyed with. His color range exploded into hues of red, blue, bright green, purple, and orange, often mixed together to produce startling effects. Pieces bearing these glazes are among his most treasured objects.

But perhaps more important were his forms, thrown paper thin and manipulated with twists, crinkles, dimples, and folds. Few people could have crafted pots so thin, and no one else thought to alter them in such bizarre ways. The most expensive of Ohr's pots, and the most desirable to collectors, are those that combine bright, imaginative colors with intense manipulation of form.

After about 1900, Ohr decided not to glaze his pots. "God put no color in souls, and I'll put no color on my pottery," was his explanation for the choice. These last of his creations are in many ways the most important of all his output. While no glazes adorn them, the natural colors of the clay interacting with the heat of the kiln provide decoration enough.

More seasoned collectors covet the bisque pieces, but the work takes some getting used to. While the pots don't bring nearly as much as extravagantly glazed vessels, the best of them can cost above $10,000 each.

Ohr stopped potting in about 1907. Because he was difficult to deal with, and because his work was so odd, nearly his entire body of work, totaling almost 10,000 pieces, remained unsold until after his death.

Twisted Red Glazed Vase, c.1900

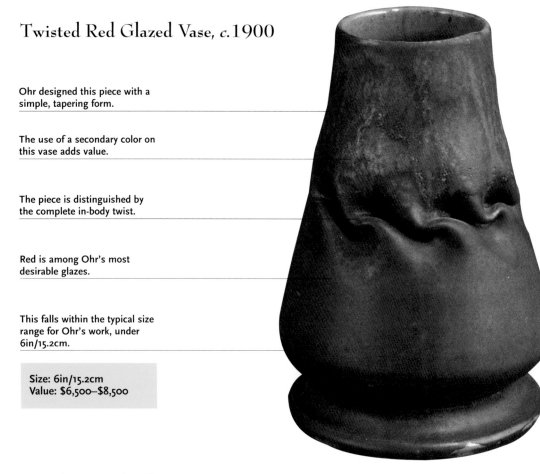

Ohr designed this piece with a simple, tapering form.

The use of a secondary color on this vase adds value.

The piece is distinguished by the complete in-body twist.

Red is among Ohr's most desirable glazes.

This falls within the typical size range for Ohr's work, under 6in/15.2cm.

Size: 6in/15.2cm
Value: $6,500–$8,500

Red Blistered Glaze Vase, *c.*1900

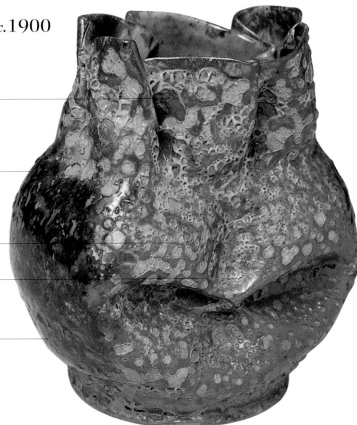

The pleated top and collapsed body add vitality to this unusual form.

This piece exhibits a more complex form than the example opposite.

The rare red blistered glaze combined with a blistered secondary glaze adds value to this piece.

Notice the paper-thin body.

This is a "complete" piece, blending exceptional glazing and form.

Size: 5in/12.7cm
Value: $35,000–$45,000

• Ohr's best pieces were usually his thinnest, which apparently allowing him more latitude for manipulation of the form.
• Great glazes do not necessarily make great pots, but rarely will a collector find an exceptional Ohr piece with a boring finish.
• Even Ohr's best glazes worked better when he mixed them with secondary and tertiary finishes.
• Ohr worked best in hand-size pieces. The more he could manipulate the entire surface at a single time, the more unified the object became. Larger pieces, necessarily hand-worked in steps, often seem at odds with themselves.

Key Facts

George Edgar Ohr was born in 1857 in Biloxi, Miss., of French-Alsatian descent. In 1879, with practically no education and a history of only brief stints at many different jobs, he accepted the invitation of a family friend, Joseph Meyer, to move to New Orleans and learn the potting craft. He stayed on for about two years. Wanting to expand his knowledge of ceramics, Ohr undertook a trip to the East Coast and the Midwest, visiting every pottery he could find. He returned to New Orleans in 1882, where he worked briefly for the William Virgin Pottery, and possibly for Meyer again.

In 1883, he moved back to Biloxi and with meager savings set out to build a pottery. He built everything himself, dug his own clay from a nearby river, and produced mainly bisque-fired utilitarian ware such as stove pipes, water bottles, and flowerpots, which he then sold door-to-door from a pushcart. He started throwing art ware for the upcoming 1885 World's Industrial and Cotton Centennial Exposition in New Orleans.

He spent all his savings setting up at the exposition, bringing his wheel and some 600 pieces, and performing throwing tricks for tourists. A dishonest shipper, hired to cart what was left of his inventory (probably most of it) back home, took off with the pots, never to be seen again.

In 1886, Ohr married Josephine (Josie) Gehring. Shortly thereafter, he built a shop—the Biloxi Art and Novelty Pottery—where tourists could buy his wares. In the late 1880s, Ohr returned to New Orleans to work with Meyer at the New Orleans Art Pottery (later the Newcomb College Pottery). He stayed less than a year; he returned home a true art potter.

George Ohr Pottery— Two-Handled Vases

George Ohr explored many different designs, some apparently for short periods of time until he "worked them through." Certain designs persisted throughout his career, however, and tall, two-handled vases were among them.

Some of Ohr's best work was lavished on such vases. They tended to be taller than most of his other pottery, and the glazes were often more striking. Judging by the marks they bear, he produced these for a long period of time, and some development of style is evident.

As with any of Ohr's work, modern collectors are most interested in striking colors and manipulated forms. Taller is definitely better in terms of desirability. A careful study of his two-handled vases shows great diversity in the types of handles, the shapes of the vessels, and the manipulations that alter them.

Damage affects the value of such Ohr pieces less than the work of any other potter. They are, after all, one-of-a-kind pieces. As Ohr himself said, "God created no two souls alike, and I'll make no two pots alike."

Looped Two-Handled Vase, c.1900

This vase is larger than most Ohr pots.

While the glazing is dark, it is enhanced with a metallic flambé effect.

This simple form is thicker than most of his ware.

Ohr used simple looped handles.

Ohr introduced no manipulation to the surface.

Size: 10in/25.4cm
Value: $20,000–$30,000

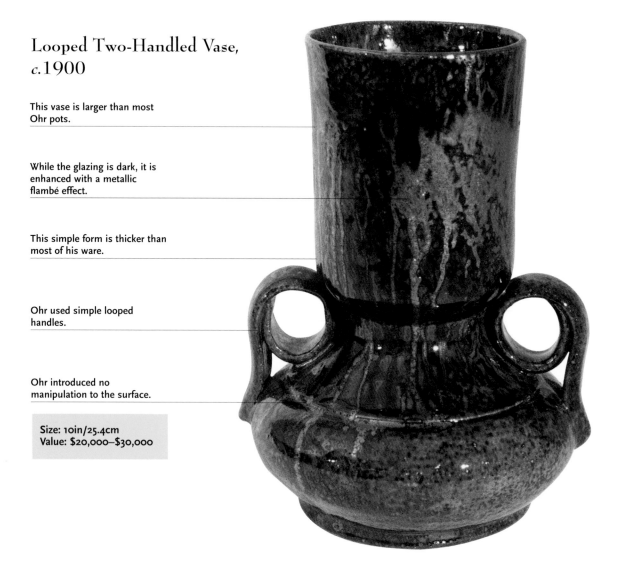

Double-Gourd Handled Vase, *c.*1900

The manipulated rim on this piece is classic Ohr.

This vase is larger than most Ohr pots.

Ohr used a more complex double-gourd form on this piece than on the example opposite.

Both the thinly potted body and the double-loop handles add to the vase's value.

Notice the excellent red glazing.

Size: 10in/25.4cm
Value: $40,000–$50,000

• *Ohr's two-handled vessels have always been a favorite of collectors.*
• *Ohr seems to have enjoyed this design form, saving some of his most extravagant glazes and manipulations for these.*
• *Minor damage has little impact on the value of his two-handled vases. These are rare, unique, and in demand.*
• *Prices for these pieces begin at about $10,000, and some are worth as much as $100,000.*
• *The best of these date to the late 19th century.*

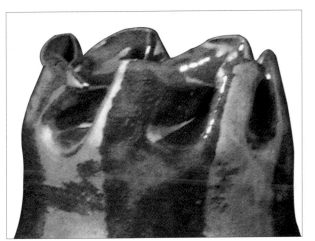

◀ *Note the manipulated rim of the two-handled vase, shown here. Any such manipulation on the body of a vessel significantly increases its value.*

George Ohr—Teapots

Ohr seemed to understand that to be considered a complete potter, he would have to perfect the teapot form. Similar to his exploration of the two-handled vase, the teapot became a leitmotif of Ohr's career, and he played with the form like no other potter in the United States. A true potter, he explored the teapot form as a botanist would study variations of hybrid roses.

Some of Ohr's most memorable vessels were, in fact, teapots. They provide a glimpse into his love for his craft. The Smithsonian collection, for example, includes an Ohr coffee-teapot, with the teapot facing one way and the coffeepot facing the other, each equipped with its own lid, spout, and handle, and pouring in a different direction. He also created cadogans, or bottom-loading trick teapots, that poured while being held upright, each with a totally different surface and glaze treatment.

Most teapots were of simple body form, "merely" thrown—albeit masterfully so—and covered with bright glazes of purple, scarlet, and blistered red. Occasionally, some were created with lids fused in place, rendering them unusable. It was, after all, the development of form and idea that drove Ohr, not necessarily the function of the piece. Actually using his teapots must have seemed a sacrilege to him.

Sizes ranged from miniature, about 3in/7.6cm, to large, about 8in/20.3cm tall and more than 12in/30,5cm across. About 20% of his teapots show some extraordinary body manipulation.

Today, Ohr's teapots, which come in many shapes and sizes, start in price at about $3,000, and the best of them sell for nearly $100,000. Average pots retail in the $5,000–10,000 range.

Multiglaze Teapot, *c.*1895

This is an average-size teapot for Ohr ware.

The applied kink handle and serpentine spout add appeal to a sedate form.

Ohr made good use of color here, incorporating five glazes.

The double-gourd form adds visual interest to the hand-thrown, simple piece.

Size: 6in/15.2cm
Value: $6,000–$8,000

Teapot with Serpent, *c.*1895

Like the example opposite, this is an average-size teapot.

The applied snake is extremely rare and adds great value to the pot.

The serpentine spout was probably slip cast and applied to the body.

The rare and desirable violet and black glazing increases this piece's value considerably.

Size: 5½in/14cm
Value: $20,000–$30,000

- *Ohr made several hundred teapots during his career, exploring the idea continuously.*
- *The best of them are usually extravagantly glazed, some with blistered red and blue finishes, dripping reds and creams, or vibrant blues and yellows.*
- *Rarely, Ohr's teapots are adorned with applied snakes. Each is hand-formed by the master and affixed to the surface before glazing.*
- *Simple design elements are what combine to create a masterpiece. While aggressive glazing is an obvious benefit, less striking touches like an interesting handle or an uncommon spout can add considerable value.*
- *While teapots were less manipulated than most of Ohr's other forms, the ones that have been twisted or otherwise "tickled" will always sell for a premium price.*

Key Facts

George Ohr attended the Chicago World's Fair in 1893, where he went unnoticed but studied ceramics from all major European and domestic potteries. A year later, a fire blazed through Biloxi, completely destroying Ohr's Pot-Ohr-E, its large inventory, and the Ohr home. Ohr immediately built a larger structure, this one with a five-story tower—Biloxi Art Pottery Unlimited—that would attract tourists.

Ohr exhibited at the Cotton States and International Exposition in Atlanta, Ga., in 1895. His works were also displayed at the Paris Exposition Universelle in 1900 and the Pan-American Exposition in Buffalo in 1901. That same year, Ohr announced formally through a letter to the *Crockery and Glass Journal* that his entire collection of art ware was for sale, but would not be divided. Not wishing to part with his "mud babies," he did so rarely and reluctantly.

In 1903, Ohr stopped glazing his pots and concentrated on purely bisque forms. At the Louisiana Purchase International Exposition in 1904, he won a silver medal but did not sell a single piece and could not afford his trip back home. He took a teaching position in St. Louis until he earned enough money to cart his inventory and himself back to Biloxi.

Between 1906 and 1910, George and Josie were caught in a drawn-out lawsuit, during which he was arrested a couple of times. He stopped potting around 1907, frail, in debt, and bitter. He gave the building to his sons Leo and Oto, who transformed the Biloxi Art Pottery into the Ohr Boys Auto Repairing Shop. The elder Ohr stashed the precious pottery in the shop's attic.

George Ohr died of cancer in 1918, in Biloxi, at age 61. His entire pottery collection was sold to an antique dealer from New Jersey in 1972.

George Ohr Pottery— Bisque Ware

In the early days of collecting art pottery, around 1975, Ohr's unglazed pots were thought to be "unfinished." These were difficult to sell, and the best of them could be easily purchased for under $100 each. Collectors eventually figured out, however, that Ohr considered his unglazed pottery his most mature work.

Ohr's statement, "God put no color in souls, and I'll put no color on my vases," suggests that Ohr saw this as a step forward. While the relative austerity of these objects doesn't immediately appeal to the American collector, they possess a subtlety that is seldom approached in period American art pottery.

For example, while bisque pieces bear no glaze color, they are not bereft of hue. In some cases, the heat of the kiln nudged the iron in the clay to form black spots or ridges against the soft brown ground. Ohr left about 2,500 pieces of his 10,000-piece cache unglazed.

More important are pieces bearing scroddled clays, where muds of different colors are blended to create a swirled effect. This is pure Arts and Crafts potting, in which the materials integral to the construction of the object become elements of its decoration. No contrived adornment is necessary.

The bisque ware provides an excellent opportunity for serious collectors with limited funds. While far more expensive than ever before, the best pieces can be had for a fraction of what glazed examples would cost. They are also easier to find because even with all the information available today, many collectors either do not understand them, do not like them, or both.

Scroddled Clay Bisque Vase, c.1906

This is a typical, hand-size vase.

Ohr used a severely manipulated form to distinguish this piece.

Scroddled clays create the swirled effect that enhances the value of this piece.

No longer recognizable as a vase, the piece simply becomes sculpture.

Size: 6in/15.2cm
Value: $10,600–$14,400

Bisque Face Vase, *c.*1905

The crimped top accentuates the otherwise simple form.

This is a typical size for a bisque vase.

Notice that Ohr relied on clay color only, with no scroddling of mixed clays.

The "face" decoration is quite unusual.

Size: 5in/12.7cm
Value: $4,250–$5,750

• *Most of Ohr's unglazed pieces bear his large, script signature mark. Relatively few have the die-stamp designation.*

• *The brittle, unglazed bisque pieces are prone to damage, and minor flaws have little to no negative effect on value.*

• *Once again, Ohr's work even here is mostly small in scale. The best pieces are hand-size and severely manipulated.*

• *The bisque ware often represents the most mature expression of Ohr's work, and some of his heavily tortured vessels are masterpieces of modern design.*

• **Be careful!** *Nearly all of the fake "Ohr" that continues to circulate through the marketplace has, as its base, an original Ohr bisque vase with a new glaze. Done some time in the 1970s by an ill-advised pair of New Jersey imitators, these enameled finishes lack in quality what they do not have in beauty.*

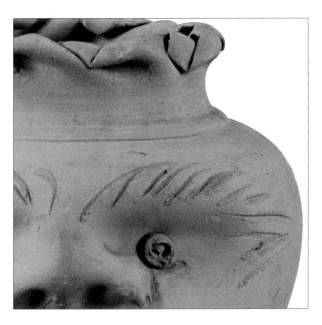

◀ *Note how the "face" decoration is rendered with incised lines for the eyebrows and applied clay "eyes." These face vases are extremely rare.*

J.B. Owens/Empire Floor and Wall Tile

While the Owens enterprises are better known for their pottery, some of the decorated tiles made by the J.B. Owens Pottery, the J.B. Owens Floor and Wall Tile Company, and the Empire Floor and Wall Tile Company are among the finest Arts and Crafts or faience tiles ever produced in the United States. Beginning in 1885 with the production of flowerpots in Roseville, Ohio, J. B. Owens Pottery soon became one of the country's most successful potteries, competing directly with Roseville, Weller, and Rookwood.

Tile manufacturing began in earnest fairly late in the company's history, around 1905. For several years, Owens produced faience tiles of exceptional quality in the Arts and Crafts style. The Arts and Crafts tiles and panels were made of wet clay thickly pressed in *cuenca* molds (a raised-line process). They featured stylized designs typical of the period, such as oak branches with acorns, and grapevines. The more important, larger panels depicted beautiful landscapes. All these tiles were covered in fine matte glazes and are as collectible today as those produced by Van Briggle, Wheatley, Rookwood, and Grueby.

The tile plant was sold in 1909. Owens quickly rebuilt and started over, this time as the J.B. Owens Floor and Wall Tile Company, which would become the Empire Floor and Wall Tile Company in 1914. John Owens moved into more three-dimensional designs, with such simplified forms as leaves or papyrus blossoms. The raised design was often covered in a contrasting matte glaze. Later, tiles were decorated in *cuerda seca*, a wax-resist technique that results in a depressed black outline.

One *cuerda seca* line stands out for the size of its tiles (12in/30.5cm square) and the labor-intensive work involved. These elaborate tiles depicted nursery rhymes. Produced in small quantities and installed mainly in concrete settings, these are seldom seen today and are thus in high demand, ranging from $750 to $1,000 a tile.

Arts and Crafts Landscape Tile, *c.*1905

The large format adds value.

The *cuenca* (raised-line) technique is typical of the Owens wares.

This beautiful mountain landscape is an exceptional design.

The condition is excellent.

A frame would increase the value further.

The tile is covered with fine matte glazes, some with speckling.

Size: 12in/30.5cm square
Value: $2,000–$2,500

Large *Cuerda Seca* Empire Panel, c.1922

The lighthouse in this island landscape originally spanned two tiles.

Some of the painting (for example, on the clouds and house) is rather crude.

The large format is a desirable feature.

The *cuerda seca* (wax-resist) technique has been executed imprecisely.

The panel has both matte and glossy glazes.

While it is a later addition, the Arts and Crafts frame increases the panel's value.

Size: 11 x 14in/
28 x 35.6cm
Value: $950–$1,250

• *All tiles were of white faience body; some were decorated in* cuenca *with Arts and Crafts motifs—acorns and grapes—and covered in rich matte glazes ($250–$350).*
• *Some large panels depicting mountainous landscapes were available in 12in/30.5cm squares or large vertical rectangles ($850–$1,500).*
• *Owens produced 6in/ 15.2cm tiles molded in relief with abstracted floral patterns, covered in two contrasting matte glazes ($200–$350).*
• *Later (Empire) tiles bore simplified floral or geometric designs in* cuerda seca, *with semi-matte glazes (now worth up to $200 for tiles measuring 2–6in/5.1–15.2cm square).*
• *A series of oversized tiles introduced after 1923 featured nursery rhymes, also done in* cuerda seca, *and covered in a mix of matte and glossy glazes ($750–$950). Transfer-printed, dust-pressed tiles are of little value today.*

Key Facts

John Bartle Owens II opened his first pottery in Roseville, Ohio, in 1885, producing flowerpots and stoneware. In 1891, he moved the pottery to nearby Zanesville; by 1893, he employed 60 people. Rockingham-type pottery appeared in 1895. Within a decade, Owens' roster of artists grew to include the best in the country.

The lines produced at Owens either borrowed from, or were imitated by, the local potteries with whom they competed: Roseville, Weller, and Rookwood. The artists experimented with the lines, mixing elements to create eccentric results. The factory also produced commercial ware, including cuspidors and gas logs.

A fire devastated the premises in early 1902, but production resumed by August of that year. Meanwhile, Owens purchased a pottery in Corona, N.Y., and published the trade journal *The*

Owens Monthly. He won four gold medals and a grand prize at the Lewis and Clark Exposition in Portland, Ore., in 1905, at which time he expanded into the Zanesville Tile Company and phased out commercial ware.

Owens sold the tile company to investors in 1907, but apparently remained in charge of production until 1909, when the tile plant was sold to William Shinnick of Mosaic Tile in Zanesville. Owens then founded the J.B. Owens Floor and Wall Tile Co., in Zanesville, which produced art pottery and tiles. He opened still another plant in 1914 in New Jersey, and the firm became known as the Empire Floor and Wall Tile Co., expanding its facilities many times. In 1917, Owens developed the J.B. Owens Continuous Tunnel Kiln. A fire destroyed the Zanesville plant in 1928. That and the Great Depression ended the business.

Pewabic Pottery

Mary Chase Perry's work at the Pewabic Pottery spanned several decades, during which she matured as an artist and became an innovator in American decorative ceramics. Although she began with her interpretation of the matte green ware produced by a hundred other companies across the United States, she evolved as an experimenter and teacher and, in the process, defined her own path. (Her earliest work concentrated on china painting on ceramic bodies, but it is rare and relatively unattractive.)

While Perry's dark green matte ware is in the spirit of Grueby and the New England Arts and Crafts potters, it is distinctive enough to spot from across the room. Always thrown by hand, and usually decorated only with her rich, enamel matte finishes, Perry's work was distinguished by her selection of form and the use of slightly off-kilter colors—brown, buff, and yellow.

Decorated examples, usually with stylized organic designs cut deeply into the thick, heavy clay body, are quite rare and eagerly sought by collectors. Perry's matte ware was produced for only a short period, and such pieces usually bear a single glaze, although several multifinish matte pieces have been found. The scale of these was rather small, the average size being 6–7in/15.2–17.8cm tall.

Pewabic was in business for a long time, and its output is not rare. Because of this, more typical pieces with even modest damage lose at least half their value. As with any pottery, however, extraordinary pieces (of which the pottery made more than its share) do not lose significant value due to minor damage.

Most of Perry's prized matte ware has been located and remains in private and public collections, a true indication of how valued the work has continued to be from its creation.

Feathered Matte Glaze Vessel, *c.*1915

This piece was rendered in a typical, simple form.

Like the example opposite, the vessel was hand-thrown.

Notice the unusual feathering and slight iridescence to the glaze.

Decorated only with matte glaze, this piece exhibits no hand-tooling.

It is typical in size for early Pewabic ware.

Size: 7in/17.8cm diameter
Value: $1,275–$1,725

Flared Matte Glaze Vase, *c.*1907

The flaring form of this piece is unusual for Pewabic.

Notice the hand-tooled decoration at the rim.

The artist finished this work unusually with two contrasting matte glazes.

The vase was hand-thrown.

This piece is large for early Pewabic ware.

Size: 11in/28cm
Value: $10,200–$13,800

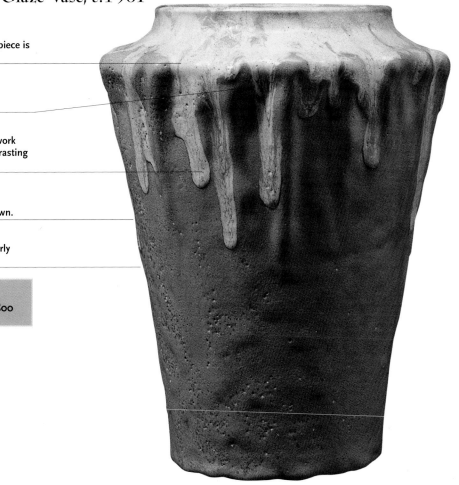

• *All Pewabic pottery was hand-thrown, except its tiles, which were molded.*
• *Early pieces of this ware were finished in matte glazes and usually bear the "maple leaf" mark.*
• *While any matte glazed piece of Pewabic is rare, tooled and modeled examples are the hardest to find.*
• *Most early pieces come in a single matte color, although two-glaze pieces may occasionally be found.*
• *Because matte pieces were produced for less than a decade, when the company was at its smallest, they are extremely rare.*

Key Facts

After studying china painting at the Art Academy of Cincinnati in 1888–90, Mary Chase Perry returned home to Detroit to open a basement studio in her family's home. She was approached by their neighbor, Horace James Caulkins, about traveling the country to demonstrate china painting on vessels to be fired in his new Revelation kiln.

Perry and Caulkins founded the Revelation Pottery in 1903 and changed its name to Pewabic in 1905. Originally, Perry produced only vases covered in matte green glaze, much in the style of William Grueby of Boston. She did all the designing and decorating, and both partners worked on glazes. By 1904, brown, buff, and yellow glazes were added. Later, orange, blue, purple, and white would be added as well.

William Stratton designed a larger new pottery for Pewabic in 1906, and tile production began around 1907. In 1909, Pewabic introduced the beautifully lustred glazes that would become its trademark. The Persian Blue Glaze followed several years later.

Perry won a national competition to supply tiles for the new St. Paul's Cathedral in Detroit. Many commissions followed. She married in 1918. Horace Caulkins died in 1923. Perry stayed at the helm of the pottery until her death in 1961 at 94 years old.

Pewabic Pottery—Iridescent

At some point around 1910, Mary Chase Perry's experiments with iridescent glazing became the main focus of Pewabic Pottery's production. This was a radical departure from the matte glazed ware and largely responsible for the pottery's longevity and modern-day popularity. While Perry was not the only American potter to experiment with and develop nacreous finishes, she was arguably the most successful in range, quality, and diversity.

Most iridescent pieces are glazed in variations of blue or green, usually with surfaces rendered silky flat. The more vibrant the color and textured the surface, the more desirable the pot. Perry's range of colors was nothing less than extraordinary, including flaming reds, frothy pinks, shimmering chartreuses, and scintillating, gold-lustred flambés. One extraordinary piece, located years ago, looked as though a handful of orange crayons had been blowtorched above it and allowed to crawl down the surface of the vase.

Most Pewabic was finished, in one fashion or another, with an iridescent surface. Nearly all pieces were marked, though the active glazes often obscure, or completely hide, the circular, die-stamped moniker. Those that were produced after Perry's death leave off the Pewabic name.

Baluster Iridescent Vessel, *c.*1920

This baluster form is typical for Pewabic ware.

The vessel was glazed in a fine, but standard, blue iridescent gloss.

Because the glaze surface is smooth, this piece is less valuable than the example opposite.

The hand-thrown form is taller than most Pewabic.

While the iridescent glaze is smooth, the "feathering" in the body adds interest and value.

Size: 12in/30.5cm
Value: $2,550–$3,450

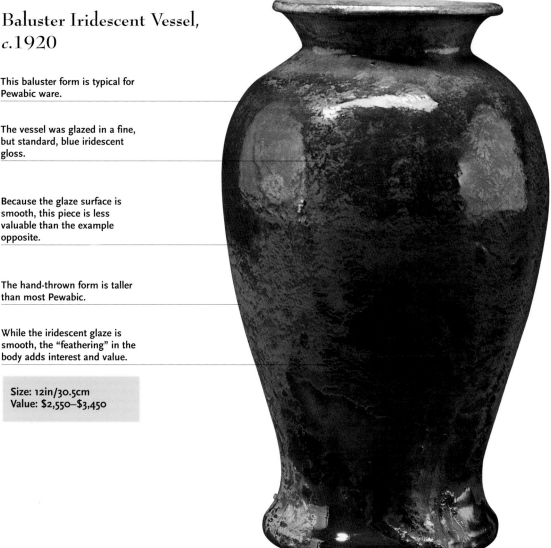

Flambé Vase, *c.*1920

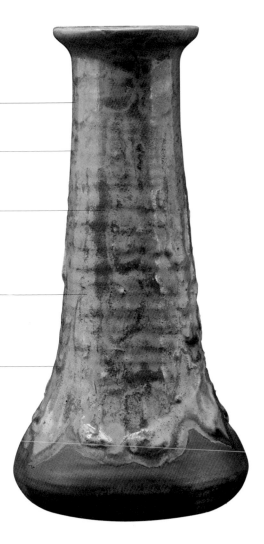

This unusual form adds to the piece's value.

The form is hand-thrown, like the example opposite.

The vase displays a fine, two-color flambé glaze.

The semivolcanic texture of the surface makes the piece worth more than if it were smooth.

The vase is typical in size for Pewabic ware.

Size: 10in/25.4cm
Value: $3,400–$4,600

• *Most Pewabic pieces bear iridescent finishes, and almost all are marked with a circular die-stamp.*

• *Most iridescent pieces bear a single glaze, although two- and three-glaze combinations are not rare.*

• *Blue and green glazes predominate. Golds, and especially tones of red, are rare.*

• *The average height of a Pewabic vessel is about 8–9in/20.3–22.9cm.*

• *Recent pieces by Pewabic Pottery—which remains in business today as a museum, studio, and adult ceramic center—are also usually iridescent.*

• *The "PP" designation in the center of Pewabic's die-stamped mark is an indication of recent vintage.*

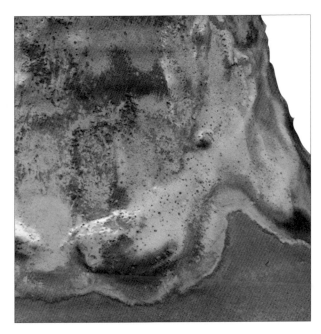

◀ *A close look at the two-glaze flambé on this vase reveals a pleasing confluence of color, lustre, and texture. This and the example opposite rank among the best of Pewabic's later iridescent work.*

Pewabic Pottery Tiles

With her Detroit pottery in full operation, and in search of further inspiration, Mary Chase Perry went to Zanesville, Ohio, for tile instruction around 1905–06. Zanesville and Trenton, N.J., were the most important pottery centers in the United States at the time. Perry probably learned the mass-production, dust-pressed process while there but decided against its use in her studio. She considered the end product too mechanical and "perfect." Her first tiles were pressed from wet clay and used for a fireplace surround in a house designed for her by architect William Stratton, whom she later married. He also designed a fine, large Tudor Revival building for the pottery, which commenced operation by 1907 and saw the firm's ascendance to one of the nation's foremost producers of decorative tiles (1909–66).

From about 1909, tile production moved to the forefront of Pewabic's business. When Detroit, Mich., boomed during the 1910s and 1920s, new buildings were erected throughout the city. Perry was approached around 1910 to enter a nationwide competition to create tiles for the new St. Paul's Cathedral in Detroit. Despite her lack of experience in ecclesiastical tiles, Perry won the competition and a commission to supply tiles, panels, and plaques for the important structure. Other church commissions followed this highly publicized achievement, including one for the National Shrine of the Immaculate Conception in Washington, D.C., in 1924. Demand for Pewabic tiles burgeoned nationwide. During the next four decades, the pottery's ware graced hundreds of theatres, office buildings, casinos, schools, private homes, and clubs (including the Detroit Society of Arts and Crafts).

In 1966, the company became the property of Michigan State University and suspended production. Two years later, it came to life once more as a pottery school and museum.

In 1981, the pottery became a National Historic Landmark. Today, the pottery's modern tiles are more widely available in the collectors' market than the vintage ones, which are fairly scarce. Examples found at antique fairs and auctions are often small and uninspired: thick, with rounded corners and crude etched design, but usually covered with a rich lustred glaze.

"Ali Baba and the Forty Thieves" Bisque Tile, c.1915

This is a rare large tile panel, perhaps part of a fireplace surround.

The body is of unglazed red clay, which generally decreases the value of a tile.

Glazing would have dulled the elaborate hand-carving of this particular piece.

The mint condition of this piece adds to its value.

The stamp "Pewabic/Detroit" appears on the reverse side of the tile (not shown).

Size: 11 x 9in/ 27.9 x 22.9cm
Value: $450–$650

Goose, Chick, and Egg Tile, *c.*1930

This is a fairly rare embossed nursery faience tile.

Notice the fine Persian Blue Glaze with white contrast.

An Arts and Crafts frame enhances this tile (not shown).

The design is crisp and playful.

Like the piece opposite, this piece bears the stamp "Pewabic/Detroit" on the back.

Size: 4in/10.2cm square
Value: $300–$400

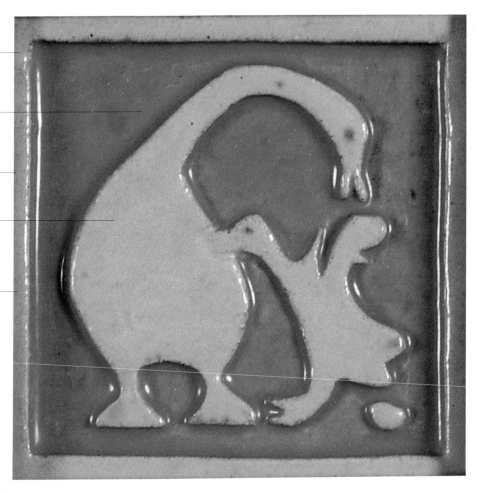

• *Typically, Pewabic created tiles pressed of wet clay (faience) in hand-carved molds, and covered with iridescent glazes, sometimes combined with matte glazes or with bisque areas.*
• *The pottery made glazed and buff mosaics to be set into tables, floors, or fountains.*
• *Large panels were assembled in jigsaw-puzzle fashion, the outlines grouted to resemble leaded-glass windows.*
• *Some hexagonal trivets were made of glaze test tiles, in matte polychrome glazes.*
• *Floor tiles were produced using Henry Mercer's technique of half-glazing, leaving the relief portion of the design unglazed.*
• *Pewabic's basic tiles (most often found) were small squares with rounded corners and uneven surfaces done in a single-color iridescent glaze.*

Ecclesiastical Triumph

Perry's greatest achievements in tile are to be found in the many churches, mausoleums, and memorials she decorated. Perhaps due to the Moresque quality of the lustred glazes, the tiles—whether on floors, on walls, or set into altars—add a glowing and festive touch to these buildings. Most Pewabic tiles were produced for specific installations.

Perry designed installations resembling Oriental carpets, with several concentric rows of plain or geometric tiles, sometimes interspersed with mosaic, and jewel-like accents. After her commission for St. Paul's Cathedral in Detroit, she was awarded contracts by many other religious establishments. These included St. Patrick's Cathedral in Philadelphia; Memorial Jewish Institute in Detroit; St. Matthew's Cathedral in Laramie, Wyo.; Christ Church Cranbrook in Bloomfield Hills, Mich.; and the Shrine of the Immaculate Conception in Washington, D.C.

Rhead Pottery

Frederick Rhead's odyssey as an art potter through the United States ended in California, where the confluence of exceptional clay deposits and natural inspiration encouraged him to create his best work. Although he remained in the ceramics industry for years afterward, he later gave himself far more to the work of a designer than that of a decorator.

Santa Barbara, Calif., was a resort and artist's colony prior to Rhead's arrival, and he became a fixture there during his short stay. His company, named the Rhead Pottery, was also referred to as the Pottery of the Camarata (meaning "friends" in Italian). His work in Santa Barbara had little to do with his past decorative work and much in common with his increasingly understated style. Surviving examples of his work there show that he used techniques he developed elsewhere, including incising, excising, inlaying, enameling, and simple glazing.

Unlike his more florid designs at the Roseville, Weller, and Avon Potteries, however, Rhead's Santa Barbara ware was stylistically closer to his production at the Jervis Pottery in Oyster Bay, Long Island. Some pieces display a bright, organic flair, but most pieces express simple, stylized floral designs or are covered with one or more of his favorite glazes. Rhead prized his stark, glossy black finish, although modern collectors are less enamored.

Judging by remaining examples, pieces were either hand-thrown or molded. Rhead had no fondness for throwing vessels himself, so he hired assistants for that task. His wife, Agnes, and others helped him with decoration, while he took chage of design and glaze experiments. Over time, he concentrated more and more on Oriental finishes. Rhead also taught ceramics classes at the pottery.

Rhead made his work available in myriad shapes and sizes. One known example measures over 24in/61cm tall, while the majority are smallish pots under 7in/17.8cm in height. Forms include tea sets, floor vases, jardinieres, low bowls, and plain old vases. They were decorated with flowers, or more unusually, with stylized landscapes, or scarabs and other winged insects.

These pieces are so rare that collectors are happy to find them in nearly any condition. Minor damage will reduce the value of a piece by only about 10%. Nothing short of a full-body crack will cut value by 50%.

Rhead pottery is almost always marked, usually with a die-stamped circular designation showing a potter at a wheel. Because the bottoms of Rhead's pots are often covered with glaze, the shallow mark may be obscured. Because of this, these pieces more than occasionally show up at flea markets and general line antique stores, especially in Southern California.

Squat Ovoid Bowl, *c.*1915

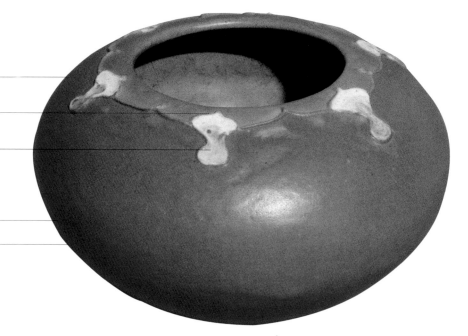

This piece used a simple hand-thrown form.

The decoration was applied with squeezebag.

The stylized floral design typifies Rhead's work.

The work employs a matte glazed ground.

While not signed by Rhead, this is almost certainly his work.

This piece is average in size.

Size: 5 x 8in/
12.7 x 20.3cm
Value: $8,500–$11,500

California Landscape Vase, *c.*1915

The design was enameled and incised.

The fine California landscape decoration adds to the piece's value.

Notice the combination of matte and glossy glazes.

The vase was not signed by Rhead, but it is certainly his work.

Perfectly designed and executed, this vase constitutes an art pottery masterpiece.

It is taller than most examples.

The piece has a simple, hand-thrown form.

This vase is from the collection of James Carter.

Size: 12in/30.5cm
Value: $25,000–$35,000

• *Rhead's many decorative styles include such techniques as incising, excising, inlaying, squeezebag, enameling, and simple glazing.*
• *Pieces appear on both hand-thrown and molded blanks.*
• *Santa Barbara pieces are the rarest of Rhead's hand-decorated work.*
• *While Rhead seldom, if ever, signed his work, it is safe to assume that he had a hand in the production and decoration of every piece.*
• *Several different clays were used during Rhead's stay in Santa Barbara, the most common being either a buff or a soft rose.*

Key Facts

From a family of ceramists, Frederick Hurten Rhead worked at numerous U.S. potteries, beginning in 1902 at age 22. From Vance/Avon Faience Pottery, Ohio, he moved to Weller Pottery and Roseville Pottery, Ohio; Jervis Pottery, New York; University City Pottery, Missouri; and Arequipa and Steiger Potteries; California.

He eventually established his own company in 1914. The pottery was probably associated with the nearby Gift Shop of the Craft-Camarata.

In 1915, Rhead won a Gold Medal at the Panama California Exposition in San Diego. A year later, with the help of Edwin A. Barber, he began publishing the monthly magazine, *The Potter*, to address all aspects of modern ceramics production. When Barber died, the magazine died, as well.

The pottery closed in 1917 due to lack of funds, and Rhead moved back to Zanesville. There, he became director of research at the American Encaustic Tiling Company. After a decade, he left AETCO to join the Homer Laughlin China Company, and he is credited for designing the wildly popular Fiesta Ware line.

Robineau Pottery

Adelaide Robineau's high-fire porcelain work was of such high quality and small production that she almost transcends the medium. Unlike most of her contemporaries, she was perhaps more important as a teacher of the ceramic arts than she was as a craftsman, though she was memorable as both.

It has been said that she produced only about 600 examples of her porcelaneous art ware during her tenure, some of which she destroyed because it did not meet her lofty standards. Regardless of the accuracy of that number, her work is extremely rare and most of it very small, under 6in/15.2cm tall.

Nevertheless, important examples seem to surface at the oddest of times, from the oddest of places. Valuable examples have been located from homes in California, Missouri, Connecticut, and Colorado, and lesser ones from all points across the continent. Many of the existing pieces are small "cabinet" vases with various flambé and crystalline finishes. The prevailing belief is that these are "glaze tests." Rarer and more valuable are larger pieces with consistent glazes of red flambés and various snowflake crystalline finishes.

Robineau's most prized work, however, is her hand-tooled ware. She championed "excising" decoration into the ceramic surface, by which the body was cut away, leaving the original surface as design and the negative space to define it. Much of this work is geometric and sparse. The best examples use decorative renderings of flowers, insects, or animals.

Firing flaws occurred often in the form of underglaze cracks on Robineau's vases, probably owing to the highly experimental nature of her work and the difficulties of working with a relatively crude kiln. Otherwise, the porcelain bodies are very hard and seem to have resisted most post-manufacturing damage.

Her mark, excised into the underside of her ware, is a work of art in itself, often accompanied by a date. The scarcity of her work means it loses little value from minor damage. Her most famous, the Scarab Vase, is valued at one million dollars, in spite of numerous firing flaws.

Golden-Brown Futuristic Vase, *c.*1915

Notice the futuristic vase form.

This piece is typical in size.

The porcelain body is hand-thrown.

This displays an exceptional snowflake crystalline glaze.

The unusual golden-brown ground offers good contrast to the crystals.

Size: 6in/15.2cm
Value: $6,000–$8,000

Indian Basket, *c.*1906

The "Indian basket" form of this piece gives it visual interest.

This is larger than most Robineau pieces.

It is unusual to have so many colors accenting the tooled decoration.

This exceptional excised surface design is probably of Native-American influence.

The titanium glaze ground is excellent.

Size: 6in x 8in/
15.2cm x 20.3cm
Value: $35,000–$45,000

• *Robineau is among the rarest of American art potteries.*
• *While Robineau did some work with earthenware, the bulk of her production was in porcelain.*
• *Robineau porcelain was usually only glazed. Such pieces were often handsome flambés or had snowflake crystalline finishes.*
• *Any hand-tooling on her work is extremely rare.*
• *Hand-tooling, usually in the form of excised design, is most valuable when describing a flower, insect, or animal. Design elements include elephants, elk, poppies, scarabs, and even Viking ships.*
• *While some of her pieces were rather large, her normal scale was under 6in/15.2cm.*
• *Robineau's porcelains were always hand-thrown. They were also painstakingly marked with her "AR" cipher. This mark is often obscured by the rich glazes that flowed over the bottom during firing.*

Key Facts

Adelaide Beers Alsop, born in Middletown, Ct., in 1865, taught herself how to paint on china at St. Mary's Hall school in Faribault, Minn. She taught others there for several years.

After several moves, Adelaide arrived on Long Island, N.Y., to study painting with William Merritt Chase. The watercolors she produced in this time were included in two National Academy exhibitions. She returned to china painting to earn a living.

In March 1899, Adelaide married French émigré Samuel Edouard Robineau. In May of that same year, the couple published the first issue of *Keramic Studio*, a monthly magazine for the china-painting trade. The following year, Adelaide exhibited her china-painted vases at the Paris Exposition.

The Robineaus moved to Syracuse in 1901, and Adelaide made her first pot in Charles Volkmar's studio. A series of articles on high-fire porcelain in *Keramic Studio*, written by the Frenchman Taxile Doat of the Sevres Porcelain Works, provided further

impetus for Adelaide. In the summer of 1903, she took a class with Charles F. Binns at the School of Clay-Working and Ceramics in Alfred, New York. The Robineaus built a studio and a house, which Adelaide named "Four Winds."

A year after taking her first pottery classes, she exhibited pieces at the Louisiana Purchase Exposition in St. Louis, Mo. The following year, Tiffany & Co. in New York carried her wares.

In 1910, the Robineaus joined the University City Pottery in St. Louis, and worked alongside Taxile Doat and Frederick Hurten Rhead. That year, Adelaide created the *Apotheosis of the Toiler*, which earned the grand prize at the Turin International Exposition in 1911. She exhibited at the Musée des Arts Decoratifs and at the Paris Salon and earned the grand prize at the Pan-Pacific Exposition in San Francisco in 1915. In October of 1928, several of her porcelain vases appeared in an ceramics exhibition at the Metropolitan Museum of Art in New York and were very well received.

Rookwood Pottery—Vellum

Rookwood Pottery's enduring success was based primarily on the creativity and adaptability of its wares. The producers never stopped experimenting and exploring new decorative styles and techniques that kept them at the forefront of their field.

One of their earliest innovations was a derivative Victorian ware called Standard Brown Glaze, with hand-painted designs in slip relief under a rich, glasslike brown overglaze. Rarer are portraits painted in the style of old masters or studies of Native Americans. While these were not the pottery's most creative works, they established a level of excellence maintained for over three-quarters of a century. Standard glazed ware enjoyed great popularity during the 1960s and 1970s, but its desirability and value have decreased, making it now worth the least of all Rookwood's decorated lines.

About 10 years after Standard Brown ware appeared, Rookwood introduced several new lines, including their Vellum ware. The Vellum Glaze diffused the painted decoration it covered, giving it a decidedly Impressionist appearance. Nevertheless, substantial clarity of design still appears on Vellum ware.

Rookwood produced most of its Vellum ware prior to 1915, and pieces from that time period are usually crazed. After 1915, the pottery used a different clay composition, which resulted in uncrazed ware from that time on. Uncrazed examples made prior to 1915 are rare and sell for a premium.

Vellum landscapes are not rare, but there are variations within the genre. Some designs are "banded," or framed within horizontal incised lines that incorporate only a fraction of the vase's surface. These usually sell for less. Variations such as "Green Vellum" or "Yellow Vellum," on which the gauzy overglaze is in tones of green or yellow rather than the usual misty clear, are rarer and usually command premium prices.

For years, Rookwood produced a quantity of wall plaques, almost entirely glazed in Vellum, featuring rolling, tree-filled landscapes and river scenes. They are among the most expensive of Vellum-glazed pieces.

Vellum Mt. Fuji Vase, c.1916

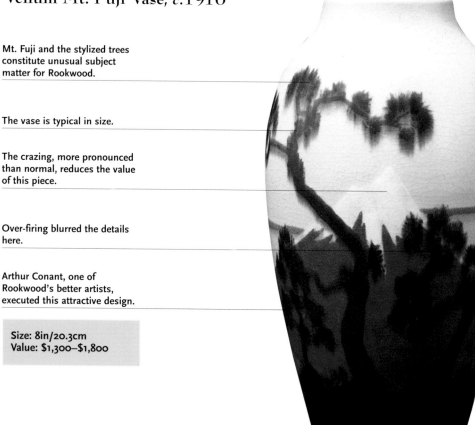

Mt. Fuji and the stylized trees constitute unusual subject matter for Rookwood.

The vase is typical in size.

The crazing, more pronounced than normal, reduces the value of this piece.

Over-firing blurred the details here.

Arthur Conant, one of Rookwood's better artists, executed this attractive design.

Size: 8in/20.3cm
Value: $1,300–$1,800

Vellum Vase in Mauve and Pink, c.1915

This vase was produced with unusual subject matter in a stylized Arts and Crafts design.

The unusual color choice of mauve and pink makes this piece rare.

Slightly less crazing than usual increases the value of the piece.

The vase will command a higher price because it is taller than most.

Sara Sax, one of Rookwood's finest artists, executed the piece.

This has great decoration, well suited to the form.

Size: 15in/38.1cm
Value: $10,200–$13,800

- *Most pieces appear in shades of cream or blue. Pieces in pastel colors, such as pink, yellow, sky blue, and light green, command a premium.*
- *Crazing will reduce the value of Vellum ware by 30–40%.*
- *The majority of Vellum ware was decorated with flowers; landscapes are second in frequency; all other subjects follow a distant third.*
- *Damage decreases this pottery more dramatically than any other pottery. A single chip will drop the price of a piece by as much as 50%.*
- *All pieces of Vellum ware are clearly marked with the company's "RP" flame designation, dated in Roman numerals, and incised with a "V" to denote Vellum Glaze.*
- *The average size of Rookwood ware is about 8in/20.3cm tall. Pieces of Vellum ware well in excess of 10in/25.4cm are unusual and will sell for higher prices.*

Vellum War

The world-famous Rookwood Pottery of Cincinnati, Ohio, was the most important producer of American art pottery in terms of quality, innovation, longevity, and volume. Rookwood was the project of a lady of means, Maria Longworth Nichols, who, along with other Cincinnati ladies, had enjoyed painting china blanks. Impressed by the pottery displays at the Philadelphia Centennial Exposition, she was one of the first artists in this country to successfully produce underglaze-painted ware in the late 1870s (along with Mary Louise McLaughlin and T.J. Wheatley).

Mrs. Nichols opened the Rookwood Pottery in an old schoolhouse in 1880, and ran it for about 10 years. She and her husband moved abroad in 1890 and left the pottery in the capable hands of its administrator, William Watts Taylor. Until World War II, Rookwood remained one of the leading producers of art pottery. Its more than 50 staff artists created lines that would be imitated by companies all over the country, especially their Limoges and Standard Glazes.

Collectors loved Rookwood long before art pottery became the popular art form it is today. This was due primarily to Rookwood's adherence to the highest standards of quality and artistry throughout its history.

Rookwood Pottery— Iris Glaze

About the same time the Rookwood Pottery introduced Vellum ware, the producers also developed the Iris glaze, a clear glossy finish that allowed for a photorealistic display of decoration. Introduction of the Iris Glaze in 1900 marked Rookwood's aesthetic high point. It should come as no surprise that Iris Glaze ware is the most valuable and collectible of Rookwood's hand-decorated ware.

Once again, most of the decorative motifs displayed under the Iris Glaze were flowers and plants. Rarer are examples showing birds and animals. Landscapes and seascapes are the scarcest subjects found on Iris pieces. The rarest Iris pieces are rectangular wall plaques, often featuring seascape vistas. The producers of Iris Glaze ware shaded the backgrounds from light to dark and used grays and creams, pink, green, blue, and yellow.

Iris pieces offered Rookwood's best interpretation of Art Nouveau design, boldly colored and decorated with sinewy flowers rendered in this vibrant new style. In better examples, hand carving augments the depth and detail.

Iris pieces are sometimes confused with other lines because of the colors used. To identify an Iris piece, look at the underside color of the clay. Rookwood's clays are usually white. Iris pieces have pure white bottoms.

Landscape Iris Glaze Vase, c.1910

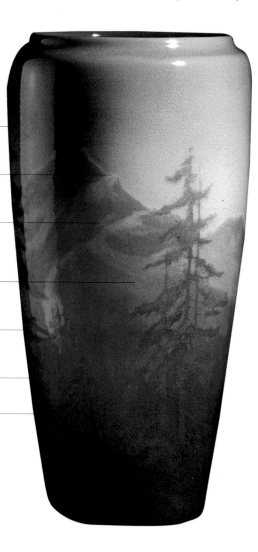

Like the example opposite, this is a slip-cast form.

Notice the underglaze, slip-decorated design.

This unusual subject matter adds to the value of the work.

The artist shaded the color toward ground in keeping with the decorative subject.

Less than average crazing increases this piece's value.

The clear gloss finish creates a lovely effect.

The vase is larger than most.

Size: 16in/40.6cm
Value: $15,000–$20,000

Shaded Iris Glaze Vase, *c.*1905

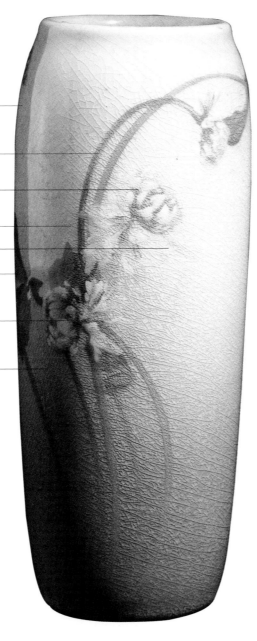

This vase was made in a slip-cast form.

It was designed with an underglaze and slip-decorated design.

The artwork is of middling quality.

This piece shows slightly more than average crazing.

Note the clear gloss finish.

The piece is typical in size.

Flowers such as these were the most common decoration.

The shaded background, from light to dark, is typical.

Size: 8in/20.3cm
Value: $850–$1,150

• *Iris ware has been a favorite of Rookwood collectors since the late 1970s, a fact unlikely to change anytime soon.*

• *It is considered the apex of Rookwood's production in terms of beauty and creativity. Probably created for its appearance at the Paris Exposition of 1900, this line helped Rookwood win the Medal D'or.*

• *Crazing will reduce the value of most Iris pieces by 30%–40%, though exceptional examples will diminish in price less.*

• *Even minor damage has great impact on pricing. One chip can drop the value of a vase by half.*

• *Nearly all Iris pieces were made between 1898 and 1910.*

• *Some of the best Iris pieces were both surface-painted and boldly carved.*

◀ *The decoration on this vase was not only painted with color but was also given texture by mixing ground clay into the pigment. The painted surface was then covered with a clear, high-gloss finish.*

Rookwood Pottery— Arts and Crafts

Along with its Vellum and Iris work, Rookwood responded to the growing interest in the Arts and Crafts movement. The pottery produced several decorative lines using matte glazing and hand-modeled designs. While this was not Rookwood's strongest product, its remarkable artists and chemists still produced work nearly as good as any in the United States. Even so, pieces from this period are uneven from a collector's point of view, with some examples selling for thousands of dollars while others remain fairly inexpensive.

There are two distinctly different types of Arts and Crafts Rookwood. Both, however, are covered with the same rich matte glazes that the company developed. It is also worth noting that relatively few of their artists decorated in the Arts and Crafts style.

Hand-carved ware was one Arts and Crafts adaptation. The work is hand-modeled, sometimes deeply so, yet the blanks themselves are usually slip cast—an odd combination. Flowers and plants almost always decorate these pieces, though sea creatures and the rare human form appear.

Matte-painted ware is Rookwood's other Arts and Crafts innovation. Pieces in which rich matte overglazes are used to paint decoration are among Rookwood's rarest work; rarer still are pieces that were successfully fired. Using overglaze to paint fine details is tricky, because the overglaze runs so freely under the heat of the kiln. Too often, such pieces are blurry and unsuccessful. But the ones that survived the test of fire proclaim Rookwood's mastery at development and experimentation.

Hand-Carved Arts and Crafts Vase, *c.*1908

The piece began with a simple, molded form.

Artist Albert Pons painted this piece in matte glazes.

The hand carving appears in high relief.

This piece exhibits decoration typical of matte glaze ware, with focus placed on flower forms.

The value of this work is enhanced by the decorative details, which are more expressive than most.

The colors are unusually vibrant.

This piece is typical in size for this line.

Size: 12in/30.5cm
Value: $3,400–$4,600

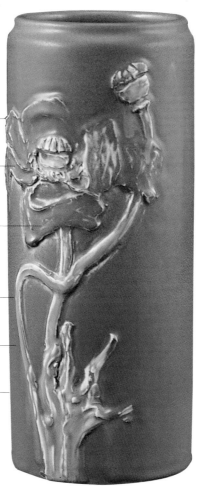

Painted Arts and Crafts Vase, c.1905

Harriett Wilcox painted this simple molded form in matte glazes.

Only the surface has been decorated, with no modeling.

Notice the typical floral decoration.

This piece exhibits excellent definition for a matte-painted piece.

The effect here is richer and brighter in color than most.

This vase measures slightly smaller in size than is typical.

Size: 8in/20.3cm
Value: $13,600–$18,400

• *Only a handful of Rookwood artists used the painted matte style of decoration. Included were: Albert Pons, H.E. Wilcox, Olga G. Reed, Sallie Toohey, Albert and Anna Valentien, and Kataro Shirayamadani.*
• *The matte glaze is one of the only Rookwood glazes that rarely, if ever, crazed.*
• *Such work dates from about 1900–10.*
• *Damage, especially nicking to the high points of deeply modeled work, has less of a negative impact on pricing here than on other Rookwood.*
• *Rookwood also introduced production ware at this time. Much of it has the appearance of their hand-decorated Arts and Crafts pottery. But artist ware bears the decorator's signature and the usual array of company marks.*
• *There are no specific glaze markings for Arts and Crafts ware, though impressed "triangle" designations occasionally appear.*

Key Facts

Experimental work on matte glazes at Rookwood started when Artus Van Briggle returned from Paris in 1896. By 1898, a couple of successful examples were sent to the Hermitage Museum in Leningrad, but production of this process was far from established. The following year, Rookwood's director, William W. Taylor, focused energy on this project, intending the glaze for use on tile. Late in 1900, after the firm's great success at the Paris Exposition, glaze results had become predictable enough for glaze to be offered for sale to the public.

For the first few years, all matte-glazed pottery was marked with a serial number ending in "Z." After June 1904, the numbering changed to incorporate matte-glazed items in the regular cataloging system.

That year also brought a most important development in matte finishes at Rookwood: the Vellum Glaze. An overglaze consisting of tightly packed miniature bubbles, the Vellum finish gave a soft and hazy look to the scenes painted underneath, as opposed to the crisp, vitreous, clear overglaze of the Iris vases.

As with the division that produced pottery, the architectural faience department—which produced garden ware and tile—made great use of this new development. The tile makers produced matte-glazed items for several decades, long after the Arts and Crafts period declined in popularity.

Rookwood Pottery—Porcelain

Although interest in factory-produced art pottery waned after World War I, Rookwood created a high-quality, decorated, porcelain-based ceramic, which it perfected during the 1920s. At this time, the firm still employed several top-flight decorators, including Jens Jensen, Kataro Shirayamadani, Sara Sax, Ed Diers, Carl Schmidt, and Arthur Conant. Some of their work during this time ranks among the best Rookwood ever produced.

Rookwood last created superior art ware from about 1920 to about 1930, using both a denser earthenware and a high-fire porcelain. The durability of this body allowed for richer enameled colors and little, if any, crazing. Line innovations included French Red, Sung Plum, and modifications of the Vellum ware.

This was also a time off stylistic experimentation. Work explored the lines of Art Deco and Modern, as well as Oriental and Persian design. Because crazing is rarer during this time, the premiums paid by collectors for uncrazed ware are significantly lower.

Most desirable are the odd creations of Jensen, the enamels of Sax, the dreamlike landscapes of Conant, and the crisp florals and scenics by Schmidt, and Diers.

Shirayamadani Vase, c.1925

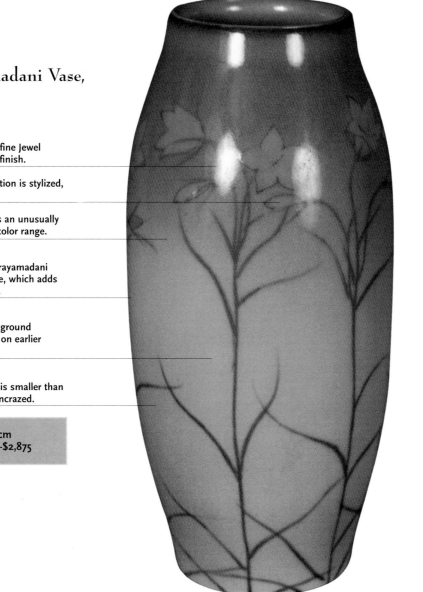

This piece has a fine Jewel Porcelain glossy finish.

The floral decoration is stylized, if sparse.

This piece shows an unusually vibrant modern color range.

Artist Kataro Shirayamadani created this piece, which adds to its desirability.

The shaded background resembles those on earlier work.

The vase, which is smaller than most, remains uncrazed.

Size: 7in/17.8cm
Value: $2,125–$2,875

French Red Vase, c.1925

With typical precision, Sara Sax boldly designed this piece in the Modern style.

The bright enameled flowers exhibit rich, saturated colors.

This is fine example of Rookwood's French Red line.

Notice the crisp detailing that resulted from surface modeling.

The artist defined the negative space with stark, matte glazing.

Size: 5in/12.7cm
Value: $25,000+

▼ The bright enameled colors of the decoration appear even sharper next to the matte glazing of the negative space.

• Some pieces from this period bear a mark with a sideways "p" to indicate porcelain. These are rare, although not particularly more valuable. More often, the clay bodies used fell somewhere between porcelain and the softer earthenware.
• A harder, more porcelaneous body was introduced in about 1915.

• About 80% of Rookwood ware produced after 1915 was uncrazed.
• Rookwood had a smaller corps of artists after World War I, owing in part to the decreasing demand for hand-decorated work. These included some of their best artists, such as Kataro Shirayamadani, Ed Diers, E. T. Hurley, Jens Jensen,

and Sara Sax.
• Because the new clay body was denser, it was more resistant to damage. Roughly 10%–15% fewer of these later pieces suffered post-manufacturing flaws.
• The denser body allowed for higher kiln temperatures, resulting in richer and more vibrant glazing.

Rookwood Pottery— Brown Glaze

The first ware produced by Rookwood that established its professionalism as an art pottery was Standard Brown glaze, an underglaze-painted Victorian line. Decoration centered mostly on representational floral designs covered with a brown overglaze, giving all colors a yellow-brown hue.

This line first introduced Rookwood's growing team of artists, and work by many of the pottery's most famous decorators worked in this medium. While this line spoke more of what Rookwood was than what it would become, production values set a high standard of quality that remains. The glazes were hard and clear, the quality of painting excellent, and the pottery crisp and well finished.

Artists decorated most pieces with flowers, usually concentrating on one side of the work and introducing just a wisp of decoration on the reverse. Later pieces offered renditions of famous Native Americans, historical figures, and American statesmen. During the 1890s, the pottery collaborated with the Gorham Silver Company in ware covered with an Art Nouveau/Victorian silver overlay that framed slip-decorated floral designs.

Standard Brown Glaze ware is highly collectible today because it can be obtained for such reasonable prices. A nice 7in/17.8cm Standard Glaze vase, perfect and decorated with flowers, sells for about $400. The same piece in Vellum would bring twice that, and in Iris, about three times the price.

Damage greatly diminishes Standard ware prices, as it does with nearly all Rookwood pottery. A single chip may reduce value by 40–50%.

Two-Handled Standard Glaze Vase, c.1895

This vase is a two-handled molded form.

The background shades from light to dark.

The vase shows an underglaze decoration of autumn leaves.

The rich, limpid brown overglaze influences the colors of the design.

The vase has suffered the light crazing typical of these pieces.

The vase is fully marked with the cipher of the artist, company, and date (not shown).

Size: 7in/17.8cm
Value: $350–$450

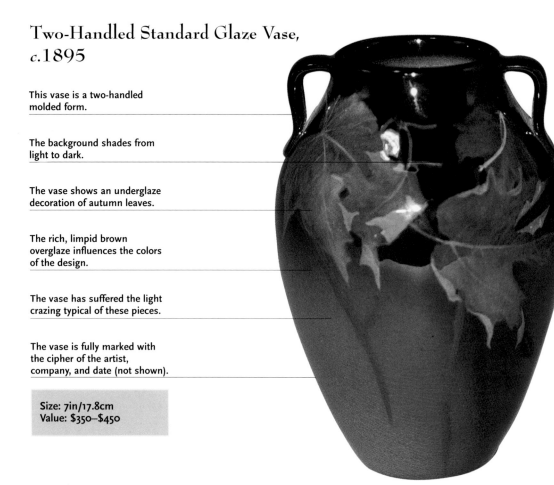

Two-Handled Chalice Vase, *c.*1895

The unusual, tall, two-handled chalice form adds to the value of this piece.

The background shades from yellow to light orange, a more appealing and valuable variation than on the example opposite.

Kataro Shirayamadani, one of Rookwood's best artists, painted this piece.

The piece was fully marked with the cipher of the artist, company, and date (not shown).

While there is no crazing at the top, heavy crazing has occurred at the bottom.

Size: 15in/38.1cm
Value: $1,000–$1,500

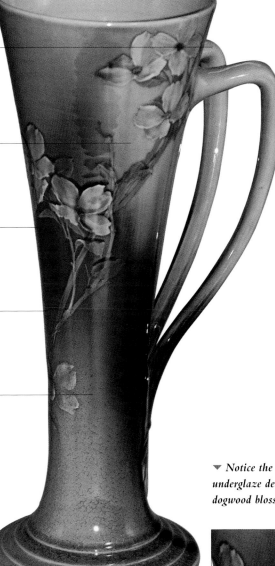

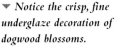

▼ *Notice the crisp, fine underglaze decoration of dogwood blossoms.*

• *With the exception of a few early Standard Glaze pieces, c.1885, Rookwood always employed molded blanks.*
• *Most of this ware was produced on a white clay body (though the underside will appear yellow/brown because of the overglaze). The occasional piece reveals a body of red or sage green clay.*
• *About 90% of these pieces are decorated with floral designs. Rarer subjects include portraits of historical figures and American statesmen, Native Americans, ghosts and spirits, and various animals.*
• *More Rookwood artists worked in Standard Glaze than any other line, in part because it comprised the bulk of the pottery's production.*
• *The average size for this ware was about 7in/17.8cm, although examples range from tiny cabinet vases to mammoth floor vases.*
• *Shape selection varied widely to include umbrella stands, tea sets, pitchers, bowls, candlesticks, and even wall tiles.*
• *Like any decorated Rookwood, these pieces almost always bear marks which designate artist, year of production, type of clay, type of glaze, and size.*

Rookwood Pottery Tiles

Tile production at Rookwood Pottery started around 1901. While a few painted plaques had been made previously, they were not usually considered tiles, but rather flat vases, or even fine art. Pressed tiles came along with Rookwood's architectural faience division, at the height of the Arts and Crafts movement. Made of a coarse faience body, they were embossed, excised, incised, painted, or done in *cuenca* or *cuerda seca*. These early tiles were covered in fine matte glazes and mostly marked with a "Rookwood Faience" stamp or a catalog number starting with a "Y." On rare occasions, hollowware artists such as Charles Todd or Albert Pons would make one-of-a-kind tiles and add their signatures on the backs.

The tiles were made to order, and customers would select the color combinations they wished. For that reason, Rookwood tiles of a single design appear in widely different color schemes. The architectural faience department worked with architects, supplying stock designs or making tile to order. After opening a New York showroom in 1903, Rookwood's faience came into high demand. The tiles are featured in important sites all over the country, including certain stations of the New York City subway system, hotel lobbies, restaurants, office buildings, and schools.

At some point before 1915, as orders for faience declined, Rookwood started offering trivets, or "tea tiles," of high-fired porcelaneous clay. The trivets, with their mass-produced feel and Art Deco pastel colors, were a later, inferior alternative (worth $100–$300) to the architectural faience tiles. A few of the trivets have strong graphics: one such, designed by William Hentschell, shows a crane with a fish in its beak and glazed in blue and black on white—Japanese in style and valued at $450–$600. Another favorite shows a rook against a grid ($500–$750).

After 1925, there were fewer and fewer orders for finely crafted faience tiles. A hefty back-tax bill in 1928, and the start of the Great Depression the following year, left the company in dire straits. The architectural faience department closed in the 1930s, while the pottery changed hands several times. Fortunately, many buildings covered with Rookwood tile remain. The Rookwood Pottery buildings still stand on Mount Adams in Cincinnati and are open to the public.

Cuenca Tile with Apple Picker, *c.*1915

One of a pair, this tile was probably an early design but appeared in the 1925 catalog.

The pre-Raphaelite scene of a young maiden picking an apple is sweet, soft, very decorative, and strongly stylized.

This is a rare, valuable, and desirable size in mint condition.

Notice the Arts and Crafts-style matte glazes.

The *cuenca* (raised-line) mold creates crisp, excellent delineation.

Size: 12in/30.5cm square
Value: $3,000–$4,000

Square Trivet with Parrot, *c.*1920s

This tile was produced on high-fired white clay. Collectors should study the surface of such a trivet for signs of wear, which will lower its price.

Parrots were to Art Deco what peacocks and oak trees were to the Arts and Crafts movement; its pastel colors are also typical of the Art Deco movement.

This tile is smaller, later, and less interesting than the example opposite.

Size: 6in/15.2cm square
Value: $300–$350

• *Hand-painted plaques were decorated in Standard Glaze and Vellum. Sold in frames as fine art they bring from $1,500 to more than $50,000.*
• *The pottery department produced a few 6in/15.2cm tiles. Tooled and marked with "RP," the flames, and artist's initials, these command prices in the $1,000–$3,000 range.*
• *About 145 production tiles, made mostly in* cuenca *or with embossed designs, were glazed to order. Today, the 4in/10.2cm geometric tile might bring $20, the ship medallion $4,000–$5,000, and the 6in/15.2cm nursery pattern tile $500–$1,200.*
• *Rookwood's most collectible tiles have Arts and Crafts designs and fetch several thousand dollars, with many potential buyers waiting.*
• *Friezes of 12in/30.5cm tiles with scenic motifs can bring more than $5,000 per tile.*
• *The trivets with parrots or Dutch scenes turn up fairly often for about $300. More unusual ones will bring $450–$800.*

Subway Tiles

The New York City subway system offers one of the most visible, prestigious, and beloved displays of Rookwood tiles. Designed by the firm of Heins & LaFarge, the project was divided into two parts. Contract One included the stations that opened in 1904, four of which featured Rookwood faience: 23rd, 79th, 86th, and 91st Streets. Contract Two followed in 1908, with Rookwood tiles in two stations: Wall Street and Fulton Street.

The tiles of the Contract One stations—modeled by William P. McDonald—included the faience cornices, mezzanine panels, shields, and corbels of the 23rd Street station; and the cornices and numeral plaques of the 79th, 86th, and 91st Street stations. *House and Garden*, in 1904, described the work as "suited to the workaday heart of 'down town,' where the daily rider will be quickly swung to his office on these smooth curves and as gaily spirited away." While offering an overall restrained appearance because of the dominance of plain white tile, the ornaments are organic and Classical, embossed with fruit, flowers, and cornucopia.

Contract Two stations—done by either John Dee Wareham or Clement Barnhorn—are much more elaborate and include cornices, floral plaques, and Greek fret panels. The descriptive "Clermont" steamboat plaque stars at the Fulton station, and the famous picket wall and Dutch house grace the Wall Street station. Subway lore has it that the stations were outfitted with faience plaques describing those particular locations so that illiterate immigrants using the I.R.T. would be able to recognize a particular wall and associate it with its location. The chief of design refuted that theory.

Roseville Pottery—Rozane Ware

Roseville pottery, from Zanesville, Ohio, has the largest collecting base in the United States. Ironically, its continued popularity centers on the production ware, which was made mostly after World War I. Even though such pottery was mass-produced, it was so well designed and production standards were so high that it has become the U.S. collectible pottery of choice.

It was in response to the growing demand for decorated art ware that Roseville introduced several hand-painted art ware lines at the turn of the century under the name "Rozane," hoping to capitalize on the fame generated by the Rookwood Pottery, of Cincinnati, Ohio.

While Roseville was simply copying the work of others, its Rozane designs were predictable and production quality passable. By 1905, however, the firm introduced a series of lines that were wholly its own, enlisting the services of such men as Frederick H. Rhead and Frank Ferrell. Roseville's art pottery production included unique lines such as Della Robbia, Fudji, and Crystallis.

In today's market, hand-painted pieces, especially rare and beautiful examples, hold much of their value, even when damaged. A 12in/30.5cm Della Robbia vase with a few chips, for example, will only lose about 20% of its value. A softer clay was used to make this hand-painted and modeled line, and the deep cutting involved in much of the decoration invites edge chips and flakes.

Still, for all but a few exceptional hand-decorated pieces of Rozane ware, the big money goes to Roseville's production ware. A transfer-decorated Tourist wall pocket recently sold at auction for $15,000.

Fudji Vase, *c.*1909

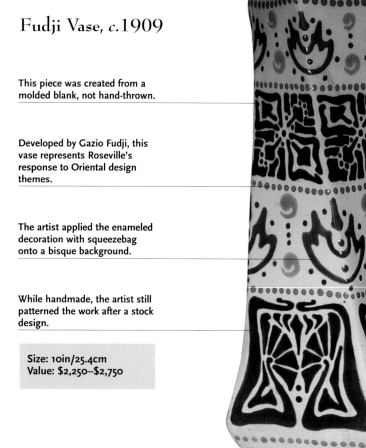
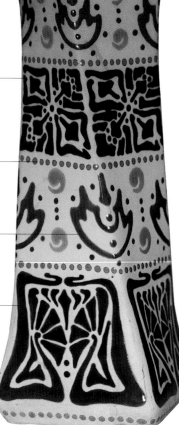

This piece was created from a molded blank, not hand-thrown.

Developed by Gazio Fudji, this vase represents Roseville's response to Oriental design themes.

The artist applied the enameled decoration with squeezebag onto a bisque background.

While handmade, the artist still patterned the work after a stock design.

Size: 10in/25.4cm
Value: $2,250–$2,750

Della Robbia Vase, *c.*1906

Like the example opposite, this vase came from a molded blank.

The decoration includes incised design.

Excised design adds to the piece's visual interest.

The artist chose to use enameled design, as well.

The piece exhibits a strong Arts and Crafts/Art Nouveau influence.

Frederick Rhead developed this design.

The monumental size of this piece adds significantly to its value.

Size: 20in/50.8cm
Value: $30,000–$40,000

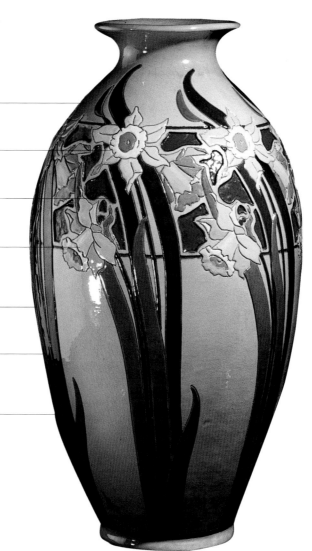

- *Virtually all Roseville is made from molded ware.*
- *The firm produced various art lines under the heading Rozane from about 1900 to 1907. Some of these copied Rookwood pottery: Rozane Royal light, Rozane Royal dark, Azurean-replicated Iris Glaze, Standard Glaze, and Aerial Blue Glaze.*
- *Original Rozane creations included Fudji, Della Robbia, Woodland, and Crystallis.*
- *Roseville introduced production, or mass-produced ware, about the time of World War I.*
- *Early pieces made prior to c.1907 were marked about 50–60% of the time and bore a Rozane ware wafer underneath.*

Key Facts

The Roseville Pottery was begun in 1890 for the production of utilitarian stoneware and painted flowerpots, in the buildings formerly occupied by J.B. Owens in Roseville, Ohio. By 1898, the company had acquired the Midland Pottery of Roseville, and shortly thereafter, its Linden Avenue plant of Zanesville, both former stoneware facilities.

With John Herold as art director, production of underglaze slip-painted art ware began in the Zanesville plant in 1900, under the name of "Rozane" (for *Roseville* and *Zanesville*). The

pottery competed head-to-head with ware from Rookwood Pottery in Cincinnati, J.B. Owens and Weller. Competition between Roseville and Weller became particularly fierce, and the new company presented its own versions of many of Weller's lines, while hiring away some of its decorators.

By 1904, Roseville had acquired the services of English potter Frederick Rhead, a former Weller designer. In 1917, Frank Ferrell joined as a designer and remained until 1954. Under Ferrell, production moved from art ware to commercial florist ware.

Roseville Pottery— Production Ware

When Roseville first introduced mass-produced pottery, the designers used transfer decoration (decals), sometimes augmented with hand-coloring on molded pottery vessels. During the 1920s, the company molded pottery with embossed decoration that a "decorator" then embellished with appropriate colors. Early production lines, such as Sunflower, Dahlrose, and Blackberry, came in only one color scheme. Some of these early production lines, including Sunflower, Ferrella, and Vista, are strikingly handsome in spite of their mass-production, illustrating that not all production ware was created equal.

As the Roseville Pottery matured in its manufacture and marketing of production ware, it added more sophisticated lines, such as the Art Deco–style Futura, one of the most popular lines ever. Later lines were made with two, sometimes three background colors, usually blue, pink, and green, with brown sometimes used in place of pink or green.

Because production ware is available in multiples and is always slip cast or molded, prices for damaged pieces are considerably lower than for perfect examples. A 12in/30.5cm Sunflower vase would be worth about $1,750, while the same piece with a single chip would bring only about $900.

Some of Roseville's earliest production ware has remained very popular among collectors. Included in this work are the Sunflower, Futura, Ferrella, Falline, and Windsor lines. They are never marked, although some pieces retain the silver, triangular "Roseville Pottery" label.

"Tourist" Production Vessel, c.1915

This work is from one of Roseville's rarest and most valuable production lines.

The vase is unmarked, typical of the time and line.

The design was applied by transfer, or decal, with some hand-coloring added by the decorator.

This piece came from one of the most popular early production lines, Tourist, depicting touring cars.

The piece was created from a molded blank.

Size: 4in/10.2cm
Value: $1,200–$1,600

"Sunflower" Production Vessel, *c.*1925

One of Roseville's middle-period production lines, Sunflower remains among their most popular today.

Like pieces from most earlier production lines, this example was available only in this basic color scheme.

Notice the molded decoration, with color added by the "artist."

While mass-produced, this line bears the highest standards of design and production.

Like the vase opposite, this piece began with a molded blank.

Size: 6in/15.2cm
Value: $800–$1,200

• *Restorers have long practiced their craft on Roseville ware, making it among the most successfully and extensively repaired pottery in the market.*
• *Slightly later versions of Rozane ware bore the "Rv" ink stamp. Still later examples, from the 1930s, were marked with an impressed designation. The latest and generally least valuable examples bore a raised mark.*
• *Even the most common and least desirable lines can be valuable in rarer forms. The most common forms are small vases and bowls; the least common are wall pockets, hanging baskets, tea sets, sand jars, and jardiniere and pedestal sets.*

◀ *Notice the molded, or embossed, decoration shown here on the Sunflower production vase. The definition is crisp, a product of good molding and hand-painting. Unlike hand-tooled decoration, however, the edges of flowers and leaves, as well as the pebbled ground, are all rounded rather than sharp.*

Saturday Evening Girls Club —Paul Revere Pottery

There are as many styles of Arts and Crafts pottery as there are potteries. While each company's work is unique, all were united by the philosophical ideas that defined the movement. The Paul Revere Pottery of Boston, Mass., with its adjunct, the Saturday Evening Girls Club (originally a club), was one of the more curious of the Arts and Crafts producers.

One reason why SEG ware has always been so popular is its charm. Typical subjects include farm animals or simple landscapes. Colors are soft and pretty, much like those used to decorate Easter eggs, and the finishes are usually a dead, porous matte or a soft gloss. This combination of quality and a sophisticated simplicity have made SEG ware a collector favorite for decades.

As with most Arts and Crafts ware, the more the enthusiast learns about it, the more enjoyment it provides. This may be truer of SEG than of any other producer.

The ware is rather brittle, and because it was produced mainly for utilitarian purposes, it is often damaged. Still, damage severely decreases the value of SEG ware, except the most minor damage on the most important pieces.

Because of the abundance of utilitarian ware produced by SEG, collectors find its vase forms most desirable. They also gravitate to designs that cover more of an object's surface, since most SEG decoration appears in bands or as borders. Hand-decoration that shows gentle modeling or the *cuerda seca* technique to delineate colored areas is always superior to pieces that are simply surface painted.

Paul Revere Pottery Vase, *c.*1925

This vase is decorated with a band that demonstrates the technique by which painted decoration was applied to Paul Revere ware.

The design was outlined with a thick line of wax and manganese glaze. The wax burned away in firing, leaving the black outline.

The decoration is covered with an unusual and lovely textural glaze.

This late piece was decorated by Edith Brown, head of the art department.

The monumental size, rare especially for Paul Revere pottery, adds significant value to the piece

Size: 16in/40.6cm
Value: $12,750–$17,250

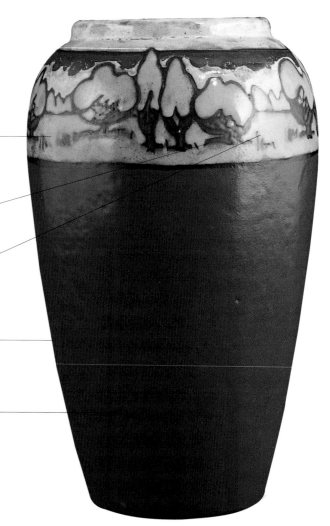

Early Saturday Evening Girls Egg Cup, *c.*1915

This has a typical porous matte finish.

The rabbit design is hand-painted.

Banded decoration such as this is typical of SEG ware.

"Easter egg" colors are typical of SEG ware.

The molded form is utilitarian, intended for everyday use.

This piece is smaller than most examples.

Size: 2.5in/6.4cm
Value: $170–$230

• *SEG/Paul Revere pottery was usually decorated by hand, although a production line also appeared of simply glazed pieces, mostly dinnerware.*

• *The company was in business until the early 1940s, but its post-Depression work was the worst it produced.*

• *While the decorative work was usually inspired by farm animals, a number of more unusual motifs appeared, as well. These included camels, witches on broomsticks, windmills, and beautifully rendered forest scenes.*

• *A design that covers most or all of the surface will bring three times or more the price of the same design restricted to a simple band or border.*

• *Collectors usually prize duller finishes over high-gloss or semi-gloss examples.*

Key Facts

Brainchild of philanthropist Mrs. James Storrow, the Saturday Evening Girls Club started meeting at the North Branch of the Boston Library in 1899. Dedicated to the teaching of arts and crafts, and comprised chiefly of Italian and Jewish immigrant girls, the club provided an aesthetic alternative to unemployment or factory work.

In 1906, the club acquired a small kiln. By 1907, it opened a pottery, headed by Edith Brown, for the production of vases, tableware, lamp bases, and toilet sets. The girls were paid for decorating the pottery and taught every aspect of the craft, from design to chemistry. For further edification, someone read aloud to them while they worked.

In 1908, the pottery moved to a new location near the Old North Church in Boston—of Paul Revere and the lantern signals fame—and became the Paul Revere Pottery. By 1915, the business required a new, larger pottery, which was commissioned by Mrs. Storrow and designed by Ms. Brown in Brighton, Mass.

World War I precipitated a divergence in the pottery's work; with trade lines to Europe closed, the pottery launched the production of doll's heads. Unfortunately, the necessary wigs and eyes were unavailable because of the same trade problems, and so the project was abandoned.

Edith Brown, who produced most of the pottery's great pieces made after 1920, died in 1932. The pottery continued to be funded by Mrs. Storrow until it closed in 1942.

Teco Pottery—Geometric

Teco pottery is the pottery of the Prairie School, the streamlined and forward-thinking offshoot of the American Arts and Crafts movement. While several important Chicago luminaries, such as Frank Lloyd Wright, played a hand in creating designs for Teco, the pottery's connection to the Prairie School ran deeper.

The British Arts and Crafts ideal eschewed the use of the machine in the production of their art ware. Americans were less reticent about power tools, believing they could reduce aspects of the toil involved in hand-craftsmanship. The Prairie School, going one step further, positively embraced the machine.

We can see this move toward a compromise between handcrafting and mass production when we examine pieces of Teco ware. Most of this pottery was completely molded, while the most interesting pieces were partially molded and partially handcrafted. The glazing on Teco pieces is exceptionally fine and the quality control as consistent as any producer's in the United States.

There were two primary expressions in Teco ware—geometric and organic pottery. Both are very desirable today and are recognized as important contributions to the ceramic arts. Some of the original pieces exhibit elaborate shapes that required time-consuming and expensive hand-finishing. Such ware was soon phased out. All pieces were made of Illinois or Indiana clay.

Teco's geometric ware is an Arts and Crafts/Prairie School hybrid, maintaining the angular lines of the former while incorporating the streamlined, futuristic elements of the latter. It is the only such work produced in this country, and extravagant examples are found in the best of collections.

Buttress-Handled Geometric Ware, c.1910

The angular buttressed handles are the only geometric element.

The fact that the handles are restricted to the top of the vase reduces its value.

Notice the fine green matte finish.

The form is good but overly rounded for a geometric piece.

Some curdling in the glaze is typical, but it has some negative impact on value.

This vessel is average in size for Teco.

Size: 7in/17.8cm
Value: $1,700–$2,300

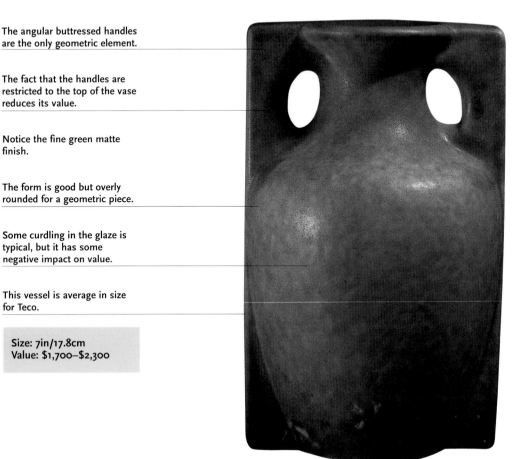

Long-Handled Geometric Vase, c.1910

This piece is monumental in size for Teco, adding significantly to its value.

Gentle charcoaling heightens the impact of the detail.

The geometric handles span the length of the vase, strengthening the visual impact of the piece.

This is one of Teco's most famous and desirable forms.

Size: 14in/35.6cm
Value: $12,000–$16,000

• Teco's geometric ware is very compatible with Arts and Crafts interiors. The soft matte glazing, often green, works well with period furniture.
• The angularity of these shapes reinforces the straight lines of the Arts and Crafts style.
• Most Teco ware is relatively inexpensive, with many pieces available for under $1,000. Better pieces, which are prone to minor damage because of the angularity of the handles, are often available with flaws for a fraction of the cost.
• Teco in off colors can also be inexpensive. While some colors, such as brown, are very popular, blues and maroons have proven less so. Pieces with these colors have the same quality of manufacture as green ones and are considerably rarer.

Key Facts

In 1893, Chicago lawyer William Day Gates attended the World's Columbian Exposition in Chicago, where he encountered the new matte glazes used by French potters. By 1902, he offered to the public the Teco line of art pottery. This pottery consisted of molded vases of architectural or organic shapes designed by Gates, as well as by the finest professional designers and architects of the time.

Gates exhibited a green micro-crystalline glaze in St. Louis in 1904, for which he was awarded the highest honors. This became his only glaze until 1910, when he added different shades of green and other colors. Mass marketing began in earnest in 1904.

Teco Pottery—Organic

Organic Teco is a blend of Art Nouveau and Prairie School, often bold and striking, but occasionally poorly designed. The best such pieces have leaf-like handles, added after the mold, creating a whiplash effect over the surface of the vessel.

Nearly all organic pieces are covered with Teco's stark, porous, matte medium green finish. Some pieces are augmented by a secondary glazing of a metallic black, which is best when left in the lowlights. Teco ware also came in a variety of other colors, including brown, blue, yellow, pink, and cream. These, however, seldom attract the same attention paid to—or the prices paid for—Teco matte green ware.

Most Teco ware was sculpted in clay, cast in molds, and sprayed with glaze. Simple and refined in its form, the work fulfilled the pottery's stated objective: ". . . to produce an art ware that would harmonize with all its surroundings . . . adding to the beauty of the flower or leaf placed in the vase, at the same time enhanced by the beauty of the vase itself."

Teco's best organic ware employed swirling handles, curving reticulations, and whiplash buttresses to reinforce the organic nature of a vessel, occasionally accented by embossed floral designs. While these details imparted visual strength to the pieces, they were often thin and willowy. As such, they are subject to postmanufacturing defects.

Gourd and Tendril Organic Vessel, c.1910

This piece is taller than most pieces.

The vase displays a fine green matte finish with charcoal lowlights.

This form is a little static and straight.

The designer made tendril-like ends to the handles.

Notice the gourdlike lobes on the bottom.

Size: 13in/33cm
Value: $8,500–$11,500

Whiplash-Handled Organic Vase, *c.*1910

This vase is exceptionally tall in relation to other pieces by this maker, adding significantly to its value.

The slight swell to the body reinforces the upward flow of the design.

The fine green matte finish shows charcoal lowlights.

This is a classic piece of Teco organic ware.

The hand-tooled whiplash handles are typical of Teco's most important pieces.

Size: 18in/45.7cm
Value: $60,000–$70,000

• *Organic Teco designs combine aspects of the Art Nouveau movement and the Prairie School. The best have expressive whiplash or tendrillike handles.*

• *Some damage is acceptable on Teco. While it is molded ware, some of the forms are extremely rare, and the clay is not extremely hard when fired. Furthermore, many pieces have handles that are easily chipped or cracked.*

• *As with geometric Teco, organic pieces are usually matte green but also come in a variety of colors. A touch of charcoal in the lowlights is always desirable. Non-green examples tend to be less expensive.*

• *Bigger is almost always better, and Teco seemed to lavish their most extravagant designs on larger pieces.*

◄ *Notice that the whiplash handles are more delicate than they may first appear. These are seldom found without at least minor damage in the form of flat chips or short hairline cracks.*

Tiffany Pottery

Louis Comfort Tiffany is best remembered for his colorful Art Nouveau lighting fixtures. A true Renaissance man, however, Tiffany's interests also included painting, metalwork, enameling, leaded windows, and art pottery. While much of his ceramic work centered on providing lamp bases for his leaded glass shades, he sometimes explored his interest in natural designs through his pottery, with occasional studies of flowering plant forms and—rarer still—reptiles or amphibians.

Pieces of Tiffany's pottery were often left with unglazed exteriors, revealing a white, bisque-fired clay. His best pieces are those bearing one of his excellent glazes. It is worth noting that while his glazing selection was consistently high in quality, he seemed to lavish the largest selection on his lamp base forms.

Tiffany's better ceramic work remains quite rare, with choice examples coming to market perhaps only a few times a year. A strong form with a good glaze appears rarely. Less common still are such examples without

damage, because the ware's relatively soft biscuit seems unusually susceptible to hairline cracks.

The lamp bases seldom bear organic designs. Usually, they are broad, squat pots, occasionally adorned with handles, and covered with Tiffany's most interesting glazes. Although limited in range, the best of these include glossy caramel flambés, intense blue crystalline flambés, and gunmetal to brown metallic flambés.

Ideal pieces of Tiffany pottery are at least 8in/20.3cm tall, covered rim to rim with embossed organic designs, and glazed with the trademark "old ivory" finish: shellac-colored glosses with traces of spinach-green semi-gloss in the low areas. Such pieces will sell for about $6,000.

The market for Tiffany has remained fairly constant for the last 25 years. Glass and lamp collectors seeking to round out collections pay the highest prices. Pottery-only collectors usually settle for one good, descriptive example.

Considering its scarcity, Tiffany ceramic ware seems reasonably valued at present. The record price for a Tiffany pottery piece is $20,000.

Pedestal Compote, *c.*1910

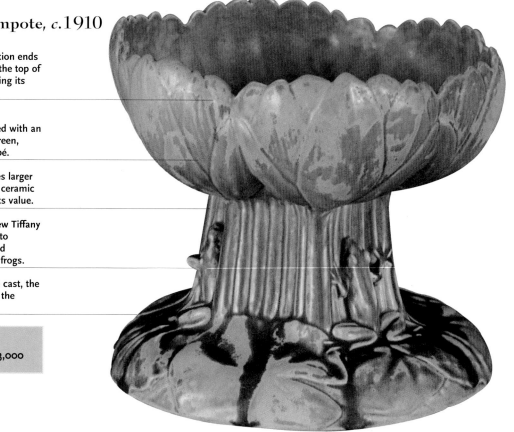

The embossed decoration ends with a jagged edge at the top of this compote, reinforcing its organic nature.

The compote is covered with an exceptional, flowing green, matte-crystalline flambé.

This example measures larger than most of Tiffany's ceramic creations, increasing its value.

This is one of only a few Tiffany ceramic forms known to incorporate flowers and creatures, in this case frogs.

While this piece is slip cast, the molding is strong and the decoration crisp.

Size: 9in/22.9cm
Value: $17,000–$23,000

Weed-Embossed Vase, c.1910

The decoration, which ends evenly at the top of the vase, would be more interesting if reflected in the rim's shape.

This follows a general rule that the more cylindrical the form, the less valuable the example.

The embossed weed design here is good and typical of Tiffany decoration.

The molding on this piece is softer than average, and the decoration does not "pop" off the surface.

Tiffany's shellac-colored finish, seen here, is one of his best glazes, marked with an incised, underglaze "LCT" cipher (not shown).

The chalky white clay body shows through the thin glazing, adding color and depth.

Size: 11in/28cm
Value: $4,250–$5,750

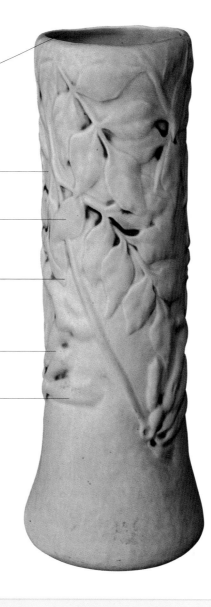

• *Tiffany pottery is almost always molded, so there is some duplication in forms.*
• *Despite the molding process, production seems to have been limited, and even the most common shapes can be considered rare.*
• *Most of Tiffany's ceramics have unglazed exteriors, leaving a chalky white, bisque-fired surface. The interiors, however, are almost always glazed glossy green.*
• *About two-thirds of the pottery does not have embossed decoration. Such pieces are used as glazed lamp bases for Tiffany's decorative shades.*
• *Tiffany's ware is almost always marked.*
• *While Tiffany's lamp base forms are usually larger in size, his vases usually measure under 8in/20.3cm in height.*

Key Facts

Tiffany Pottery was made in Corona, N.Y., from about 1904 to about 1920. The pottery products were originally intended to provide lamp bases for the designer's famous leaded glass shades, but they evolved into a decorative pursuit in their own right. Introduced at the 1904 St. Louis World's Fair, they were first sold through Tiffany outlets in 1905, including the well-known New York City retail store.

It has been suggested that because Louis Comfort Tiffany rotated stock in his sales outlets every 3 months, unsold pieces were likely returned to the Tiffany Studios and possibly destroyed. This might help account for the ware's scarcity.

Though all signed pieces bear the "LCT" cipher, there are sometimes additional markings such as "Favrile Pottery" (a handmade designation) and "Bronze Pottery" (denoting pieces covered with a metal jacket). Fakes are becoming more common, with the cipher scratched into the bottom of some pieces and incised under glaze in new forgeries.

Van Briggle Pottery—Floral

The Van Briggle Pottery is the only company from the original art-pottery period still in business. While its contemporary ware is of a higher standard than most commercially produced pottery, today's collectors focus entirely on the earliest work.

Artus and Anne Van Briggle were in love, and the ware they created during their short time together has always been the collector's choice. They opened their pottery in Colorado Springs, Colo., in 1900. Artus made slip-cast vases embossed with floral or figural patterns, reflecting the Colorado flora and fauna in his choices of shapes, matte glazes, and clay. On the open market, a piece from his first year would challenge all records for this maker.

Production in 1901 was still limited; perhaps only a few dozen pieces bearing this date have been identified. Examples from 1902 are extremely rare too; only slightly more available are pieces from 1903 and 1904, the year Artus died. One prominent collector has suggested that only about 400 pieces total were made prior to his death.

Scarcity alone does not account for its popularity, however. Van Briggle pottery brings together elements of Art Nouveau, Native-American design, superior creative glazing, and a smoldering sensuality—all manifestations of the rather torrid and ill-fated relationship against which they were created. It never lacks a market. Nowhere else in the world of art pottery is so much of the emotion and beauty between two partners displayed in their work.

Although Van Briggle decorated for 20 years, his best work was produced between 1902 and 1904. Consistent with Arts and Crafts sensibilities, the Van Briggles employed natural colors and textures to augment their organic designs. While they molded their ware, their studio operation saw only limited production. Their intention was to use molds to duplicate forms but introduce postmold tooling to increase definition and artistry.

Anne created fine pieces after Artus's death, from about 1905 to 1912, when other potters took up the work. The last pieces of collecting merit date to 1932.

Mixed Color Vase, c.1902

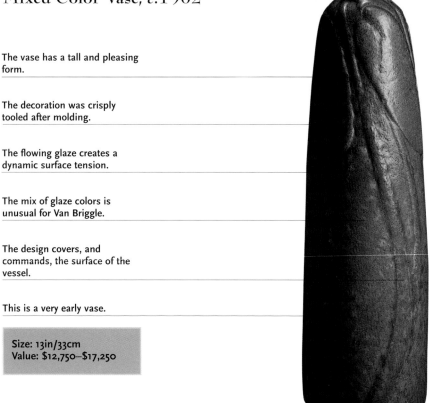

The vase has a tall and pleasing form.

The decoration was crisply tooled after molding.

The flowing glaze creates a dynamic surface tension.

The mix of glaze colors is unusual for Van Briggle.

The design covers, and commands, the surface of the vessel.

This is a very early vase.

Size: 13in/33cm
Value: $12,750–$17,250

Pod Vase, *c.*1903

The embossed decoration shows good detail.

Additional color on the pods adds minor contrast.

This maroon color is more common than the color on the example opposite.

The good design covers most of vase surface, increasing the work's value.

This interesting form is larger than most Van Briggle ware.

This is an early vase.

Size: 10in/25.4cm
Value: $6,400–$8,600

• *Van Briggle's ware was molded, but output was limited and employed a good amount of hand-detailing. Production standards were of the highest order.*
• *Matte green is the most common color on early pieces, followed by tones of blue, then maroon. Browns, ochres, purple, and cream are among Van Briggle's rarest glazes.*
• *Occasionally, multiple glazes are employed. Rarer still are iridescent finishes, used mainly during 1904, and probably from a single test kiln.*
• *The early figural vases, including Lorelei, Lady of the Lily, Dos Cabezos, Climbing for Honey, and Despondency, have always commanded the highest prices.*
• *Van Briggle ware is very durable: pieces are usually either in perfect condition or completely shattered from a fall.*

Key Facts

Born in Felicity, Ohio, in 1869, Artus Van Briggle apprenticed under Karl Langenbeck in 1886–87, and studied at the Cincinnati Art School. He joined the Rookwood Pottery in 1887 where he worked in underglaze painting.

In 1893, Van Briggle studied in Paris and first encountered the Chinese Ming Dynasty matte glazes that would launch his quest for their formulae. In Italy in the summer of 1894, he met Anne Lawrence Gregory of Plattsburg, Penn., there on an art study program; they became engaged to be married.

Back in Cincinnati in 1896, he set to work on dead matte glazes. Within a couple of years, he produced his first Lorelei vase, modeled with a veiled nude wrapped around its shoulder.

Tuberculosis forced Artus to move to a warmer, dryer climate. He left for Colorado Springs in 1899. Successful experiments led him to exhibit matte-glazed vases at the Paris Exposition Universelle of 1900, as part of the Rookwood display. He opened the Van Briggle Pottery in 1900. His initial show met with tremendous enthusiasm and proved to be a great success.

The pottery was officially named the Van Briggle Pottery Company in 1902, the year, he married Anne Gregory. He won medals in the 1903 Paris Salon, and the 1904 Louisiana Purchase Exposition. Sadly, he died of tuberculosis in 1904, at age 35. Anne became president of the reorganized Van Briggle Company at that time.

Van Briggle Pottery—Figural

When Artus Van Briggle set up his own Cincinnati studio in 1896, he toiled to find the secret of the lost "dead" glazes of the Ming Dynasty, relegating his work for Rookwood Pottery to a part-time occupation. The tuberculosis that eventually took his life forced him to the more propitious climate of Colorado Springs in 1899. But once settled in and somewhat recovered, Van Briggle resumed his experiments on matte glazes with the help of a new acquaintance, Professor Strieby, who headed the Colorado College department of chemistry. The success of his glaze experiments and his skill as a designer gave Van Briggle the courage to send Rookwood a collection of pieces to be exhibited with theirs at the Paris Exposition Universelle in 1900.

Van Briggle's wares created such a sensation that William Taylor, the president of Rookwood, wrote Van Briggle to ask him for his glaze formula. Believing his death to be imminent, and apparently intent on leaving a legacy, the ailing potter sent his recipe to Taylor at once. Van Briggle survived that bout of tuberculosis, but not before Rookwood had begun its own experiments with his dead matte glazes.

Later that year, Van Briggle established a workshop. He produced slip-cast vases either embossed with floral patterns or wrapped with languid figures that appeared to have been born from or grown out of the vessels. He covered the pieces with smooth, airbrushed glazes in one or two colors that flowed into each other. A true artist and craftsman, he preferred to throw his wares by hand rather than cast them. However, their shapes were so sculptural that his only choice would have been to carve them one at a time. He therefore opted to cast a small number of vases in each mold and finish them with undercutting.

In terms of the value of Van Briggle work, older is better. The Van Briggle figural masterpieces were first conceived and best rendered during Artus's lifetime, which ended in 1904. A Lorelei pictures a lithe and lovely woman, shrouded in filmy cloth and wrapped around a vase. Suggesting a different mood, Despondency depicts the full figure of a man in repose, his forehead resting in his hand and his body limp. Proceed carefully on a piece that seems to be dated 1900. Most of these are actually from 1906, with the "6" partially glazed over so that it's easily mistaken for "0."

Lorelei Vase, c.1902

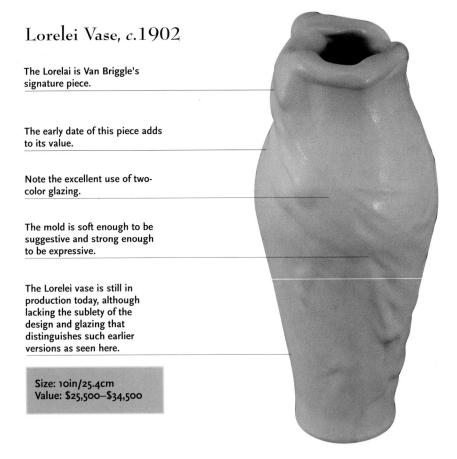

The Lorelai is Van Briggle's signature piece.

The early date of this piece adds to its value.

Note the excellent use of two-color glazing.

The mold is soft enough to be suggestive and strong enough to be expressive.

The Lorelei vase is still in production today, although lacking the sublety of the design and glazing that distinguishes such earlier versions as seen here.

Size: 10in/25.4cm
Value: $25,500–$34,500

Climbing Bears Vase, *c.*1906

This whimsical design features bears searching for honey.

This fairly early example was produced after Artus's death.

In this piece, the decoration is too strong, competing with the vase form.

While the brown glaze is unusual, it appears flat rather than vibrant, taking away from the visual impact.

This tall vase form is one of Van Briggle's larger figurals.

Size: 14in/35.6cm
Value: $8,500–$11,500

• *Pieces of Van Briggle pottery are clearly marked with a cojoined "AA" in a rectangular box.*
• *Early pieces, through 1907, are marked with hand-incised, four-digit dates. While these dates can be obscured by glaze, dental X-rays have proven effective in revealing them. Other markings on early pieces include die-stamped numbers referring to shape and letters denoting size.*
• *Pieces from 1907–12 often bear incised numbers on both sides of the "AA" mark and an incised number below "Van Briggle." All three numbers should be visible if one is to be certain it dates from this period.*
• *Later pieces are occasionally dated or bear other marks. Prices are most affected by designations on pieces made prior to Anne Van Briggle's departure in 1912.*

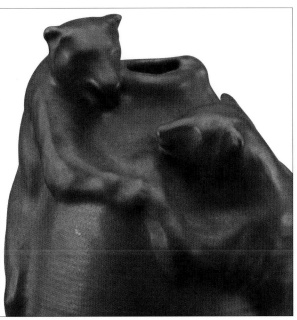

◀ *The bears were actually molded, but details were sharpened by hand prior to glazing. This technique allowed the Van Briggles to produce a quantity of ware without wholly sacrificing craftsmanship.*

Van Briggle Pottery Tiles

Anne Gregory Van Briggle, involved with Van Briggle Pottery's operations for several years, took over as president when her husband died in 1904. Although tile production may have been on Artus's mind, it began only after his death. The decision to make tiles seems to have been primarily based on economics. They could be produced quickly and inexpensively, and the pottery was coping with the stresses of rapid expansion and competition.

Whatever the motivation, beautiful hand-pressed tiles were made from 1904 until 1920, decorated with Anne's stylized Arts and Crafts and Art Nouveau designs, and covered in matte glazes. The tiles were apparently very popular with local builders, who were busily erecting the many new homes going up in Colorado Springs at that time. The tiles also adorned the facade and interior of the

new pottery that Anne opened in 1908, built as a memorial to her husband.

Collectors of fine Arts and Crafts tiles might be frustrated in their search for Van Briggle tiles. Possibly because of the size of the work force, or because of the time involved in making anything by hand, a very limited quantity of these tiles was made. To add to the frustrations, most of these tiles were architectural (and still remain where they were first set), many were designed in friezes, and few were marked with the company name. Because of their utilitarian nature, the glazed tea tiles produced often show surface abrasion.

All this is to say that when Van Briggle tile panels or friezes turn up, they cause a feeding frenzy and cost the lucky purchaser tens of thousands of dollars. Single, 6in/15.2 floral tiles regularly go for over $3,000.

Six-Tile Panel with Trees, *c.*1905

This is an extremely rare and large panel with a strong design of stylized trees that were cropped in interesting manner at the top.

The fine matte glazes appear in at least four colors here.

The panel is decorated in *cuenca* (raised line).

Framing allows this spectacular six-tile panel to be displayed as a single art piece on a wall.

Size: 18 x 12in/
45.7 x 30.5cm
Value: $20,000–$25,000

Architectural Tile, c.1907

Although rare, this tile appears more often than the panel opposite.

The Art Nouveau design recalls English tiles from the turn of the 20th century.

The work exhibits fine matte glazes in four colors.

Like the example opposite, the tile is decorated in *cuenca.*

The Arts and Crafts frame exhibits this tile as a single work of art, as opposed to being a part of a building or larger design.

**Size: 6in/15.2cm square
Value: $2,750-$3,250**

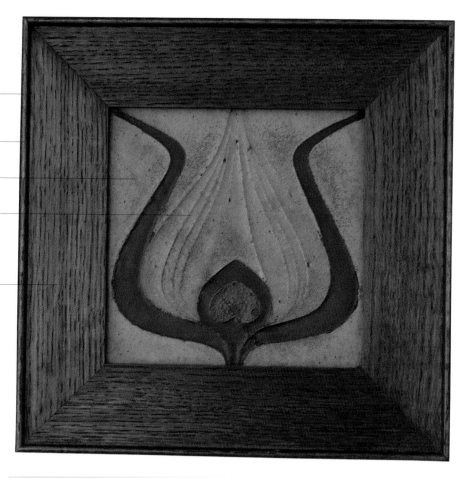

• *Fine, hand-pressed faience tiles were produced from 1904 to 1920 in relatively small quantities, covered in fine matte glazes.*
• *These tiles were either decorated with matte painting on a dark bisque ground, hand-pressed in* cuenca, *painted in wax-resist* cuerda seca, *or modeled in relief.*
• *The tiles were seldom signed; look for "VBPCo" stamped on the underside.*
• *Architectural tiles were either sold from stock or custom designed.*
• *Van Briggle produced tea tiles of red or dark clay with carved bottoms for home use.*
• *Tiles feature sophisticated, stylized Arts and Crafts designs of abstracted flowers of Art Nouveau influence, partial trees, and birds and geese in illustrative style.*
• *Tiles and architectural faience for fireplaces were sold as kits and offered in Van Briggle catalogs.*

Van Briggle Tile Installed

Several hotels and institutions around Colorado boast lovely displays of Van Briggle tile. The most spectacular one, however, has to be the old Van Briggle Memorial Pottery (now the Colorado College Physical Plant), built in honor of its founder by his widow.

The memorial plant, designed by the Dutch architect Nicholas Van den Arend in his national vernacular, was built in 1907 on the corner of Glen Avenue and Uintah Street. Its red brick surface was embellished with elaborate tile installations that complemented the exterior with their warm blue-green and yellow glazes. Even the kiln chimneys are enhanced with blue brick and bear decorated tile. Other chimneys throughout the structure are enhanced with three-dimensional dogwood tile and swirling faience.

Inside the memorial plant, the original director's office remains intact, replete with tile on the floor, the walls, and a stunning full-height fireplace. Outside the office is another tiled floor and fireplace surround worthy of inspection.

The Van Briggle Art Pottery plant now occupies a sprawling, mission-style building from 1887, where commercial versions of Artus's great vases are produced. Tiles are also being pressed from old molds (or copies of old molds), and while a little brighter than the ones produced a hundred years ago, they are as handsome as any new crafted tiles on the market. The largest public collection of original Van Briggle pottery and tiles can be viewed at the Colorado Springs Pioneers' Museum.

W.J. Walley

William J. Walley was probably more important for his philosophy than for the pottery he made, although it would be impossible to separate the two. Walley was a pottery purist, believing there was more integrity and aesthetic merit in a brick—formed, decorated, and finished by one person—than in the best possible example of molded production ware.

Walley pottery was always hand-thrown. The man was nothing if not a stickler for craftsmanship.

Walley's studio in Sterling Junction, Mass., was the kind of philosophical beacon that so often marked the Arts and Crafts movement. In addition to pursuing his own vision and creating his own style, he was involved with the local Worcester State Hospital, introducing patients to the rehabilitative aspects of arts and crafts.

Walley's production was fairly small, although typical of a studio outlet. Most of his work was simply glazed, with the remainder bearing some level of decoration. His best work imitated the style of the Grueby Pottery, with tooled and applied leaves. He also used incising and sculpting on some of his pieces. His glazes, best when matte, appeared in tones of green and brown. He created high-gloss finishes of a high quality, although these seem curiously inconsistent with the otherwise organic notions of the Arts and Crafts movement.

Walley employed a red clay that was fairly dense. Even so, it is prone to chipping and nicking around the edges. A few flaking chips around the bottom rim will not bring the price down by much, but Walley pottery loses about 35% of its value with the first real chip.

Glossy Green Vessel, c.1910

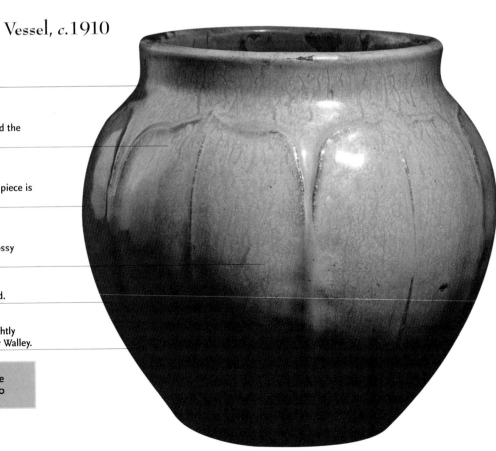

The shape is simple and unforced.

Walley tooled and applied the leaves.

Like all Walley ware, the piece is hand-thrown.

Note the light green, glossy finish.

Only one glaze was used.

The piece measures slightly smaller than average for Walley.

Size: 5in/12.7cm wide
Value: $1,700–$2,300

Matte Glazed Vessel, *c.*1910

The form of this piece is more interesting and dynamic than the example opposite.

Walley employed matte glazes to finish this piece.

He used a two-tone finish that augments the visual effect.

The vessel is larger than average in size.

The tooled and applied leaves typify Walley's style.

The form is hand-thrown and appealingly organic.

Size: 9in/22.9cm
Value: $3,000–$4,000

• *While the best Walley pieces were finished in his trademark matte glazes, he employed a range of glossy coverings, as well.*
• *Much of his pottery is simply glazed, but the best pieces were decorated with tooled and applied leaves, much in the manner of Grueby.*
• *Walley's decorative techniques included incising, tooling, and applied work.*
• *On at least one famous Walley form, called the "devil mug," he added garnet eyes to the modeled, impish face.*
• *Like most Arts and Crafts ware, minor damage has little negative impact on the value of Walley's work.*

Key Facts

William Joseph Walley was born in 1852 in East Liverpool, Ohio. His father was a potter in the area. Upon his premature death, the younger Walley went to England, presumably with his mother, and was apprenticed before he was ten at the Minton Pottery in Stoke-upon-Trent.

After learning every facet of the potter's trade for 11 years, he returned to the United States and settled in Portland, Me. By 1873, he was trying to produce art pottery of his own.

The Portland experiment did not prove to be successful, and in 1885, Walley moved to Worcester, Mass., about 40 miles west of Boston. He purchased an emery-wheel business owned by Frank B. Norton, the grandson of one of the founders of the Bennington Pottery in Vermont. The buildings had originally housed a pottery run by Norton and Frederick

Hancock, also a Bennington alumnus, and Walley hoped to revive it.

After achieving only lackluster results, Walley moved his studio operation up the road to Sterling Junction, into what had once been the Wachusetts Pottery. This, too, had been turned into an emery-wheel factory, but once again he aimed to revive the original business. He started producing art pottery, vases, mugs, tiles, and candlesticks, all hand-thrown of red clay and usually covered in green or brown glaze. A staunch believer in the craftsman philosophy, Walley presided over a company of one.

In 1904, Walley became a member of the Society of Arts and Crafts in Boston. He exhibited there in 1907 and was awarded Master status in 1908.

William Walley's death in 1919 marked the end of his pottery.

Weller Pottery— Slip Decoration

Zanesville, Ohio, played an historic role in the story of American decorative ceramics. Much of the activity there centered around the Roseville Pottery, renowned for both its hand-decorated and commercial ware. However, Roseville might not have achieved such acclaim without an equally creative and tenacious crosstown rival, the Weller Pottery.

Samuel Weller pursued a personal vision that moved his operation from traditional flowerpot and sewer tile producer to majolica manufacturer, and finally to art pottery maker. Weller Pottery's growth was similar to Roseville's in that its earliest work approximated that of Rookwood, and not very well. To replicate Rookwood Standard Glaze and Roseville Royal dark, Weller created Louwelsa. Rookwood Iris and Roseville Royal light elicited Eocean from Weller. Also like Roseville, Weller did not really establish itself as a serious venture until its designers created wholly original lines.

Even in such pursuits, Weller Pottery marched in lockstep with its crosstown rival. Roseville hired Frederick Rhead to create Della Robbia. Weller lured him into its camp to develop Jap Birdimal, a squeezebag-decorated line. Roseville won this battle. Weller brought Jacques Sicard over from the south of France to cover Weller pots with his scintillating metallic nacreous finish. Roseville responded by developing Mara ware. In this case, Weller won the day. And so it continued.

Weller also moved into production ware as the demand for hand-painted pottery decreased and associated costs rose. In some instances, this line equaled Roseville's creativity. Lawn figurines are among the most curious and compelling production pieces made in the United States. Other figural lines, incorporating animals, frogs, and children, are similarly popular today.

However, Weller floral patterns, with few exceptions, never had the bite of Roseville's. Whether Weller lacked commitment to this mass-produced ware or simply could not attract the designers that established such high standards at Roseville, today's collectors know the difference. It is relatively easy to sell just about any Roseville production line, while most of Weller's ware sells for considerably less. The exceptions, such as Coppertone, Muskota, and Selma, enjoy a deep collecting base.

Louwelsa Flat Pitcher, c.1900

The hand-painted underglaze typifies this early Weller line.

The molded form was made in a late Victorian shape.

Weller's version of the brown overglaze was used on this.

The flowers were hand-painted in slip relief.

Detailing of the flowers here is good, but not great.

This measures slightly smaller than the average Weller.

Size: 3in/7.6cm tall
Value: $125–$175

Eocean Floor Vase, c.1905

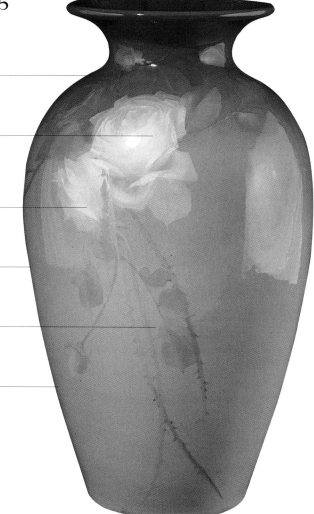

This is an unusually large form for Weller, increasing its value.

The detailing of the flowers is good, but not great.

Like the example opposite, the flowers have been painted in slip relief.

The piece displays Weller's version of a clear overglaze.

The blue background color makes this piece attractive and desirable.

The artist signed this show piece (not shown), another value factor.

Size: 24in/61cm
Value: $7,500–$10,000

- *Weller's hand-painted ware, like Roseville's, is almost always a step down from Rookwood quality. Weller and Roseville produced a slightly lesser work for a cheaper price.*
- *The quality of the overglaze is also not on the same level as Rookwood's. In addition to lacking Rookwood's clarity, it is also susceptible to heavy crazing and buckling.*
- *Well-glazed examples always bring premium prices.*
- *The best artists working in slip relief included Hester Pillsbury, Mae Timberlake, and Albert Haubrich.*
- *The two lines seen here are directly influenced by others made famous by Rookwood.*
- *Relatively minor damage will reduce value on all but the best of pieces by 50%.*

Key Facts

Samuel A. Weller began his pottery business in Fultonham, Ohio, in 1872, with utilitarian pots that were unpainted and plain. He next went door-to-door with a line of pots that he had painted with house paint, then added stoneware. Within a decade, he needed a larger location. Ten years later, he had leased extra warehouse space, built his own new pottery, and bought an additional plant. His pottery lines included jardinieres, painted flowerpots, hanging baskets, umbrella stands, and additional pieces.

Only in 1893 did Weller begin to produce art ware. Inspired by Lonhuda ware at the Chicago World's Fair, he lured William Long to the Weller Pottery and was soon producing Lonhuda himself. Artists—Charles Babcock Upjohn, Jacques Sicard, and Henri Gellée—came and went, contributing their talents and art ware.

By 1915, Weller Pottery claimed to be the largest art pottery in existence. Production ware replaced Weller's better lines at the end of World War I, and at this time, Weller began his one-for-one replication of Roseville Pottery's wares. Weller Pottery continued to operate until 1945, but its heyday was long since over.

Weller Pottery—
Embossed Decoration

A great disparity exists between Weller's earlier attempts at production ware and later, less labor-intensive, efforts. Even at the firm's creative peak, the company introduced vessels with embossed decoration that artists extensively augmented. This had the net effect of producing pottery that appeared more hand-decorated than it actually was.

It is unlikely that Samuel Weller was prescient enough to know that, eventually, he would be forced to produce ware that was decorated almost entirely in-mold. Nevertheless, it seems clear that these earlier technique experiments marked the beginning of his approach to reconciling beauty and cost.

Some of the most striking early examples of Weller's art ware—such as the Sicardo floor vase shown on the opposite page—combined superior design and molding with equally high-quality decorating. Usually, the designs molded into the pot were enhanced with decoration like the embossed grapes and painted leaves seen here.

Artists at Weller Pottery enhanced their early objects with some of Weller's best glazes, the Standard Brown and lustrous sheens of Jacques Sicard being prime examples. While later production vases did not enjoy the same benefit, the best of them had a charm of their own, especially such popular lines as Coppertone, Selma, and Woodcraft. But Weller never matched the Roseville Pottery's flair for producing top-grade commercial ware. Now, with only a few notable exceptions, the company does not have the broad collecting base enjoyed by its perennial competitor.

Malvern Embossed Vessel, c.1935

This is an example of Weller's Malvern pattern, a later line created in response to Roseville's production ware.

The design was embossed in the mold.

A moderately trained worker added the colors by hand.

The odd pillow shape is typical of the post–Art Deco period.

Size: 7in/17.8cm
Value: $125–$175

Sicardo Embossed Vase, c.1905

This is an example of Weller's Sicardo line.

Although Sicardo ware was usually hand-painted, this piece employs a design that is both embossed and hand-painted.

Bold, iridescent metallic colors of magenta and silver enhance the value of this piece.

The work represents a bridge between Weller's early hand-decorated ware and its later production pottery.

Jacques Sicard was regarded as highly for his painting on pottery as for his glazing, making this an unusual design for him.

Size: 20in/50.8cm
Value: $6,400–$8,600

- *Production pieces were almost always molded.*
- *Weller attempted to compete with Roseville's popular production ware but seldom matched its rival's designs and production standards.*
- *Included among Weller's most popular production lines are Coppertone, Woodcraft, Selma, and a series of curious large lawn figures.*
- *Artists routinely added colors to the molded decorations on the production pieces.*
- *Production ware almost always bore one of the company's numerous marks.*
- *Because these pieces were created with molded, repeated designs, even minor damage greatly reduces value.*
- *In general, production lines with designs using animals and creatures are the most valuable and salable.*

◀ *While the embossed grapes and leaves shown here were part of the molded form, the rich, lustrous glazes that cover them came from the hand of master designer and decorator Jacques Sicard.*

Wheatley Pottery

Thomas J. Wheatley began his pottery work at T.J. Wheatley Pottery by copying the Cincinnati style—which itself replicated the Haviland Limoges style—of painting designs, mostly floral, in high, thick relief on vigorously painted and colored backgrounds. This might have been acceptable had he not claimed personal credit for the technique and patented it. Fortunately, he was not able to bar his fellow Cincinnati potters from continuing their work in the underglaze process.

About 20 years later, he emerged as the principal in another Wheatley pottery, making mostly very good copies of work already made famous by Grueby and, to a lesser extent, Teco. These pieces, with thick matte glazes covering organic or architectural forms, were nearly always slip cast, with embossed decoration, or simply glazed.

Despite his questionable ethics, Wheatley enjoyed reasonable success in both ventures. The quality of his later matte-glazed ware, seen here, was very good, as far as it went. And his Limoges style ware was certainly on a par with the work produced by such noteworthy rivals as Rookwood, Rettig and Martin, Matt Morgan Art Pottery, and the Cincinnati Art Pottery.

Wheatley's matte ware was versatile in design, often mimicking the severe Arts and Crafts lines of Grueby ware, with spade-shaped leaves and small ovoid buds. A smaller percentage of Wheatley's Arts and Crafts work was architectural in ways similar to Teco ware, usually visible in straplike handles and angular hollowware forms.

The easiest way to distinguish a Wheatley matte glazed vase from a similar Grueby example is to look for throwing marks on the interior of the pot. Because Wheatley is nearly always cast, there will be no horizontal, concentric rings lining the walls. Wheatley is also lighter in weight by about 20%. And Wheatley pottery does not have a foot ring, while a doughnut ring of glaze around the bottom edge often defines Grueby's. One may also be able to differentiate between molded floral and leaf decoration (Wheatley) and the sharper, hand-modeled variety.

Because Wheatley matte ware is molded and repeatable, damaged examples will diminish in value more than most Arts and Crafts pottery. Small nicks on embossed decoration have little negative impact, but a rim or base chip might reduce value by as much as 35%.

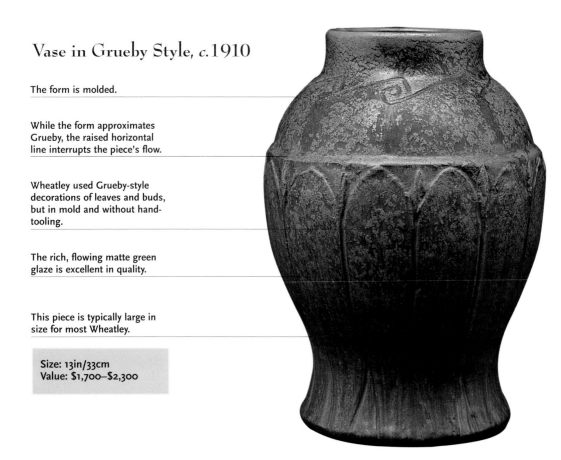

Vase in Grueby Style, c. 1910

The form is molded.

While the form approximates Grueby, the raised horizontal line interrupts the piece's flow.

Wheatley used Grueby-style decorations of leaves and buds, but in mold and without hand-tooling.

The rich, flowing matte green glaze is excellent in quality.

This piece is typically large in size for most Wheatley.

Size: 13in/33cm
Value: $1,700–$2,300

Replica of Grueby's Kendrick Vase, c.1910

This piece is large, like most Wheatley ware.

Like the example opposite, the form is molded.

In this work, Wheatley created a nearly exact copy of Grueby's Kendrick vase, a plus for value on the collector's market.

Notice the rich green matte glaze, another of the vase's virtues.

The detail in the decoration is muted, a consequence of molding rather than modeling.

The vase's proportions of form seem clumsy and top-heavy, lacking the grace of the Grueby prototype.

Size: 13in/33cm
Value: $3,500–$4,500

• *Nearly all Wheatley matte ware is molded. A few hand-thrown examples exist, but they are usually simple forms with matte glazes.*
• *There appears to have been some hand-sharpening of decoration on pieces bearing leaf and/or floral design.*
• *The most successful (and valuable) pieces of this work are those that most closely replicate Grueby ware. As such, they offer a good quality decorative product for one-half, one-third, or even one-fifth the price of Grueby.*
• *Most Wheatley ware was probably marked with the pottery's die-stamped "WP" cipher, but the thick glazes often cover the bottoms, obscuring the mark.*
• *This work was often produced on a larger-than-average scale. The typical size approaches 12in/30.5cm in height, and some examples exceed 30in/76.2cm.*

Key Facts

The history of American art pottery is dotted with its share of scoundrels. But none seemed as consistently predisposed to borrowing the ideas of others as did Thomas J. Wheatley.

Thomas Jerome Wheatley was one of the earliest figures in the American art pottery movement. In 1879, he experimented with underglaze-painted wares at Cincinnati's Coultry Pottery, where Mary Louise McLaughlin had been building her reputation with a similar type of ware since 1877. Wheatley formed the Cincinnati Art Pottery in 1880 to provide capital for his venture at Coultry.

Wheatley started the Wheatley Pottery Company in 1903 with Isaac Kahn. The wares produced there were entirely different from the ones he had done previously and are often referred to as the "poor man's Grueby." Vases and lamp bases were slip cast with relief patterns, mostly floral—designs borrowed directly from other potteries of the time, such as Grueby and Teco. Most were covered in thick, textured glaze of green, blue, or ochre that imitated these potteries' wares, but with a matte, almost "dry," finish that tended to bubble in the firing. Wheatley's were some of the largest pieces produced at the time.

While interesting and organic, the glazes with which Wheatley covered pottery did not compare to the extraordinary matte enamels of William Grueby.

Wheatley Pottery Tiles

Thomas J. Wheatley may be remembered for his free use of others' good ideas. And he may be judged for using glazes that could not compare to the works he copied. However, the glazes used on his tiles were altogether different. Wheatley tiles, modeled or decorated in *cuenca* or *cuerda seca*, were covered with perfect Arts and Crafts enamels, separated in "curdling," with a matte finish, and in a variety of rich colors.

The production standards of Wheatley's tiles equal the very best of Grueby, Van Briggle, Rookwood, or Mueller, molded with fine, precise *cuenca* and covered in exceptional glazes. Unfortunately, Wheatley never found an artist of the caliber of Addison LeBoutillier to create first-rate images for the tiles. Besides a handful of strong, stylized Arts and Crafts designs, now worth about $1,500 for a 6in/15.2cm tile, Wheatley created a line of rather uninspired designs of superior quality.

The most successful Wheatley tiles had strong Arts and Crafts graphics and were probably among the earliest to be designed. Variations on trees or flowers, made in short supply, are ardently pursued by collectors today. In perfect condition, these are worth more than $1,000 apiece.

The company had the capacity to produce great tiles, a potential that went largely unfulfilled. The majority of the tiles feature moderately interesting geometric, heraldic, or floral patterns, along with some zodiac signs and animals. Large rondelles embossed with ships were competently done and covered with attractive glazes. But those glazes were sometimes applied too thickly, which had the effect of masking the more subtle details.

Floral *Cuenca* Tile, c.1915

The flat rendering of the flowers suggest Japanese wallpaper.

This is an unusual size and design that makes good use of the space, which increases its value.

Note the precise delineation of pattern, perfectly fired and without any glaze overflow.

This glaze separation, or "curdling," is a desired effect in the texture of Arts and Crafts pottery.

Size: 6in/15.2cm tall
Value: $400–$600

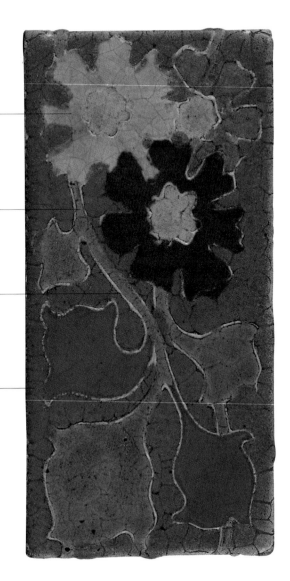

Geometric *Cuerda Seca* Tile, c.1915

This is a fine example of a geometric tile.

Cuerda seca, or "dry cord," was well executed to create the dark outline.

Desirable "curdling" is a feature seen also in the example opposite.

The superior glazing is in gorgeous colors.

Because geometric designs are the more common among Wheatley tiles, the value of this near-perfect tile is decreased.

Size: 4in/10.2cm square
Value: $90–$110

- *Wheatley produced exceptional* **cuenca** *(raised-line) and modeled tiles, covered in matte glaze and textured with "feathering," "curdling," and crackling.*
- *Like most decorated-tile manufacturers, the firm also offered a line of plain tile (its bread and butter) and architectural faience.*
- *Wheatley's inserts are difficult to date because many of the early designs were still being produced in the late 1920s and were offered in the 1928 catalog.*
- *A line of ecclesiastical plaques, designed by Henry D. Dagit & Sons for the Church of the Transfiguration in Philadelphia in the 1920s, was put into general production.*
- *Wheatley produced the famous Christ Child, by Luca Della Robbia, and a Paschal Lamb identical to one made at Mueller's in Trenton, N.J.*

Key Facts

Thomas Jerome Wheatley perfected his own version of the underglaze painting used in Limoges, France, while at the Coultry Pottery in Cincinnati. Coultry, in business since 1859, had recently been brought to the public's attention by the much-publicized experiments of Mary Louise McLaughlin. Wheatley would have seen the Limoges technique at the 1876 Philadelphia Centennial Exposition three years earlier.

In 1880, he left Coultry's and opened the T.J. Wheatley Pottery. There, he built a kiln and did his own preparation of clay, molding, glazing, and firing. He received a patent for his improvement to underglazing in the same year, although McLaughlin claimed to have developed it first. In that year, four companies produced underglaze-painted pottery in Cincinnati alone: Coultry's, which now employed Rettig and Valentien to teach classes; the Dallas Pottery, home to the Cincinnati Pottery Club headed by McLaughlin; T.J. Wheatley &

Company; and the Rookwood Pottery. Only the last of these would still be in business by 1882.

In 1897, 15 years after closing his pottery, Wheatley went to work for Samuel Weller in Zanesville, Ohio. He returned to Cincinnati in 1900 and opened the Wheatley Pottery Co. in 1903, where he produced his own line of art ware. In 1910 a fire destroyed the pottery. After rebuilding, it appears that art ware was discontinued. It was then that Wheatley began concentrating his production on architectural faience, tiles, and garden pottery.

T.J. Wheatley died in 1917. The Cambridge Tile Manufacturing Co. of nearby Covington, Ky., purchased the Wheatley Pottery in 1927 and reincorporated it as the Wheatley Pottery and Tile Co. Cambridge also formed the Cambridge-Wheatley Co. to represent both its dust-pressed tiles and Wheatley's faience tiles. The new company had headquarters in New York and Chicago by 1930, but both tile companies were dissolved in 1936.

Sources & References

Where to See and Buy Art Pottery

Looking at art pottery has never been easier. There are several reputable auctions that focus on high-end decorative ceramics, while offering good service and solid guarantees. A handful of major dealer shows across occur the country, hosted by the finest purveyors in the land. And a growing number of museum collections in major cities, have holdings ranging from worthwhile to spectacular. To follow are our recommendations.

Major Conferences and Shows

Grove Park Inn
Asheville, North Carolina

Usually the third week of each February, this is the best of all period events. Every year, thousands of Arts and Crafts enthusiasts descend on this lovely town in the Smokey Mountains for four days of pottery, wood craft, and conversation. Do stay at the Grove Park Inn, although you'll have to reserve your room at least a year in advance. This is the best period antiques show in the country. About half of the show focuses on art pottery. In addition, the event sponsors numerous lectures, hands-on workshops, displays by publishers, and more. If you have time for only one event, this should be it.

Zanesville Art Pottery Lovers Festival
Zanesville, Ohio

This is the oldest, and, arguably, the most famous, of all pottery-related events. Usually the second to third weekend in July, it takes place in the town that was once the art pottery capital of the world. The emphasis here is strictly on art pottery, and dealers set up in rooms at the local Holiday Inn and Quality Inn. There is also a well-managed show and sale in a local exhibition hall the second weekend of the event. The Festival has been watered down in recent years by a few pottery auctions that are held during the Festival and timed to profit from the crowd. Unfortunately, these unrelated auctions have the effect of draining revenue from what would otherwise have been spent in support of the dealers who make this show possible. Consequently, the dealers do less business and have less incentive to return. If you go—and you should—give the dealers your support, or you may not see them there again.

American Art Pottery Association Annual Convention

The AAPA celebrated its 20th anniversary in the year 2000. The association is dedicated to maintaining high ethical standards in the art pottery business and disseminating knowledge about American decorative ceramics. The organization publishes a professional bimonthly newsletter, which is included in the membership fees. There is an annual convention, usually in April, that moves throughout the United States.

Bay Area Pottery Show

This is one of the more enjoyable pottery-only events, held every February in San Jose, California, and managed by the affable Steve and Martha Sanford. This is a quality event offering a broad range of hand-decorated and production art pottery.

Glendale Art Pottery Show

One of the oldest pottery-only dealer shows, the Glendale Art Pottery Show is held every October at the Glendale Civic Auditorium in Glendale, California. The size show varies, but the quality and variety are as good as any in the country.

Museum Collections

Several important museums have been building their art pottery collections for years. The increased popularity of American decorative ceramics has resulted in more frequent exhibitions at these institutions, as well as better permanent displays of their holdings. Here are our recommendations.

Los Angeles County Museum of Art (LACMA)
Los Angeles, California

The Los Angeles County Museum of Art has been the most aggressive museum in the United States in developing a premier collection of Arts and Crafts and art pottery. Their efforts have paid off. If any questions remain about what happens when you combine knowledge, taste, money, and passion, you'll find the answers here. This is a great permanent installation with some of the finest examples of art pottery visible anywhere. Go there.

Newark Museum
Newark, New Jersey

The Newark Museum is one of the only museums in the United States that purchased art pottery directly from the people who made it, while they were still making it. Consequently, they boast an exceptional collection not only for the quality of the ware, but for the stories associated with the acquisitions. Under the direction of Ulysses Dietz, this museum is a charming experience of how a serious museum can and should be run.

The New Orleans Museum of Art
New Orleans, Louisiana

This is yet another institution that has made the commitment to assembling a first-rate ceramics collection. Under the direction of curators John Bullard and John Keefe, the Museum has pursued some of the more esoteric works, in addition to such usual suspects as Rookwood and Grueby. A magnificent new wing, completed just a few years ago, provides a clean and well-lighted space to view this institution's intelligent assortment of objects.

The Syracuse Museum of Art
Syracuse, New York

The location of this Museum was especially fortuitous, because it made it possible to represent in an exceptional way the local hero Adelaide Robineau. The Syracuse Museum has the biggest and best collection of this luminary's work to be found anywhere. Thanks to the direction and insight of former curator Barbara Perry, the museum also boasts a handsome array of work by Robineau's contemporaries.

The Metropolitan Museum of Art
New York, New York

In an institution of this magnitude, it's easy for art pottery to be overwhelmed. In spite of this, curator Nonnie Frelinghuysen has maintained a commitment to 20th century decorative art, providing us with beautiful placement in their relatively new wing, as well as scores of pieces in nearby study cabinets. This collection offers both beauty and brains.

The Cooper Hewitt Museum
New York, New York

Housing the collection of Bill and Marcia Goodman, and the subject of Vance Kohler's book, *American Art Pottery*, this charming New York institution has been a stalwart supporter of decorative ceramics for decades. The collection and the Museum are small enough to view in a single visit, and serious enough to warrant the trip.

Other museums are building collections as this book goes to press. Keep an eye out on the *Mint Museum* in Charlotte, N.C., where Barbara Perry is currently providing expertise, and the *George Ohr Museum* in Biloxi, Miss., which, while still on the drawing board of world-famous architect Frank Gheary, promises to be memorable in many ways.

Other Sources of Information

Andersen, Timothy; Moore, Eudorah; and Winter, Robert. *California Design 1910*. Pasadena, CA: California Design Publications, 1974.

Barber, Edwin AtLee. *The Pottery and Porcelain of the United States (third edition) and Marks of American Potters*. New York, NY: Feingold & Lewis, 1976.

Evans, Paul. *Art Pottery of the United States (second edition)*. New York, NY: Feingold & Lewis, 1987.

Hawes, Lloyd E. *The Dedham Pottery and the Earlier Robertson's Chelsea Potteries*. Dedham, MA: Dedham Historical Society, 1968.

Hecht, Dr. Eugene. *After the Fire: George Ohr*. Lambertville, NJ: Arts & Crafts Quarterly Press, 199.

Kaplan, Wendy. *The Art That Is Life: The Arts & Crafts Movement in America, 1875-1920*. Boston, MA: Museum of Fine Arts, 1987.

Koehler, Vance. *American Art Pottery*. New York, NY: Cooper-Hewitt Museum, 1987.

Kovel, Ralph and Terry. *Kovels' American Art Pottery*. New York, NY: Crown Publishing, 1993.

Maurer, Christopher and Iglesias, Maria Estrella. *Dreaming in Clay on the Coast of Mississippi*. New York, NY: Doubleday, 2000.

Monsour, Peter. "California Faience: A West Coast Pottery of the American Arts and Crafts Movement." *Journal of the American Art Pottery Association*, Vol. 12, No. 9, 1996.

Sigafoose, Dick. *American Art Pottery: A Collection of Pottery, Tiles and Memorabilia 1880–1950*. Paducah, KY: Collector Books/Schroeder, 1998.

Taft, Lisa Factor. *Herman Carl Mueller: Architectural Ceramics and the Arts and Crafts Movement*. Trenton, NJ: New Jersey State Museum, 1979.

Weiss, Peg. *Adelaide Alsop Robineau: Glory in Porcelain*. Syracuse, NY: Syracuse University Press in association with the Everson Museum of Art, 1981.

Glossary

Applied design: decoration attached to the surface of a piece of pottery.

Baluster: art pottery having a bulbous middle and a flared top and base.

Bisque: art pottery left unfinished after firing.

Brocade: a rich cloth or tile panel with a raised design that often tells or alludes to a story.

Charcoaling: copper crystal blackening.

Cloisons: raised outlines on tiles made by the *cuenca* process *(see below)*.

Crazing: gentle crackling of the glaze that occurs when the body and the glaze expand at different rates in the kiln.

Crystalline glaze: glaze with a surface lustre sheen resulting from recrystallization of particles during the cooling period.

Cuenca: Spanish tilemaking process whereby wet tiles are impressed with raised outlines before firing and the resulting inner sections glazed.

Cuerda seca: Spanish tilemaking process whereby dry cord is used to outlilne flat color sections; these outlines become black during the firing stage, when the cord burns away.

Earthenware: a lightly fired pottery whose porous body is often sealed with a glaze.

Embossed design: raised surface decoration.

Enamel: a glossy, opaque, hard protective coating.

Encaustic: a heat process by which a design is inlaid.

Faience: earthenware decorated with colorful, opaque glazes, from the French for "handmade."

Glaze: the coating applied to seal the porous body of earthenware.

Granite ware: stoneware that has a speckled appearance.

Green tile: flat, wet tile as yet undecorated.

Ground: the basic body of a piece of pottery on which the decoration is applied.

Incised design: engraved or carved decoration.

Intaglio: a design that is carved, incised, or engraved, rendering it below the surface.

Natural process: a technique developed at J. & J.G. Low Art Tile Works whereby a delicate object, such as a leaf or a piece of lace, was placed between two unfired tiles, covered with tissue paper, and pressed to produce two separate tiles with an impressed natural design.

Overlay: application of surface or overglaze decoration to a piece of pottery.

Plastic sketches: technique developed by John Low at J. & J.G. Low Art Tile Works whereby tile panels were made from wet or plastic clay, as opposed to damp dust.

Porcelain: a high-fired ceramic ware with varying degrees of thickness and translucency.

Porcellaneous: exhibiting porcelain-like qualities.

Pottery: generic term that includes earthenware, clay, and stoneware products.

Relief design: decoration raised from the body of a piece of pottery or porcelain.

Scroddle: the process whereby clays of various colors are mixed together to produce a swirled effect.

Sgraffito: technique in which decoration is scratched through the surface glaze to reveal the underlying color of the clay body.

Shaped rim: decorative technique whereby the rim of a vase is given a regular or irregular pattern instead of a smooth outline.

Slip decoration: technique in which liquid clay is applied to the body of a piece to produce a raised design, usually decorated with colored glazes.

Sponging: application of color or glaze to the body with a sponge to produce a mottled effect.

Squeezebag: decorative technique whereby liquid clay, or slip, is applied in a manner similar to that used in cake decorating.

Stoneware: refined pottery having a strong, nonporous body.

Stylized design: non-naturalistic decoration, sometimes abstracted from a natural motif.

Terra cotta: unglazed, lightly fired earthenware that is reddish in color.

Tesserae: the small pieces used in mosaic work.

Index

Acknowledgments

Grateful acknowledgment is given for permission to reproduce the photographs in this volume. Permission to reproduce the photograph on page 119 was granted by Mr. and Mrs. James Carter. The piece shown there is part of the James Carter collection. All other photographs are reproduced courtesy of David Rago Auctions. The author has made every effort to ensure that all subjects are correctly and fully credited; if any errors or omissions have occurred, the publisher will be pleased to correct them in future editions.